NANNY WANTED

Lizzy Barber is a London-based author living in Islington with her husband, George, a food writer, and their son, Marlowe. She read English at Corpus Christi College, Cambridge.

She has worked as an actress and in film development, and has spent the last ten years working in the restaurant business with her brother, Jamie, as head of brand and marketing for The Hush Collection. They have a boutique group of restaurants in London: Haché, Hush and Cabana.

Also by Lizzy Barber

My Name is Anna
Out of Her Depth

LIZZY BARBER

NANNY WANTED

PAN BOOKS

First published 2023 by Pan Books
an imprint of Pan Macmillan
The Smithson, 6 Briset Street, London EC1M 5NR
EU representative: Macmillan Publishers Ireland Ltd, 1st Floor,
The Liffey Trust Centre, 117–126 Sheriff Street Upper,
Dublin 1, D01 YC43
Associated companies throughout the world
www.panmacmillan.com

ISBN 978-1-5290-6102-4

1 3 5 7 9 8 6 4 2

A CIP catalogue record for this book is available from the British Library.

Typeset in Sabon by Jouve (UK), Milton Keynes
Printed and bound by CPI Group (UK) Ltd, Croydon, CR0 4YY

Visit www.panmacmillan.com to read more about all our books
and to buy them. You will also find features, author interviews and
news of any author events, and you can sign up for e-newsletters
so that you're always first to hear about our new releases.

For George – who I will state plainly and in full is the
inspiration for *none* of the men in this book

NANNY WANTED

When I think of Kewney Manor, it's the wind I think of most.

Funny, after all that went on there, that it should be that which stirs my memories most of all.

Not that wretched house, or the people within it.

But the wind.

It will catch me at the strangest of moments: a soft whistle through trees in the park, a sprightly gust as I walk down the high street, and I am instantly transported – hairs on my arms prickling, body racked with shivers regardless of the temperature – the manor's imposing facade rebuilding itself brick by brick, encircling the secrets it worked so hard to keep inside.

That sea-salt-sucked air.

How it howled through you, up there on the exposed clifftops.

Raked through your hair and left your skin dry as bone.

How it carried on it the smell of seaweed and heather, mineral and sweet.

How it whipped up the flames, as we watched the manor burn.

2013

1

Nick and I were finally over.

I had to force myself to believe it.

Our relationship had been a vacuum; one that, over the course of five years, had sucked from me my friends, my sense of self, my freedom – everything, in fact, that wasn't his and mine intertwined. The moment I shut the door on our suffocating Brixton flat – knowing that I would never return – felt like the first time in five years I could take a full breath.

When I finally extricated myself from him, I did so in the only way I could see how.

I wasn't stupid. I knew I had to get away. Get as far away as possible, as quickly as possible. No sign, no trace; nothing to implicate that there was still an 'us'.

But when you have to get away; when you have no ties to anyone, or anything – Mum dead; Dad little more than a footnote, a biannual call from Australia, or Stockholm, or Taiwan, or wherever he'd last stuck a pin into a map – where do you go?

Sequestered on the other side of London, the curtains in my dingy hostel room drawn tight, I inhaled the freedom of the damp air and sticky carpet as I trawled websites in incognito mode, hands shaking, anticipating at any moment the knock on the door, the sign that it was all over.

But no one came.

And then a listing caught my eye:

NANNY WANTED, CORNWALL.

Cornwall.

I googled it. Ran my finger over images of pretty fishing villages and lush scenery.

And, lured by the healing promise of the sea; of dramatic clifftops; of, crucially, a distance far enough from London that no one could come after me in a hurry, I thought, for the first time, maybe I can actually do this.

Parcelled up my skills, such as they were – a good-to-middling History degree, six months of a PGCE teacher training degree (abandoned at Nick's derision), plenty of online tutoring and enough teenaged babysitting experience to garner me the nickname 'Super Nanny' – and sought change.

Showered. Dressed. Braved daylight to find a cafe frequented by international backpackers, perfectly suited to my need for anonymity.

Got in contact – a video call, at her request – and through the shaky screen ('The cliffs, I'm afraid, terrible reception!'), I was introduced to Laurie's bright eyes and natural smile for the first time.

And there was something about the prospect of it, of being folded into this family, of the children, dark-haired and pretty, who popped into the corner of the screen with energetic waves, that made my heart beat steadily. This was it, this was the answer – the distance, the rejuvenating sea air – the way to make the spectre of Nick, his bruises, both seen and unseen, fade for good.

A day later, I was on my way to Kewney Manor.

2

She said that she'd organize a taxi for me at Truro station.

I had written down her name and contact details the moment we'd finished the call, although soon enough they were committed to memory.

Laurie Rowe.

Clutched the piece of paper for most of the journey, talisman-like, as if the name alone had the power to ward off anyone or anything that tried to stop me.

A taxi, she'd said. Which was why I hadn't been anticipating a sleek black limousine, parked most precisely at the entrance of the station's low-slung building. A driver, in one of those traditional hats with the visor (that should have been the first hint, really, that the Rowes weren't your average, common-or-garden family). My name on a board in thick black lettering – LILY STERN – making me jolt to attention after the bleary five-and-a-half-hour journey from Paddington, making me search with uneroded fear the faces of the remaining passengers clustered on the pavement. Until the board dropped uneventfully to his side.

The driver took my bags without asking, held the door open as I slid inside. Pointed out the bottles of mineral water tucked into the arm rest, and, nestled between them, a dish of white mints, in individual cellophane wrappers. A memory came to me unbidden: an early date, dinner at a local Chinese. My fingers fishing around in the glass bowl by the entrance, and Nick's quick and surprisingly savage admonishment, 'Are you crazy? Don't you know how many people's hands have been in there? Disgusting.'

Followed later by what I would learn was his signature turnaround: an arm around my shoulder, a teasing smile. 'Sorry.' A packet of Softmints slipped into my pocket and all forgotten. How might things have been different, if I'd read the runes then?

The thought was severed by the slam of the car door and I was hit with a blast of sterile air conditioning. It was only mid-April, but the country had been bathed in a heatwave, worst in the South West, and my armpits were already sticky from the few minutes I'd been outside. I pressed my head against the leather seatback, tipped my face towards the cold air and let it blow the last of the memory away.

And then we were wending. Quite quickly off the wide A-roads and onto myopic country lanes, hedgerows studded with ferns and cow parsley blinkering our view. Occasionally we'd round a corner and I'd get a glimpse of the sea, flint grey and glistening in the bright sunlight. More occasionally still, the driver would point out places of interest – 'This here's known as the Roseland Heritage Coast', 'That way's Veryan, known for its thatched houses' – but mostly we were silent, the hum of the engine and intermittent scrape of gorse against the car our only soundtrack.

Eventually we pulled into a long gravel drive curving

past a pair of floral filigreed iron gates that whined on their hinges as some unseen hand allowed our entrance. We swooped through the carriage driveway and came to a halt on a crunch of gravel under the shadow of Kewney Manor.

To say it was imposing would be an understatement. To say it was large would be stating the obvious. But when I stepped out of that car and stared up at that blank, grey facade for the first time, either of these words would have sufficed more than the only thing I could think to muster.

'Wow.'

'Big, isn't it?' The driver, sliding my case out of the boot and placing it at the foot of the wide stone steps, slipped his hands into his pockets and came to stand beside me. 'One of the finest in the area.' When I said nothing, he found a mint, crunched it loudly against his back teeth and made for the driver's seat. 'Well, good luck,' he said with an awkward tip of his cap. And he was gone.

I turned towards the house, wondering what the etiquette was for using the heavy, lion-headed door knocker, whether there was some servant's entrance I would be expected to use, when the door was suddenly pulled open and a woman's face appeared.

'Darling!' she called, opening the door fully to reveal a cornflower-blue dress, spotlessly pressed; quilted, patent-toed ballerinas. An intricate jewelled chain, with multicoloured gemstones set to look like a floral wreath, was draped around her collar. 'You made it at last! You must be exhausted.'

Laurie.

She was different, I thought, than she had appeared on screen. A certain pinchedness in her expression that I hadn't detected through the blur. The copper hair that had spilled about her shoulders in waves was now pulled into a tight chignon, a hint of shadow falling across her freckled face and limpid grey eyes. But her wide mouth was the same, and when those thin, dark rose lips pulled back into an easy smile, and she stretched open her arms, encouraged me into a hug, I felt the same rush of warmth towards her I remembered so well.

'Welcome, welcome. We're so happy that you made it.'

'So am I.'

Nick's face that night, his mottled anger. The sound of a chair crashing. The rhythm of my pulse beneath the press of his fingertips.

I wanted to press my palms against my ears, but instead I swallowed the memory down, arranged my features into a smile.

I meant it.

'Right, shall I give you "the tour"?'

I took her hand more gratefully than she realized, allowed her to propel me along, trying to keep up with her restless energy as she gave me a breathless history of Kewney and its surroundings.

'It was first mentioned in the Domesday Book,' she pitched, leading me through the door and into what I would come to learn was the Great Hall. 'Not this exact house, of course. That was rebuilt in the eighteenth century.' Our footsteps clipped on the chequerboard floor as we passed over it, the sound echoing around the high ceilings and up the scrolled double staircase. 'That's a repro,' she whispered, impish, as she watched me appraising the tall suit of armour that held pride of place opposite the door. 'But he fits in so well. His name's Steve.' At that she stopped, gave him a sharp salute. 'Keep up the good work, Steve.'

She motioned to move on, but then paused, head tilting as she inspected the suit.

'Hmm.' Her smile wrinkled. With the tips of her middle finger and thumb, she took Steve's hand in hers, moved it a quarter of an inch to the left. 'Better,' she pronounced, with a nod of her head. And then we were off.

We snaked through the ground floor, Laurie keeping up a running commentary, as seamlessly as though she had learned it by rote.

'This is the library,' she announced, leading me into a room as big as my flat in Brixton, packed floor to ceiling with books, and complete with a sliding ladder like the one Angela Lansbury uses in *Bedknobs and Broomsticks*. 'There's a secret door here that leads into the billiard room.' She gave a row of books a little push, and my eyes widened as the section gave way, revealed an entrance. 'Evelyn Waugh was staying here when they installed it.' She selected a book off the shelf, passed it to me as she ducked through. 'He thought it would be funny if they filled the shelves with books with fake titles.' She raised an eyebrow at me as I fingered the spine, *Lady Agatha's Surprise*, by Abum Hole. 'I like to think the current Rowes are a little less puerile.'

We passed through the parlour, drawing room, formal dining room, rooms I didn't know even existed outside a game of Cluedo, a dizzying labyrinth of pastel silks and hand-painted wallpaper and intricately detailed wood, such that when we finally reached the kitchen, sleek and modern with shiny black appliances, and veined marble surfaces, I was taken by surprise.

'The living rooms were one thing,' Laurie explained, seeing me blink, 'but I put my foot down on the kitchen and bathrooms. There's only so much Regency living I could take. Charles insisted on the Aga, drain on utilities that it is, because it was his grandmother's, but everything else is firmly twenty-first century. Perrier?' She yanked open the doors of a vast American-style fridge, and before I could make the mental leap in conversation, a cold green bottle was placed into my hands, the exterior already sweating as it made contact with the atmosphere.

I heard more about Charles as we continued the tour. She said that they'd met whilst she was an art student in Boston – now my ear tuned to the softened consonants I had passed off as Cornish. He'd come to America to showcase the family collection of gothic carved ivory. I didn't quite catch how she explained it, lost in the cross-continental meanings of 'school', and 'college', as she loosely described, but as part of her course she was invited to lunch with him, and he, ten years older and fresh from five years' banking in Hong Kong, swept her off her feet.

'He went back to England but we kept in touch – we just couldn't forget one another,' she added wistfully. 'Eventually I moved over, and we got married. I was twenty-three, and Charles . . . Charles was –' she sighed deeply, her face lighting up in a way that gave me a glimpse of what a teenaged Laurie must have been like '– well, you'll see what Charles is like, soon enough.'

Laurie ended the tour in my room, where some invisible caretaker had already placed my suitcase, unzipped, on a steamer trunk at the foot of the four-poster bed I couldn't quite believe would be mine, complete with decorative drapes tied back with braided gold rope. I tried to process the strangeness of it all – the long journey; the shock of leaving concrete London for Cornwall's wild fields and sea air; the grand beauty of the house – but before I could catch my breath, the children came home, barrelling off the school bus in a flurry of discarded backpacks and kicked-off shoes.

I helped her oversee their homework and prepare their dinner, both tasks I would be taking over the next day, shadowing her as she glided through the kitchen, plucking out pots and pans and rice and vegetables in a seamless ballet. And then it was bath-time, each of them chatting non-stop, firing questions at me nineteen to the dozen that I tried to answer as truthfully as I could without mentioning Nick. Wrestling each of them into pyjamas and persuading them to brush their teeth; an endless parade of fetching glasses of water and last-minute trips to the toilet and, 'Not that book, a different one,' before they would entertain the idea of sleep.

'Would you care to join us for dinner?' Laurie asked, once duvets had been tucked, a maternal hand raked softly through hair and bedroom doors firmly shut. 'Charles works late – he keeps an office in the village – so we tend to eat once he gets back.'

'I . . . actually, would you mind if I went to bed?' As intrigued as I was to meet the remaining member of the Rowe family, as soon I stepped into the child-free silence of the main staircase I found myself overwhelmed with tiredness, a dull ringing in my ear signalling the beginnings of a headache.

'How silly of me!' Laurie clapped a hand to her throat. 'You must be exhausted. Please, go to your room and get settled in. Is there something I can bring you up? A snack?'

I shook my head. 'Nothing, thank you. I'll be fine.'

'In that case, rest well.' She reached for my arm, squeezed. 'Oh – and I'm so sorry, but if you need to let anyone know you've made it safely, you're probably best to wait until the morning. The cell reception here is patchy at best, and the only good Wi-Fi signal is in Charles's study, but he doesn't really like you disturbing his things.' She gave me an apologetic grimace. 'That's why I said on our call that this position is best suited for people without a whirling social life. Trying to keep in touch can get quite frustrating, quite quickly.'

I hesitated, then gave a small shrug. 'That suits me. I have no one to call.'

She regarded me carefully for a moment, and I wondered if I had said the wrong thing. But then her expression changed, and she gave me a wink. 'There, you see: I knew you'd be a perfect fit. You'll be part of the family before you realize it.'

Alone with the silence at last, I collapsed into bed the moment I entered the room, eschewing all thoughts of unpacking until the morning. My heavy sleep was punctuated with flashes from the day – the whizz of scenery from the train carriage, the children's laughter, glimpses of the sea.

Still, despite the deepness with which I slept, I couldn't fend off the ragged thoughts of Nick that made me toss and turn, my breathing tight. At one point I was roused fully, sure I had been woken by the sound of the bedroom door clicking shut. I sprang from the bed and prised open the door, convinced that it was over, of who I would see on the other side.

But the corridor was empty, the air still. And by the time I had assured myself it was nothing more than the old house settling, that my fears were unfounded, sleep claimed me completely.

3

I had discovered a digital clock on the bedside table, a relic of the nineties, which I'd managed to get working. But when it went off the following morning, the sound was so unfamiliar, so alarming – a staccato, insistent beep – that I was shocked into wakefulness, momentarily forgetting where I was.

But one look at the carved posts that cornered my bed, at the leaf-patterned eiderdown that had slipped off in the night and now lay rumpled on the floor beside me, and my fingers relaxed their grip on the bedsheets. I was really here. I had made it.

I went over to the windows and pulled open the curtains, thick, damasked things plunging the room into daylight. Heaved up the sash to stick my head into the raw morning air, inhaling freshness.

The house was only two floors, but the double-height ceilings and vast windows afforded me soaring views across the grounds, and, beyond that, the sea. Craning my neck, I tried to situate myself, only to find that there was very little to see except for land and water: no hugger-mugger neighbours, no busy roads; little else save a few terracotta peaks across the bay to suggest the makings of a village.

In the distance, church bells clanged the hour. A caw of seagulls. And then nothing.

I thought of our old flat. The wheeze of the 137 bus as it stopped two doors down. Cars beeping, the drivers fisting the horn until whatever irritant they perceived had passed. Shops unshuttering. Clubbers, still in last night's heels, singing tunelessly on their way to the chicken shop. Nick snoring himself awake, and the feel of his hand on the small of my back as I debated whether I could pretend to still be asleep.

The hate on his face when I told him I was leaving.

I drank in the silence, turned my face to the light.

I had expected that I would find Laurie in the kitchen as I followed the children down for breakfast, but the room was empty, no sign on the surfaces of a previous presence.

'It's breakfast and weekday supper in the kitchen, weekend meals in the breakfast room, and Sunday lunch in the formal dining room, unless there's guests and then it all changes.' Bess, eight and already remarkably self-assured, had guided me when I had naively asked if they liked to have breakfast in front of the television. I wished I'd brought a paper and pen. 'Please don't mix them up. Mummy always hated it when . . . ow, my *foot*, William,' she had said, breaking off as William launched himself from the bottom three steps directly into her.

'When what?' I had called after her, but the moment was lost in a flurry of childish shrieks.

In the kitchen, I got the children settled on the leather bar stools that surrounded the marble-topped island unit, busied myself with trying to remember where to find pots and pans and pantry, as I tried to keep up with their voracious requests: two different kinds of toast, specific ratios of cereal to milk, a fried egg for William, only accepted on the second try after the first one split. I had just located the kettle and was settling onto a third stool with a mug of tea when the door opened, and a man appeared.

'Daddy!' the children chorused, doing the detective work for me. They slid from their stools, rushed to greet him, and he waded fully into the room with a child at each leg.

'Careful, William, you're getting butter on my trousers.' And then, softening. 'Give us a bite and we'll call it even.' He bent down, and I heard the crunch of toast between teeth before he stood up, faced me directly and said plainly, 'Hi.'

Somehow, after Laurie's storytelling yesterday, my brain had formed an image of Charles that was now being rapidly dismantled. Because the man before me was nothing like the bookish, formal, middle-aged father I had envisaged. For one thing, although I knew he must be over fifty – Laurie said in passing she was in her forties, he ten years older – he looked nowhere near how, with the folly of youth, I'd envisaged a fifty-year-old man to look. He wore jeans – not the suit and tie I had fictionally clothed him in – albeit good ones, dark and smoothly fitting, and a linen shirt with a fine red ticking stripe, the cuffs rolled up to the elbows. His face was darkly tanned, with a square jaw, long, aquiline nose and distinctly full lips, framed by a head of the dark curls I had rightly predicted he had passed down to his off-spring. At a certain angle, he was almost pretty.

'Hi,' I said in return. And then, realizing my station, stood, surreptitiously brushing crumbs from my skirt. Held out my hand. 'Sorry, I didn't get a chance to intro-duce myself last night. I'm Lily, the new nanny.'

For some reason I felt prompted to add, 'How do you do?', an expression I had never used and felt ridiculous saying. And he could tell, I knew; I saw the chuckle in his eyes, as he took my outstretched hand and said, 'I assumed that was the case. Either that or a kidnapper, and I thought the latter probably wouldn't have taken the risk of making them breakfast first.'

I laughed, shyly, and was suddenly struck by my new-ness, unsure of protocol – should I offer to make him coffee, breakfast?

Before I could decide a course of action, a loud trill reverberated through the house, startling me.

'The gates,' Charles offered, helpfully.

When I looked at the clock on the microwave oven, I saw that it was five to eight, the time the minibus arrived to take Bess and William to school.

'Shit,' I hissed. Then reddened. 'Sorry.' Gathered the plates and cutlery into the sink, chivvied the children into the hall to find shoes and bags, stormed up the stairs to get the swimming kit Bess had forgotten, thrusted it through the open doors of the bus seconds before it rolled out of the gate.

When I returned to the kitchen, it was empty. Surfaces wiped. Plates and cutlery in the dishwasher.

I didn't see Charles for the rest of the day.

It was strange, my first full day at Kewney. Mentally, I had been aware that Bess and William would be in school for another month or so yet, that my job would be relegated to weekends, mornings, and after school care; but that hadn't quite prepared me for the long stretch of daylight in between, the nothingness of feeling I should be doing something useful but not quite knowing what that was.

I unpacked my things, slipping clothes onto the hangers in the deep mahogany wardrobe, tucking the empty case under the bed. I padded to the children's rooms, hoping to be of some use there, but not a thing was out of place in Bess's, and I opened William's door to find a woman with grey hair and a black mole above her lip hovering over his things.

I shrieked, making the woman leap up in surprise, and then noticed the navy cleaning overall she was wearing, the vacuum cleaner at her side.

'So sorry,' I apologized when we were both calm. 'I didn't expect to find anyone in here. I'm Lily, the new nanny.'

She appraised me, the mole moving as her eyes twitched across my face.

'No English.'

And then she turned back to her work.

I hovered in my room, idly toggling the data on and off my phone in the hope of inciting some signal, but

Laurie was right: any scrap of service disappeared after a second; and besides, did I really want to see who might have called?

When I heard the church bells chiming one o'clock, I swung myself from the bed and found the kitchen, hoping I might encounter some activity there, but once again it was empty. Laurie hadn't mentioned a job, so unless she had managed to slip seamlessly in and out of the house all day, I supposed her to be somewhere in it. How bizarre, to live in a house where you had absolutely no clue whether people were coming or going.

My stomach growled. I hadn't eaten anything since the train journey yesterday, but it felt odd, rooting around in the kitchen fridge. Laurie had insisted though, hadn't she? 'Treat this place like your home!'

I made myself a cheese and tomato sandwich gingerly, washing and drying the knife and cutting board to escape detection, and then, judging the day to be clear enough, decided to take it outside.

Remembering the pair of French doors in the parlour, I made my way to the other side of the house. Balancing my plate and glass of water carefully, I fiddled with the handles of the closed parlour door, edging one down with an elbow, then turning to nudge the doors open fully with my back. When I turned around, there was Laurie.

She had her back to me, giving me the advantage of being able to observe her undetected, and I saw that she was painting; an easel was set up in the middle of the room, upon which rested a huge canvas, easily five feet in width. Her hair was pulled into a messy bun, half of it already escaping in trails down her back, and she was wearing a turquoise silk kimono, patterned across the back with a great peacock motif whose feathers fluttered when she moved an arm. She was barefoot, I saw, her feet twisting into the white drop cloth laid under the canvas and around the clutter of paint pots and turpentine and brushes. There was a rhythm to her movements, the way she threaded, seamlessly, around the debris, her body flowing, almost trance-like, with each stroke of the brush.

A small sofa, gold-edged and patterned in a trailing William Morris print, was jerked out of position beside the set-up. On it rested a coffee cup and the discarded peel of an orange, the edges drying and curled. From the little I knew of Laurie, this seemed uncharacteristically uncouth, a testament to her flow.

From the corner of the room all I could see of the canvas was blue, but when I got closer, I saw it was a landscape: the sky meeting the sea, swirls of aquamarine and periwinkle and deep indigo. The sky she was depicting seemed calm; pale and almost iridescent, with big fluffy clouds like in a children's picture book; in contrast the sea was churned up, peaks of white raked into the blue.

'Laurie.' I stepped fully into the room, speaking softly so as not to scare her. And then when she didn't answer, louder, 'Excuse me, Laurie?'

Nothing. I came towards her, touched her gently on the arm, and at that she flinched, turned around, and I realized that she had been wearing headphones, tiny wireless pods that she removed from her ears as she smiled at me.

'Lily! Sorry, I was in my own world.' She held the pods in her hand, and I recognized the muffled guitar strings of Fleetwood Mac's 'The Chain' twanging from her closed palm.

'I didn't know you were an artist?'

She wiped her brush on a rag which she tossed into the metal bin at her feet, and then, resting the brush on the easel, she retied the cord of her kimono and took a step back, standing beside me to appraise the work.

'Artist is a strong word for it.' She wiped the back of her wrist across her forehead, dislodging a stray hair but leaving in its place a streak of steel blue, almost the same colour as her eyes. 'I enjoy painting. I always have. There's a small gallery in Truro that displays my work. There's quite the market in seascapes for second homes and holiday lets, as you can imagine. They barely make more than the canvas they're painted on, but I guess that's not the point.'

'It's beautiful,' I said. And it was. There was something chilling about it, the discord between the two states, the way the sea crashed angrily into the sky, marring its pretty perfection. But there was something thrilling about it too; 'awesome', in the literal sense, the scale of it. Elemental. It sent a shiver up my spine. 'My mum was an artist,' I said softly. 'Well, an illustrator. She drew greeting cards. Not the comedy cartoon ones you see now, but beautiful ones, for children. She was working on a book, too, before.' I felt her eyes on me, seeking clarity. 'She died when I was eight.'

I swallowed the word, as I always did when I had to tell someone new, even though it was nearly twenty years ago now, the initial shock of pain dulled to a more frequent numbness. She used to draw me, too, in idle moments; pen-and-paper renditions of my mouth half-agape as I watched TV, or my hair spilling across the kitchen table as I bent over my homework. I could still picture her, pen in hand, adding the collar to my school uniform. It was what I was wearing the day they told me; I'll always remember the scratch of the sofa against my legs, bare beneath my chequered summer dress, as my world shifted. 'Mummy's very poorly.' Nan's eyes red, as she took one of my hands beneath hers. Dad's avoiding mine.

'I'm so sorry, Lily.' Laurie reached out to touch my upper arm. Her palm was warm, the skin smooth. 'It is so hard to lose a mother that young. I'm not close to my parents, but I can only imagine how distressing it must have been. I'm here if you ever want to talk. I want you to think of me as your friend.'

I wanted to brush her off, fold in on myself like I was used to doing when I mentioned Mum, but the look she gave me wasn't one of pity, but of solidarity, and I found myself nodding back.

'Thank you . . . I will.'

She noticed my lunch then, offered to keep me company. Guided me through the French doors and out onto the lawns, where a solid wooden dining table was set up on the flagstones, offering views of the orchard, where once upon a time, she told me, there had been a working cider press. A jasmine plant crept up the wall behind us, the white flowers in thick bloom, and the sweet scent clung to the air around us, perfecting the country idyll.

We talked, casually at first, about the gardens, their layout and design, the path I would take if I wanted to go down to the beach. She told me titbits about the children, their life in Kewney, but although she touched upon her own childhood in Boston, she seemed to steer clear of anything too personal, and it didn't feel right to press. In return I described Nan and Grandad's, where I'd eventually moved permanently: blackberry picking and homemade pies. Later, London, for uni, how like so many people, after I graduated I just . . . stayed.

She was a good conversationalist. Asking questions when pertinent. Knowing when to stay silent, listen. I felt myself relaxing in her company. And somehow, despite every intention to the contrary, I found myself telling her about Nick – not all of it, of course – but enough to offer some hint of colour as to how I had found myself at Kewney.

His name stuck to the roof of my mouth like peanut butter.

'You lose who you are, in a relationship like that,' she mused. 'Sometimes you have to take yourself to the darkest of places, to try and find yourself again.'

I looked up, struck by her clarity. Had I said too much?

But Laurie seemed lost in her own thoughts, staring out across the fields to where the sky met sea.

'Tell me what it was like, moving here?' I asked, using her silence to move the conversation on.

Thankfully, she took the bait.

She described seeing Kewney for the first time, when Charles's parents were still living in it: 'I thought I was walking into the pages of a novel.' How strange she had found it when they took ownership of it themselves.

'I didn't know how I'd ever get used to it. So many rooms to keep tidy, so much history to keep on top of – especially in a place like this, where you're considered an outsider if your family doesn't go five generations back. And then there was the silence. The lack of people or places to go unless you planned for it. Boston wasn't exactly Manhattan, but you still bumped into your neighbour. Charles's mother, Nancy, didn't exactly warm to me, but she kept telling me that once we had children I wouldn't have a chance to sit still. But then that took a while, and Charles was always off . . .' She stopped herself before she finished the thought, shook her head. 'Anyway, it was years before I thought of Kewney as my home.'

Before I had a chance to press her on it, she rose, her chair scraping loudly against the stone tiles.

'I should probably get back to my painting. You don't mind, do you? Only, I don't like to lose the rhythm for too long when I'm in the zone.'

'No, no, please go ahead.' I stood, gathering my empty cup and plate. 'I imagine the children will be back from school soon. I should start getting something ready for their dinner.'

I half phrased it as a question, but she didn't reply, instead leading the way back through the French doors, leaving them open for me to follow. I hesitated, unsure whether I should say goodbye or not, but when I stepped inside, she was already putting her headphones in, picking up her brush. I crossed the room and opened the door to leave the parlour, my hand resting on the scrolled brass door handle, turned to look at her one more time before I left.

She was staring at the painting with her arms by her sides, her stance wide, like a boxer about to throw a punch. She held her brush aloft, twisted it so the handle pointed down, and drew her arm back with such force I thought she would rend the canvas in two. I watched, unable to look away, but at the last minute she paused, her arm dropping to her side, blue paint dripping from the brush and onto her bare foot like a tear.

4

I didn't see Laurie again until the children were just sitting down to dinner. Her manner seemed light, whatever
cloud had settled on her after our talk vanished, and she
had changed out of her kimono and into a crisp white
shirt and full skirt in a vibrant paisley print, both wrists
encircled with heavy, beaded bracelets that jangled as she
moved.

'Darlings! How was school?' she called as she breezed
into the kitchen, pulling each child into her chest, and
running her fingers through their hair, listening patiently
as they escalated into an excited burble.

'Oh, you're not going to have dinner now, are you?'
she asked me when the children had finally settled back
down.

I looked at the portion of lasagne in front of me, fork
poised.

'I thought it would make it easier if I ate with Bess
and William? I don't want to be in Mr Rowe's and your
way?'

'Don't be silly.' She gave a little pout, her features
morphing prettily. 'Charles and I are sick of each other's
company. It would be a delight to have you join us.'

I hesitated, unsure. 'I don't want to waste all this
food . . . ?'

'Nonsense.' Suddenly she was all motion, taking my

plate over to the sideboard, pulling out silver foil, covering it. 'It'll keep for a day at least. You can have it for lunch tomorrow. I've ordered some fantastic steaks from the butcher. Go on . . . say yes?'

I acquiesced, getting the feeling I was fighting a losing battle, and when I clicked the door to Bess's room shut an hour later, arms full of dirty laundry, Laurie was waiting for me, hovering in the hall.

'I thought it might be fun to dress up. Treat tonight as a sort of celebration of your arrival.'

'Oh?'

I tried shake the feeling I was being accosted as she pulled the clothes from me, placed them in a heap by the door. 'Leave those here – the cleaner can sort them out in the morning. Indulge me, will you?'

I took the hand she stretched out for me, allowed her to lead me through the corridor and over to the east wing of the house, where she and Charles had their rooms, into what was obviously her dressing room – panelled wardrobes in a delicate robin's egg blue, an ornate, skirted dressing table overlooking the window. It smelled strongly of her – pretty pink florals intermixed with something lusher, muskier; vanilla and oak. I hadn't consciously detected it before, but now I could smell it on her skin as she placed her hands on my shoulders, moving me to the stool in front of the dresser, and realized how fitting a scent it was for how I was just beginning to perceive her: the delicate top notes of femininity only a part of her complex nature.

'I was sorting out some clothes earlier for the charity

pile and I found a dress that I thought would look so lovely on you. Indulge me: will you try it on?'

Her voice was softer in here, as if the womb-like space necessitated a certain sort of hushed tone.

'I . . . of course . . .' I found myself adjusting to it too, speaking sotto voce as I turned to watch her take an item down from a cane folding screen.

The dress was rose pink, a gauzy chiffon material patterned with a ditzy floral print and intricate covered buttons. Not overtly formal but certainly more so than the jeans and T-shirt I was currently sporting.

'I don't usually wear a lot of pink . . .' I stared at the dress, already envisaging myself tripping down the stairs and ripping a hole in it.

'Oh, go on,' she coaxed, and then, a little firmer, 'just try it. I promise if you don't like it you can wear whatever you like. It's just a bit of fun.'

She held it out to me, and I slipped behind the screen, pulling my T-shirt off and the dress over my head as I shimmied out of my jeans. The dress fell to my midcalves, with a sweetheart neckline and banded, puffed sleeves that stopped a couple of inches above my elbow. I fumbled with the buttons, growing hot from the stress of how fiddly they were, knowing Laurie was waiting for me on the other side, desperate not to rip anything in the proceedings.

Dressed, I stepped out from behind the screen, unsure how to hold myself, arms stiff. But when I turned to her, Laurie beamed, beckoned me to the full-length mirror beside the dressing table.

'See, it's perfect on you.'

She was right. The dusty rose highlighted the paleness of my skin, enhanced its contrast with my dark hair and eyes, the cut elongating my body, skimming my hips and nipping in at the waist.

'What do you think? How does it make you feel?'

I eyed my reflection. 'Good . . . I guess . . . ?' It had been a long time since I'd had cause to dress up.

She smiled, obviously pleased with herself. 'Come on. Now for the rest.'

She touched her hand to the small of my back, guiding me to the dressing table and releasing the band from my haphazard ponytail as I sat. I gave over to her, watching her work, smoothing my messy waves with her fingertips, diligently selecting blusher, mascara, lip gloss to dab, apply, sweep. It was the kind of scene I could have imagined with my own mother, and I wondered if our conversation earlier had tugged at Laurie's maternal core, had prompted this occasion.

'Gorgeous, see?' she whispered, looking at my reflection over my shoulder. 'And just in time for dinner.'

We walked into the kitchen to the melody of Frank Ocean playing over the surround sound, a deep, syncopated beat. Charles was standing over a sizzling pan, a chopping board of sliced mushrooms in his open palm. The smell of butter clung to the air.

'Ah, the chef,' Laurie greeted him, sashaying easily past the island unit's sharp corners to plant a kiss on his cheek. 'Smells delicious.'

'Mushrooms, cream, truffle . . . what's not to like.' He shrugged, wiped his forehead with the back of his hand as he added the mushrooms and the pan exploded with steam, snaked the same hand around her waist to give her a kiss in return.

He had changed, too, since that morning – a baby-pink shirt with the cuffs rolled to the elbows, navy fitted chino shorts – and was freshly shaven, his hair still wet from the shower. They looked so good together, this handsome couple in their designer kitchen; like watching people on TV. I hovered in the doorway, wondering if I had made a mistake, agreeing to dinner, when Charles looked up from the pan, turned his head towards me.

'Ah, the guest of honour. Laurie, there's a bottle of Dom in the wine fridge. Let's crack it open.'

Before I could offer to help, she was already moving, pulling down flutes and removing a dark-green bottle with a gold shield-shaped label from the second fridge I'd only just noticed, filled top to bottom with bottles. A whole fridge, just for wine.

We clinked, and I pressed the glass to my lips, tonguing the bubbles as a memory surfaced on them.

I had been drinking champagne the night I met Nick. Not like this, cold and crisp, but the too-warm, piss-yellow stuff, downed from thin plastic glasses at a house party. He'd come up with some terrible excuse for talking to me, deliberately addressing me with the wrong name, pretending he thought I was someone he knew. I called him out on it, even as he made a great show of continuing the charade, but by the time he admitted it our introduction had been made, the first seed sown.

He was like that, Nick, fond of playing the part. Consummate funny man. As long as he was the one making the joke.

'*Don't make me laugh.*' The sound of his voice, that last night, hoarse with rage. '*You won't leave me: you're a fucking joke.*' Later, the argument not forgotten. '*I'll find you, if you ever try to leave. You know that, right? Wherever you go, you'll never get away from me.*'

Suddenly the champagne smelled like vomit. My stomach turned.

'Don't you think, Lily?'

I saw Laurie looking to me, waiting for an answer.

'Sorry?' I shook my head, trying to shake the shadow of Nick's words away.

'I said that, when you drink Dom Pérignon, it makes you realize that all other champagnes are just a poor imitation; that this is what champagne should actually have tasted like all along.'

'Oh . . .' I swirled the glass. 'Well, to be quite honest with you, I know absolutely nothing about champagne. I'm just glad this has bubbles in it, so I know what it is.'

They both laughed, but it was a friendly, warm laugh, not Nick's slow sneer of derision. I felt myself relaxing, my muscles loosening as I drank thirstily, the smell vanishing, and with it, Nick's threat.

Champagne fizzed through my system.

'Well, if you want a lesson, that's one thing I can help with.' Charles topped up my glass, spinning the bottle away just before the bubbles foamed over the top. 'I consider myself a bit of a wine nerd.'

He held out the near-empty bottle to me, and I took it, fingers grazing his.

'Dom Pérignon is a vintage-only champagne.' He pointed to the looping black letters on the bottle:

Vintage 2006. 'A lot of people assume that vintage means the champagne is old, but actually it means that the grapes were all picked in a single year. Other houses only produce a vintage every three or four years and create a blend in between, but with Dom, if the grapes aren't good enough, they produce nothing. They like things to be the very best. And I like that about them.'

He was leaning over me, elbow lightly touching my upper arm, so I could smell the cologne on the nape of his neck, spices and wood, the cooking scents that clung to his shirt and hair.

'Honey, you're boring the poor girl.'

'Sorry.' Charles stepped back, gave me an abashed smile. 'I can't help myself when I get carried away.'

'The mushrooms are burning,' Laurie added, draining her glass.

He raised his glass to her. 'In that case, bring on the steak.'

I had to keep reminding myself over dinner that I was the Rowes' employee, and not their guest. They were easy hosts, the conversation always fluid, an even mix of asking questions about me and sharing stories of their own, never putting me on the spot or leaving me out. Laurie was kind, keen to point out my few accomplishments to Charles, relaying the details of my History degree, the points where it intersected Charles's own interests; highlighting my paltry Spanish GCSE when he mentioned a year spent living in Madrid. Charles made an excellent show of being interested, but I couldn't help feeling awkward, almost as if Laurie were trying to justify her reasons for hiring me, proving me to be 'the perfect find'.

We drank wine, pale-red stuff which tasted vegetal, like licking a forest floor, and then something deeper, almost spicy, finishing off with a sweet and sticky Spanish sherry that Laurie, to Charles's mock horror, insisted on pouring over raisin-studded vanilla ice cream. I never knew people ate like this – drank like this – within their own homes.

When I rose, later, much later, I found myself swaying, all the wine and food sloshing in my stomach. I hiccupped; made a too-late attempt to hide it; joined in their laughter.

'Looks like we may have rolled out the welcome wagon a little too strongly.' Laurie's hand on my back, tender. 'Let me fetch you a jug of water to take upstairs.'

It was later, much later still, after I had dragged myself to the bathroom to remove my make-up, hung the dress carefully in my wardrobe and was drifting to sleep, that a crash from the depths of the house made me rise up, my ears prick to attention.

I waited ten breaths, recited the nine times table . . . nine, eighteen, twenty-seven . . . before lifting the covers, padding softly towards the top of the stairs.

'Laurie!' Charles was calling, his voice echoing through the open corridors downstairs. 'Laurie, come back here.'

'Stay away from me.' A crash, the sound of glass breaking, followed by a cry, mottled pain and anger, the culprit unclear. I turned to my right, half expecting the children to emerge, but their rooms were buried in the west wing, far from the noise below.

'Just leave me be.' Laurie's voice was getting louder now, and I heard the quickening of her tread across the floor. When I saw her emerge into the Great Hall, I retreated to my room, face pressed against the cool wood of the closed bedroom door.

Footsteps sounded on the staircase. A second pair followed. A door closed in the distance. Silence.

When I was almost certain my path would be clear, I opened the door. Finding the corridors empty, I crept down to the floor below.

The kitchen was clear, lights off. Moonlight pooled from the bay window, casting its lemony light across the gleaming surfaces.

On the floor, in the middle, where no accidental hand of God could have let it roll, the champagne bottle lay, its neck shattered in two.

I left without determining if the dark spots beside it were blood.

5

The bottle was gone when I came down the next morning, and the memory of it ebbed as the days continued, washed away like a name written on the shoreline.

The hours in between Bess and William's departure to and arrival from school stretched out, but I organized myself into a new rhythm, one that fitted more serenely with the verdant-green views, the distance shushing of the Celtic sea.

It seemed so easy, out there on the clifftops of Kewney, to forget London, all that had happened there; and as the days rolled on, the feeling of looking over my shoulder, of the arrival of an unwelcome visitor, slowly began to fade.

Nevertheless, I set out to prove myself indispensable to Laurie and Charles, my genuine, hardwired need to please coupled with a driving fear of what would happen if they were to let me go. Each morning I would make sure to clear up after the children had left, removing any trace of my own laundry or dishes. When I was satisfied, I would wander through the gardens and down to the path Laurie had pointed out that first day, which snaked down the cliffside, arriving at the horseshoe bay below. Despite the heatwave, the sea was far too cold to swim in, but I would roll up my jeans and paddle in the shallows, toes succumbing to the water's burning numbness, watching tiny crabs skitter across the stones, and slipping shells into my pockets that I would later try to identify using the hefty coffee table books in the parlour – flat periwinkle, cowrie, dog whelk. Sometimes I would join Laurie as she painted, enjoying the lilt of our idle chatter as she mixed colours, selected brushes, but I would learn to judge her mood carefully, understand exactly when she sought company, and when she would rather be left alone.

On certain days she would have groups of women to the house – fundraisers from this or that charity she was on the board of, other mothers from school; similarly elegant and well-put-together women who infused the house with chatter and perfume.

On those days, I would help Laurie set up for lunch, always on the same theme: an array of multicoloured salads, new potatoes, a whole side of cold poached salmon or a leg of ham; at least three different cakes. It was all delivered by a caterer first thing.

'Everyone always uses Sardo's to cater these things.' I couldn't help but detect a note of irritation in her voice. 'I once asked Nancy why we couldn't just hire a cook, but apparently it's not "the done thing" around here. *"Sardo's has been around for generations."'* She affected a high-pitched tone which I presumed to be an unflattering depiction of her mother-in-law. 'People can be quite stuck in their ways around here.'

Nevertheless, she would spend hours before the guests arrived artfully arranging the food on toile-patterned serving dishes in the kitchen, layering china plates with delicate scalloped napkins, her face set with tension. The first time, I lingered, mindlessly rearranging the kitchen knives in the big wooden block that sat in the centre of the island unit as I listened to the guests arriving and chattering in the garden, when a woman, tall and thin with a dark-brown plait that betrayed streaks of grey at the temple, opened one of the doors and stepped inside.

'Just grabbing a glass of water,' she called back to the party as the door closed behind her. 'No, no, don't worry, I'll help myself. Oh.' And then stopped herself, one hand poised on the island unit, taking me in. 'I didn't know Laurie had hired a maid.'

'Oh, no, sorry.' I replaced the cutlery on the counter. 'I'm Lily. The nanny. I was just lending a hand.'

'The new nanny?' She quirked an eyebrow. I performed an uncomfortable half-nod, half-bow. I didn't like the way her eyes crawled over me, couldn't help a lingering fear that somehow she knew about Nick. 'I wonder how *you'll* turn out.' I opened my mouth, wanting to extract from her what she meant by the emphasis, but before I could muster any sort of response she stalked past the display of food, running her finger along the rim of one of the platters. 'She does try so hard to make an effort, doesn't she?'

Leaving no doubt as to whether the question was rhetorical, she turned on her heels and left. It was only after I had made myself scarce that I realized she'd forgotten the glass of water.

After that, I decided I would keep to myself when Laurie had guests, finding refuge in the cool, sun-shunned walls of the library, whose shelves I was making my way through.

One day, towards the end of my second or third week,

I lazed in there on the chaise longue, leafing through a green leather-bound copy of *Jamaica Inn*. I'd only read *Rebecca*, once – an ill-fated trip to Venice where Nick, annoyed by my split attention, ripped the book from my hands and threw it into the canal – but the library had a complete collection of Du Maurier, and in some ways I imagined that working my way through it was a way of taking back control.

The sound of the door creaking made me look up, my heart beat irregularly, as it was still prone to do at a surprise encounter. But then I saw Charles's head poking around the door, and immediately righted myself to a more appropriate position.

I had had little interaction with him bar the fleeting mornings I had stumbled upon him in the kitchen – another dinner invitation had not been forthcoming – and I found myself unsure how to act around him, a man who was nominally both my boss and my housemate. His nonchalant, steady manner only made me more flustered.

'Hi – Mr Rowe.' Heat flushed through my cheeks as I went suddenly formal, righting myself and putting the book aside. 'Are you looking for Mrs Rowe? She's on the lawn having lunch with the women from the Cornish Estates Association.'

'*Jamaica Inn*.' He stepped fully into the room, looking at the book in my hand. 'That collection was my mother's.'

'Oh?' My hands tensed on the cover. 'I'm sorry, should I have asked . . . ?'

'No, no.' He sat down beside me, reaching across my lap to take the book in his hand, running his palm over the smooth leather. 'She made claims to have nearly married Du Maurier's son – Christian, I think his name was. Although considering he went on to marry a beauty queen, I'd say that's a little far-fetched.' He snorted. 'She said Daphne herself was quite cold, thought she was most probably a lesbian, which, bigot that she was, she obviously despised.' Rolled his eyes. 'To be quite honest, I don't think she ever actually read the books herself, but it would be just like her to have them on display, to give her an excuse to share her dislike when prompted.' His finger looped over the embossed gold lettering on the cover, tracing a thought, and then he shook his head lightly. 'Please call me Charles, by the way. And Laurie would hate it if you thought of her as Mrs Rowe. Besides anything else, it would make *her* think of my mother too.'

I thought he was going to say something else, but he just sat there, looking at the book in his hands.

I swallowed. '. . . Did you want me to let Laurie know you're here?'

He blinked, as though he'd almost forgotten I was there, then turned to face me, and I noticed that his eyes weren't entirely brown, as I had thought, but had little flecks of gold in them, encircling the pupil, like one of the periwinkle shells I'd collected.

'No, no, that's all right. I didn't fancy having lunch at the office, so I thought I'd see if Laurie was free. Perhaps –' he cocked his head '– if you haven't already eaten . . . would you like to have lunch with me instead?'

I looked over at the oak grandfather clock in the

corner of the room. It was one thirty. Late for lunch, but I hadn't wanted to be in the way whilst Laurie was preparing, so I'd avoided the kitchen, figuring I'd just skip it.

I considered Charles's offer. Would it be odd, having lunch with him, just the two of us? Or would it give me the opportunity to get to know him better, in the hope I might feel more at ease with him? There was nothing inherently wrong with accepting his invitation, and yet something about the optics of it gave me cause to pause. But then again, I was living in his house; it was an entirely natural thing to do. And something about Charles intrigued me, made me want to know more. Lord, why was I making this so complicated?

I felt him looking at me, waiting for an answer.

'Well, I do owe you, from dinner, so why don't I make us both something?' I propelled myself up before I had the chance to hesitate. 'Don't get too excited though,' I warned, as we left the library, 'I'm no Nigella.'

Because the day was clear the women had taken their luncheon onto the terrace, the buffet set across linen-blanketed trestle tables, and so I presumed we would have the kitchen to ourselves.

I remembered there was leftover roast chicken in the fridge, so I set about making sandwiches, shredding strips of cold chicken and mixing it with mayonnaise and lemon, a dash of Dijon mustard, adding a layer of sliced tomatoes to lightly toasted white bread. I presented a plate to him with a small flourish.

'Ta-da!'

I took a seat opposite him on the island unit, elbows resting on the cool marble surface, fiddling with the corners of my crusts as I waited for him to take a bite, willing him to like it. I had quickly tuned to the fact that Charles didn't offer praise lightly, which reflexively made my desire to earn it acute.

'It's good!' he pronounced, finally, through a full mouth. 'Don't do those culinary skills down.'

'Thank you.' I felt myself easing, tried to take a delicate bite, wary of the sandwich collapsing in my hands. 'It's how my nan used to make them. The mustard was her secret ingredient.'

It was one of our things, me and Nan. She'd make a roast chicken on a Sunday night, the nights that Dad would call. The landline in the living room would go – Jesus, that BT ringtone; for years after I'd had a Pavlovian response to it – and my whole body would go rigid as Nan guided me towards it, closed the door behind her with a whispered, 'I'll give you some space.' I never knew what I'd be met with: trite small talk about school and the friends he'd never met, or him crying down the phone whilst I stood silently holding the receiver.

But then there was the smell of roast chicken and potatoes permeating the air from the kitchen, the promise of warmth and comfort and that things would get better, and Nan coming back to take the receiver – 'Well, supper's ready, so we'd best be off.'

Then, on Mondays, the sandwiches.

I had tried to make her roast chicken once for Nick, not long after I'd moved into his house in Peckham. It was Valentine's Day, a day he adamantly refused to celebrate for being 'a commercial, corporate holiday that just lined the pockets of greeting card companies', but he'd been working really hard, his housemates were out, and I knew he finally had the evening off, so I determined to give him a treat. I read a few recipes online, searched my memories for exactly what Nan had done to make it special, but nothing worked out the way I wanted it to: the bird was dry and stuck to the pan, the skin soggy and puckered, not crisp like hers, the onions and rosemary I'd arranged so carefully around it blackened and hard. In the end it didn't matter anyway. I waited for him, but he didn't get home until ten. He'd been out drinking with the junior doctors, returning with his coat dishevelled, scarf askew.

'*Why didn't you tell me you were going out?*' I'd asked as his voice overlapped mine.

'*For fuck's sake, what's that smell?*' And then, spying the Pyrex on the side, '*Are you kidding me? My mum bought me that.*'

'*I'm sorry, I just wanted to do something nice for you. My nan . . .*' I tried to explain – he knew what Nan had meant to me – but he was already stalking across the room, eyes on the pan.

'*It's fucking ruined now.*' It sailed through the air, missing me, but exploding on impact with the wall just beyond my head. '*Dumb cunt.*'

He apologized the next day. He always did, didn't he? Bought me flowers. And a card. A wink in his eye, because he'd got it 50 per cent off.

If I'd stayed, how many more Valentine's Days would it have taken him to hone his aim?

*

'She was obviously a hell of a cook.'

'What?' I felt as though years had passed.

'Your nan. You must have been a very lucky kid.' I felt the warmth pass between us, felt it dilute the memory of Nick.

I smiled. 'She was the best.' Took another bite, feeling my shoulders relax.

He smiled back, eyes crinkling at the corners.

'So, what else do you like to read?'

It turned out Charles was not just an enthusiastic but a voluminous reader. 'The school holidays were long. When you have access to centuries' worth of books, it becomes a sensible pastime, particularly when you were raised by parents who preferred children to be neither seen *nor* heard.' We swapped authors, old and new. Shared a love of Donna Tartt and Dickens, a loathing of Hemingway. The conversation was effortless, flowed. I liked watching the way his face illuminated when he was particularly passionate about a point, how he would lean forward in his chair to listen to you, nod along as you spoke, giving credence to what you were saying before you had even finished saying it.

It made me realize that it was the first time in as long as I could remember that I had been alone with a man who wasn't Nick. And it was empowering, that thought. Maybe this was a sign that I was going to be OK.

I don't know how long Laurie was standing there before I saw her. We'd moved on from books. Charles was telling me about his work: explaining to me about the various pubs and small hotels lining the Cornish coast he played landlord to. He was in the middle of telling me a favourite anecdote – an altercation with a renter trying to deny that she was using her kitchen as a commercial dog kennels ('Every time we heard a bark she'd cough loudly, pretend it was her asthma') – when I threw my head up, laughing, and caught sight of Laurie standing in the doorway.

Her expression was obscure, hitting an odd midpoint between pleased and pissed off. When she saw me looking, she fixed a grin on her face, although when she stepped fully into the room her eyes were cold, almost like that painting of hers: the two halves not quite adding up to a whole.

'Couldn't face another pasty then, Charlie?' She came to him, kissed the top of his head and placed a hand on his shoulder, proprietorial.

'I was actually hoping to have lunch with my wife, but it turned out she was otherwise engaged.' He wrapped an arm around her waist, pulled her close to him, but I definitely detected a layer of frost in his voice.

'Engaged in the preservation of *your* society.' She said it daintily, but I couldn't help but notice the way her fingertips danced idly across the handles in the knife block in front of them.

'Laurie, can I help clear up from your meeting?' I went to stand, misjudged my leap down from the bar stool and knocked it with the back of my ankle, causing it to wobble precariously on its hind legs. Charles caught it with a quick hand before it clattered to the porcelain-tiled floor. 'Sorry,' I stuttered when it was righted, 'let me fetch the plates from outside.'

'Well, time to get back to the office.' Charles gave

Laurie a peck on the cheek, falsely jovial. 'Any excuse to get out of the washing-up, eh?'

She touched a hand to her cheek, as though the kiss had stung.

She was waiting for me when I came back inside, my arms full of plates. Standing by the sink, a finger resting atop the picked chicken carcass. 'Lily, I would appreciate it if you'd ask, before using anything from the fridge up in its entirety.' Heat flushed through me.

'I'm so sorry.'

'Just a small point.' She held her long fingers up, placating. 'I do want you to think of this place as home but please also try to remember the rest of us in it.'

'Absolutely.' I nodded, head down like a schoolchild. 'I'm mortified.'

'Honestly, it's not a big deal.' She stepped on the foot of the pedal bin, tipped the carcass into it. It landed with a chthonic clunk. 'All that hosting's got the better of me. I think I need a lie-down. It would be a wonderful help if you could finish clearing up.'

'Yes, of course, Laurie. You must be exhausted.'

When she looked at me again, the old Laurie was there, sunshine and light.

'Thank you. You're such a great help. I don't know what I'd do without you.'

Later, in bed, the yellow light from my bedside lamp illuminated the open copy of *Jamaica Inn* on my knees that I wasn't reading. I strained my ears, listening for the sound of them below. Fighting, laughing, anything. Why did I feel like I had done something wrong? And why did I feel it was about more than just a leftover chicken?

Nothing. I heard nothing.

I must have dozed off, because when I next stirred the lamp was still on, the book fallen to the floor, sleep-discarded. The time on the bedside clock said it was just past eleven thirty.

I was thirsty. The heat rose in that old house, and on a hot day, as it had been, the air in my bedroom seemed to swell, stale as the inside of a balloon. I roused myself, taking my empty water glass in hand and setting off down the corridor to the bathroom, which fell just before the main staircase.

My fingers were just finding the grooves of the door-knob when I heard the sound of a door shutting in the direction of Laurie and Charles's wing. Not wanting to risk an awkward nightly encounter, I hurriedly pushed open the door, slipped quietly inside. But when I heard the footsteps coming closer, the creak of the wooden stairs underfoot, I eased it back open, peeped out.

Laurie was descending the staircase, dressed in a robe similar to the one she wore whilst painting, this one a soft lavender, edged in peach-coloured lace, blooms of flowers stitched down the arms and back. Her hair was loose, falling down her back in a sheet, undulating as she walked.

She was barefoot – but for the creak of the stairs you wouldn't know she was there – hand skimming the ban-ister as she glided down, and at first I thought she could be sleepwalking, her movements were so even. But when her feet found the ground floor she paused, twisted to look back up the stairs, towards her wing, and I saw that her eyes were lucid, clear. She stood for a moment – still, looking – but whether she was hoping someone would follow or wishing they wouldn't, I couldn't tell, and when no one appeared, she moved towards the front door, opened it and was gone.

Inside the house, I let the bathroom door close fully behind me, exhaled the breath I didn't know I was holding. I filled my water glass, drained it, refilled it, drank again. Listened to the antique pipes creaking in response; the funny groans and sighs of the house settling. I waited, perhaps twenty minutes, my ears tuned to the sound of the front door opening, but Laurie didn't return.

The next morning, she was there as normal, painting in the parlour. It was a new canvas: another seascape, only this one was at dawn, the streamers of clouds lit up with iridescent pinks and greys.

Charles and I didn't have lunch together like that again, and the incident with the leftovers was never mentioned. Like so many things about my early days at Kewney Manor, the event folded into the past, a neat inconsequence that I didn't think – or want – to dwell on.

6

As my days at Kewney Manor stretched first into one week and then two, I enjoyed getting to know my small charges: their idiosyncrasies, what made them tick.

Bess played the role of eldest child to a T, intelligent and headstrong but also earnest, with a consummate dread of being told off. William was the storm to her calm, a bundle of energy who regularly threw himself down the stairs and off the walls, causing me near heart attacks at every turn.

I quickly fell in love with them, protective of both their feelings and their safety – although I was sometimes unnerved by their perceptiveness, that uncanny ability children have for knowing far more than they let on.

'Remember Mummy likes the cupboard doors closed,' Bess would remind me carefully each morning as we left the kitchen after breakfast. I obeyed, already wary of Laurie's particularness, but Bess was so insistent of it that one day I asked why.

'Nina used to leave them open all the time,' William replied. 'But, this one time, Mummy slammed them all, only she didn't know Nina was there, and she accidentally caught Nina's hand in one and – *what?*' William, talking at five hundred miles an hour, juddered to a halt as his sister dug him in the ribs.

'What?' I found myself echoing.

'Mummy doesn't like it when we talk about Nina,' Beth explained slowly, more to William than to me.

I frowned.

'Who's Nina?'

They exchanged one of those secret sibling looks.

'No one,' Bess brushed me off, her expression enigmatic. 'Will you take us to the beach?'

I acquiesced, but not before clocking William, beside her, gazing down at his hand as he stretched and flexed his fingers, imagining, I was sure of it, this mysterious Nina's own fingers as a cupboard door slammed over them.

The exchange was odd, but I was becoming used to the roster of help at Kewney Manor: the caterers and caretakers, the people collecting laundry or dropping off fresh bed linens, the rotating cast of cleaners, all performing their duties with a ghost-like discretion that betrayed an undercurrent of wariness – of Laurie, I assumed. Any one of them a candidate for the unfortunate culprit William described.

And so it was easy to wave away Bess's comment, particularly as I was learning that my own minor altercations with Laurie were surmountable; a small price to pay for the safety Kewney Manor offered me in return. Indeed, the longer I stayed undiscovered in Cornwall, the more I believed this to be true: that I would happily take whatever Laurie threw at me, if I continued to be sheltered from Nick, and London, and all that had happened there.

We headed off to the beach early that morning, avoiding the savage midday sun, armed with wetsuits and an artillery of buckets and spades. We were making our way through the grounds when movement caught my eye, a rustling low in the hedgerows. I instinctively leapt back, the nerves I had tried to abandon in London now racing back to me, and saw a figure emerge; a man I hadn't seen before, in a sleeveless grey T-shirt and dirty black jogging bottoms, sporting thick green gloves and brandishing a pair of giant clippers.

'What are you doing here?' I clenched my fists, instincts flaring, Nick still on the periphery of my thoughts.

'I'm Joss.' He folded his arms in a way that instantly seemed defensive. 'The gardener.'

'Oh.' Even as I clocked the metal wheelbarrow behind him, knew that he was telling the truth, that he wasn't a threat, my body was still taut, prepared for flight.

'Who are *you*?' He scrutinized me, a thick eyebrow cocked.

'Lily, the nanny,' was what I meant to say. But adrenaline made my tongue thick, and the words got chewed up on exit, came out, 'Nily, the lanny.'

I reddened, quickly correcting myself as William guffawed beside me, delighting in my spoonerism. 'Lanny Nily! Lanny Nily! I'm calling you that from now on!'

Joss observed me with a bemused smile, dissipating the last of whatever tension was left in me.

'Well, there you go: first time we've met and I've already given you a nickname. Did you start recently?'

'A few weeks ago.' And then, trying to deflect his inquisitiveness, 'I haven't seen you, though?'

'My brother has a farm near Bodmin. He lost a farm

hand and needed repairs doing. And then, well . . . I was just dying to stick around to help with the lamb castrations.'

The way he said this – po-faced, eyes looking directly into mine – I knew he was trying to get a rise out of me.

'Charming,' I retorted, head held high. 'And on that note . . .'

I ushered the children away, but I was pretty sure we were still in earshot as Bess asked, 'What's castration?', and I was almost certain I heard his chuckle on the breeze as I bumbled through a reply.

I bumped into him again a few days later, on one of my strolls down to the beach.

'Hey,' I heard a voice calling, searched the borders for its owner, only to see his head pop up from behind a row of blousy blush-coloured peonies. He jogged over to me, smelling of soil. 'I'm sorry, about the other day, for teasing you.'

'That's OK; it gave me a wonderful opportunity to teach the children about dystopian feminist fiction.'

He snorted, a genuine, unprompted chuckle, and I saw something loosen in him, his shoulders relax.

'Touché.' And then he took off his glove, stuck a hand towards me. 'Shall we start again?'

After that, I started making note of Joss's working patterns (Tuesdays, Thursdays, every other Saturday), fabricating some excuse to myself to be in the gardens, to seek him out. After too much time alone with my thoughts, it was a relief to find a companion to escape myself with.

He was only a few years older than me – I pitted him at closer to thirty – but Joss had a confidence about him that made him seem much more than that. His father had been the gardener at Kewney before him – and his father before that, stretching back as long as he could remember. As the youngest of five children, he'd never thought the role would fall to him, but as his brothers and sisters had gradually grown up, got married or moved away, a sense of duty urged him to take up the mantle. He didn't mind. He loved gardening; could reel off the names of every plant in the grounds without a moment's hesitation, and most of the birds. He liked working outside, liked using his hands, liked the quiet (this he said wryly, a reaction to my constant burbling). In short, Joss was as melded to his work as his work was to him.

His view of the world was completely unfettered; he refused to be drawn into gossip, ignoring the bait when I probed him for information about his other wealthy clients, and as such I was very cautious to question him about our own, shared, employers.

My relationship with the Rowes continued much as it had done those initial few weeks. They were generous, kind hosts, always eager to include me in their plans, always ready to make time in their lives for me or the children.

I grew to anticipate what would set Laurie's nerves on edge, stopping a glass millimetres from touching a particular surface after I noticed her complaining about ring marks, taking to removing my outdoor shoes the moment I crossed the threshold when she asked me, not-quite-pointedly, if I enjoyed bringing the beach home with me. I still didn't know who the Nina was the children had referred to, but I for one had no intention of arousing Laurie's ire, and jeopardizing my position.

Any fears seemed unfounded, though: she seemed to delight in having me around, to 'doll about with', as she antiquatedly called it. I would often return to my room to find clothes – designer clothes, sometimes still with the tags in them – hanging from the door or parcelled up on the floor outside with a handwritten note, 'Saw this and thought of you', 'Go on, try it!'. When I questioned her, she told me she'd bought them on a whim, that they hadn't suited, hadn't fitted, that she couldn't be bothered to return them, even though I think we both knew it was a ruse. Whenever I complied, she was there with the perfect pair of shoes, a necklace that would 'just pop', brimming with compliments about how beautiful I looked, how she knew she'd saved that outfit for a reason. Soon it became habit, and I found my own tastes changing too, eschewing my standard uniform of jeans and T-shirts in favour of sundresses, taking care with my hair and make-up so that it was just so.

I realized that, with Nick, I had stopped caring what I looked like. Dressing up had become too fraught, too bound up in the threat of being labelled 'asking for it', of being questioned as to 'who exactly' I was hoping to attract. When I left our flat, the contents of my suitcase took up less than half the space they had when I had arrived; I remembered the lightness of it, as I closed the front door for good.

Laurie was right: looking better made me feel better

about myself; and after so long a period of not caring – about myself, about anything really – it was a welcome change to feel good.

I began to have dinner with them. The odd occasion to begin with, but soon it was a given. Loosened by a glass of wine, Laurie was always overtly kind to me, almost sisterly, and with her encouragement I felt any lingering awkwardness slip away.

Charles, I discovered, was fiercely intelligent: his recollection was uncanny, rattling off plots of whatever book I was reading, even though he said it had been years since he'd read it himself. He'd regale me with family lore – like the ancestor who lost a bar fight in Jamaica and requested his body to be returned to England pickled in rum – awakening in me the historian's mind I had thought long forgotten, his nonchalance eliciting in me a desire to display my knowledge, to prove to him I was worthy of his attention.

I would often find myself caught up in the whim of some conversation with him and then stop myself, guilty at the thought of Laurie being left out, but she never seemed particularly bothered, happy to indulge us whilst her thoughts seemed to run miles away.

And yet, despite this, despite the freedom I had and how amenable and lovable the children were, there was something about my life at Kewney Manor that made me uneasy. After the cacophony of the city, I found the house too quiet, the silence conversely picking up every little noise, every wrongly placed foot or noisy sneeze setting me on edge. The rare noise of the buzzer at the gate would ricochet through the house, bringing me out in a cold sweat until I was sure of who was on the other side.

The flipside of running away, of hiding, was that I never truly felt safe. The fear of discovery brought with it a paranoia that underpinned my days, an alertness that made me constantly on edge.

The days were long, despite my best efforts to use them, and at night I never slept soundly, stirred, often, by indistinct disturbances in the house. In these messy sleeps my subconscious was free to roam places I didn't want to go, and so instead, with nothing else to hook my mind on, I focused my thoughts on Laurie and Charles, wondering at the interplay of their relationship, what they thought of me, never quite able to gauge the answers.

I found myself reaching for the words to describe all this to Joss, seeking out the comfort of his company in my solitary days, but I stumbled at every turn, apprehensive of appearing churlish, ungrateful; of the look of scorn I would provoke in him, for eliciting idle chatter. But one morning – it must have been a few weeks after I first arrived, because the children were still at school – my curiosity got the better of me and I asked him, directly, 'What do you think of Charles and Laurie?'

Joss seemed surprised, although not altogether shocked to hear the question.

'Mr and Mrs Rowe?' He paused, taking a sip from his mug – I'd started bringing him tea in the mornings, and although he never explicitly thanked me for it, it was always finished. 'Why?'

'Just asking.'

He threaded his fingers around the handle – the nails always had dirt underneath them, despite the gloves, and there was something faintly comical about the contrast of his wide, soiled hands clasping one of Laurie's delicate floral blue cups – and I thought I saw him roll his eyes.

'I promise I'm not gossiping; I genuinely want to know.'

'I don't really have much interaction with them, to be honest.'

I got the sense that he was trying to avoid my gaze, couldn't resist the urge to push him further.

'You must have had some impression of them, over the years? What about your father?'

He shrugged. 'I keep myself to myself. So did he. We're a very different sort of people, us and the Rowes – we don't exactly have much to talk about – but from what I know –' he took another swig; I heard the liquid pulsing down his throat '– they appear to be the perfect family.'

I waited.

He ran a hand through his hair. He had nice hair, Joss; thick and fair, and slightly too long, falling just below his chin.

'I was just a kid when the old Mr Rowe died. Charles didn't come about much then, he was already grown up I suppose, but after Mr Rowe died he was down here all the time, and soon he'd taken over. They moved his mother to an old age home up the coast pretty sharpish, and from what I can recall, she died not long after.' He pulsed his shoulders, up, down. 'My father wasn't one to say much about his work normally, but I remember overhearing him talking to my mum once about the family – I'd come along with him, on the weekends, occasionally, help with the weeding and so on, so I knew who they were. "That family was always peculiar, Sally," he was saying to her, "and the boy might just be the worst of the bunch."'

I frowned.

'What did he mean, "peculiar"?'

Charles didn't seem particularly odd to me. If anything, it was Laurie I'd cast in that role.

'He didn't say; he caught me hovering in the doorway and stopped. 'But over the years you hear things: old Mr Rowe was a bully, and a drunk; I'm not sure the mother was much better. Both of them hyper-religious, from what I understand, almost Victorian. There was a sister, I think, much older. I'm not quite sure what happened to her.'

'A sister?' Charles had never mentioned one. But then again, I hadn't asked.

Joss nodded. 'There were rumours – and again this is probably just idle gossip; people around here have too much time on their hands – that she wasn't his sister at all, but his mother.'

I exhaled. '*What?*'

But Joss wouldn't be lured. 'I'm just telling you what people have said. I don't know the ins and outs. Mr Rowe has always been nothing but friendly to me, so whatever reason my father had to dislike him, I've never had any issues with him.'

I could tell Joss was growing tired of the conversation, and so to urge him on, I asked, 'And what about Laurie?'

He stirred the tea in his mug, stared down at the beige whirlpool as if debating whether to speak his mind or not.

'People around here are very protective of their own. Especially these big houses. Half the time you can't even own them unless you can prove you've got DNA going back to the bloody Stone Age. So they didn't like it when Mr Rowe came home with her. An outsider. And American, no less. I'd go a little loopy myself, given that.'

'What do you mean?'

Joss squirmed. I gave an encouraging nod.

'Look, I've never had much to do with her. But occasionally I'll come across her in the gardens, collecting flowers for the house, and she'll always be very polite to me, always refers to me by name. Only, one time, I found her on the path down to the sea, just standing there, staring. I called her name and she jumped, as though she'd been a thousand miles away; couldn't even remember who I was let alone what I was called. When she walked away, I noticed she was wearing no shoes, even though it must have been the middle of winter.' He stood, poured the dregs of the tea out onto the lawn, and handed me back the mug. 'But you know these rich people can all be a bit . . . as my mum would say, "eccentric". And they seem to have lots of friends here, and be very popular, so clearly she's managed to win people over. I'm sure whatever Dad said, it was just a case of him being rubbed up the wrong way.'

He picked up his spade and resumed his work without another glance in my direction.

'Joss?' I called to his back, a final thought pricking me. 'Did you ever know someone here called Nina?'

I thought I saw his shoulders tense, but when he turned his features were smooth. 'Why are you asking about Nina?'

'William mentioned her. I don't know who she is, I was just wondering.'

'Oh.' He stood, resting his weight on the spade like a crutch. 'I only met her a few times. She wasn't here that long. She was the nanny before you.'

And then he turned, thrust the spade into the ground, heaved a pile of earth from the bed.

I watched him a moment, thinking, but it was clear that I had been dismissed, so I left.

That night I lay in bed unable to sleep. There was nothing untoward about there having been a prior nanny – Laurie hadn't indicated that I was the first – but why had the children clammed up at her mention? Why had Joss?

The image of Laurie's shoeless feet loomed in my mind. There was no doubt that she was an acquired taste. I could quite easily imagine her and Nina having a falling out, an acrimonious departure. I was sure that such a thing would probably upset the children, make them wary about bringing her up, particularly if they knew it would upset their mother.

I had failed to pull the curtains closely enough to, and a shaft of light now blinked on, visible through their centre. I sat up, suddenly alert, ripped the bedclothes from me and made my way to the window, inching the curtains back to search the source. No sooner had I got there, the light disappeared. Motion sensors, I concluded, to ward off intruders – probably just a bird or something disturbing them – but just before I turned to go, I spotted movement in the gardens, a figure heading in the direction of the coastal path.

Without wasting another moment, I fetched a jumper from the bedroom floor, pulling it down over my pyjamas as I simultaneously slid my feet into trainers, moved towards the bedroom door. In the corridor I made sure I was alone before tiptoeing down the stairs, heaving open the great oak front door and letting it click shut as quietly as I could. Motion sensors, but no locks on the front door. The foibles of my employers never failed to confound me.

Outside, the air was fresh, dew clinging to the grass from a shower I had missed, spitting at my bare ankles as I carved through the grounds. Making sure to keep my distance from Laurie, I headed into the gardens and took the turn down to the coastal path, taking care to move gingerly as grass gave way to earth, watching my tread for loose stones that could cause me to stumble, alert her to my presence. It was dark, with only the pale light from the bulging gibbous moon to guide me, so I went slowly, hands braced at waist height. The hedgerows grew coarser here, unkempt, sundried branches from what I knew in daylight as blackberry bushes. They scratched at me when I veered too close to the sides, and my jumper snagged on one – my limbs twitching in fright at the sudden pull and resistance – made me send a panicked puff of breath into the night sky as I was released. I clamped a hand over my mouth, carried on.

The sound of the sea grew louder as I approached, an angry, churned-up grumble signalling the rain of earlier, and the wind picked up in chorus. I slowed my pace to a crawl, knees bent, body low to the ground. By now I was no stranger to this path, having crossed it so many times on my daily ramblings, so I knew the final bend opened onto a promontory, before descending into a steep incline, dusty earth broken by tree roots, that one could easily trip and fall on, before finally reaching the sand. It was on the promontory that I paused, standing back against the bushes to mask my shadow, and looked out onto the bay below.

There she was, my mistress, a lone figure in the moonlight. The wind was stronger here, pulled by the sea, and it blew through her loose hair, whipping it into tangles. I shivered, pulled the sleeves of my jumper over my icy hands, but she seemed unaware of the cold, moving nimbly to the water's edge with only the thin silk of her dressing gown for protection. There she stopped, staring out into the black waters, as if hypnotized by their ebb and flow. I leaned forward too, searching the waves, as though they may have written on them the answer to Laurie's strange behaviour. We stayed like this, me watching Laurie, Laurie watching the sea, for what in that dark night air felt like an eternity. But then something in her shifted, came to. Her hands moved to her waist, pulling at the cord of her robe, and then in one, swift motion she loosed herself from it, let it flutter to a shiny pile on the ground, and placed a stone to keep it still. And then she was moving, her naked body even paler against the blackness of the icy water, treading through it as painlessly as though it were bathwater. Just the thought of it sent shockwaves down my calves. Knee-deep, she paused, and I saw the rise and fall of her shoulders as she breathed, before releasing an almighty shriek that ripped through the air and reverberated around the bay.

She raised her arms in the air, fingers touching to a point, but just before she dived, I caught a glimpse of her naked back, illuminated in the moonlight. And what I saw made me flinch, sent shivers through my nerves more powerful than any cold water could.

A palimpsest of scars. Running from the middle of her shoulder blades to the base of her spine. Thin as hairs and pale enough to have been sewn by silkworms, but visible nonetheless even from my distant position on the promontory.

How, or why, or when could she have procured them? My mind began to race, the thoughts swelling within me.

But before I could look again, garner more clues for my searching soul, she vanished beneath the waves.

7

I said nothing to Laurie about what I had seen, although the image of her naked back stayed with me long after I had fled back to the house, rubbing the warmth back into my fingertips and slipping under the covers, praying for sleep. The reason for her nightly antics I mused at: perhaps, for all I knew, she simply found it invigorating? She was an artist, wasn't she? Artists have been known to have all sorts of quirks: Picasso used to carry a gun around and shoot people with blanks if they annoyed him. But the scars? Those I could not begin to comprehend.

And then half term arrived, two weeks for Bess and William's fancy private school, and my duties increased tenfold, the children thrusting themselves upon me with all the boredom and ennui that seems improbable, to an adult, in children. I had had visions of staying close to home, where I felt safe, but at Laurie's behest, I arranged trips, hauling myself into the steel-grey Range Rover that was apparently designated for my use, trying to recall the rules of the Highway Code I had memorized years before and barely used since. We visited Heligan, the rambling pleasure gardens, the children shrieking amidst the implausible Jurassic foliage, and spent a wet day stalking the Eden Project biomes, our enthusiasm for flora and fauna waning under the dull grey sky. There was a more enthusiastic trip to the little town of Looe, where I let them get hopped up on butterscotch ice cream and set them loose on the arcades. We visited countless beaches, clambering over kelp-covered rocks and slimy green sea grass in search of crabs, the children donning wetsuits as they crashed eagerly into the waves, laughing at me shivering in the shallows, lacking their hardy Cornish roots.

Still, each trip brought with it that familiar unkempt fear, lungs tightening, scanning the crowd, expecting at any moment to feel a hand on my shoulder, to turn and find myself discovered, the game over. But as each successive occasion ended uneventfully, the fear dulled, like a bruise healing, so that even the image of Nick himself softened at the edges, the thought of him relegated to a past life, a past me.

We were barely in the house those days, leaving shortly after breakfast and returning, exhausted and hungry, in time for dinner. And although I thought about Joss, missed our morning chats, considered telling him what I had witnessed of Laurie, the opportunity didn't present itself, so the inclination to do so faded away. We caught glimpses of each other, though, as I was loading my charges into the car and he was hauling tools into the gardens.

'What's a man got to do to get a cup of tea around here?' he called across the gravel one morning, waving a trowel at me.

'Make your own damn tea. We're busy.' I leaned out of the car window, stuck my tongue out. Those days I was feeling giddy, marvelling at my own good fortune, the new life I had carved out for myself. I was even beginning to sleep better.

'It doesn't taste as nice as when you make it.'

His demeanour was nonchalant, but my ears pricked up at the softness in his voice, underscoring the joke.

'See you later.' I spoke firmly, like I was telling William to put his pyjamas on. Rolled up the window and put the car into reverse, pressing my neck against the headrest as we backed out of the drive. I couldn't help a glance in the rear-view mirror, watching him watch us as we disappeared through the gates.

'Why do you look weird?' Bess, catching my eye in the mirror, blinked her eyelashes at me innocently.

'I don't,' I answered quickly. 'That's just the way I look.'

'No, it's not,' she cajoled, leaning closer, 'and now your face has gone all red, like when someone is trying to keep a secret.'

'I'm just hot – it's hot in here!' I opened the window, fiddled with the dashboard to turn the radio on.

She sat back, said nothing more, but I could feel her eyes on me as I adjusted my face, searching the scenery for distraction.

Despite the fact that I barely used my phone in Kewney, I found myself bringing it with me on these trips, out of habit, shoving it into my handbag before we left the house. Having it on my person reminded me of the comforting life raft it had once offered me: the ability to call someone or check where I was, should I get lost or need help, but apart from that, I failed to see what about this now 'foreign object' had once held me so enthralled. Now that I had been weaned off the mindless scrolling – the social media sites, the gossip columns, the 'one click' impulse purchases that played havoc with my bank balance – the thing held no power over me. I was becoming used to this quiet, analogue life. In fact, I could almost say I preferred it.

At first, on these trips, I would keep it off, not wanting to know what cacophony of beeps and buzzes I would incite, or, rather, fearing what turning it on might trigger. But soon I found myself turning the thing onto airplane mode, rereading old conversations as though they were historical texts to gloss. Whilst the children were occupied eating lunch – crab sandwiches or fish and chips perched on benches or picnic mats, feet in the sand – I would wind back through group chats to try to get a glimpse of my forgotten self, before Kewney Manor, before, even, Nick. Mostly innocuous groups – 'Hannah's Birthday Dins', 'History Grads 2009' – or individual friends whose last words had sighed their way out to me months, if not years, ago; but it was the name at the top I always looked at, the last message there, still marked unread, brief enough that I could see it there in full beneath his name, like an ironic epithet.

I'm sorry

How easy Nick found it, to type those words.

The insouciance of them. I didn't even deserve a full stop.

The date was there beside the message, but I remembered when it was sent. Right before I had returned home that last night, when he would go on to prove, like always, that he wasn't sorry at all.

We met in that liminal summer when I had just graduated university and was yet to start a job, relying on the last of my student loan and how long I could stretch a packet of pasta, filling the gaps with some online tutoring. He was a medical student, four years under his belt, and another to go before the years of placements, traineeships and specializations that would finally result in him becoming a qualified, practising surgeon. The arduous path to his noble profession that he was always so keen to remind me of should I dare complain about some comparatively unimportant element of my day.

I knew from our first meeting that he was funny: the life of any party, and I was drawn to that – to his wit, his quick answers. The sharp tongue that only later, in the thick of it, would I identify for what it truly was: a slick of humour that was used to patch over the underlying cruelty.

He had a very 'take charge' attitude that I was drawn to, liking, at first, the way I didn't have to think when I was with him, just 'do' – although my friend, Jade, in one of the last comments she made before our friendship died, told me that this was indicative of my so-called 'daddy issues'.

He flattered me. Always telling me how gorgeous I was, how funny, how clever, how kind. He had the ability to make me feel like a fucking goddess.

Fumbling about in the no man's land I was in at that time, he tethered me, made me feel my worth.

And, I'll admit it: he was sexy, with dark floppy hair

that was always falling into his eyes, full lips, a dimple on one cheek that made his face irresistibly kissable. Unlike previous boyfriends, he wasn't shy about physical displays of affection. He always reaching for me, hugging, tickling; pulling me into alleyways, barely able to stop himself from taking me then and there. The sex, in the beginning, was phenomenal. It was only later I would learn that tactility and possession make common bedfellows.

We lived near each other: me with three university friends in the charming but marginally inconvenient Dulwich Village (salubrious, I know: the house had been purchased years ago, as a buy-to-let by one of the girl's property-developer parents), he in Peckham with two Geography grads who had advertised a spare room on Facebook. He took me on dates to Peckhamplex cinema, arm looping around me in the dark; to hipster cocktail bars in railway arches near Queen's Road; restaurants on rooftops in Rye Lane; fingers fumbling under tables, knees touching, always leaving early so that we could go home, be alone, take each other's clothes off.

When he said, more times than not, that it 'just made sense' for us to stay at his instead of mine – there was nothing to do in Dulwich (or as he pronounced, 'Dull-witch'); and besides, he 'had an early start' – I didn't have much reason to contest it. A bed was a bed, as far as I was concerned, and I'd rather be in one where Nick was.

Soon I was staying over several nights a week, often returning home just to wash my hair somewhere with decent water pressure, to grab a change of clothes. And when the girls clamoured that I never saw them any more, asked why Nick always waited outside if he was picking me up, why he was never interested in hanging out with them too, I fobbed them off.

All my life I had craved family, craved belonging.

I became high on Nick. High on being an 'us'.

Before I knew it, six months had passed, and I was cramming my belongings into the spare room in Peckham. I'd got funding for my PGCE course, taking on more tutoring to supplement it. '*I could do with help on the rent, it's not cheap, saving people's lives.*' (By now the dates were less frequent, as were his offers to pay for them.) '*Besides, you're never even at yours.*' It would be another six months before we moved out of there, into the flat in Brixton, the first place since my mother's death that I had considered 'mine'. It is only really with hindsight that I can see how myopic our world became, how he had zeroed in on the two of us, blacking out any other frame of reference.

He kept a skeleton in his room – a requirement, as I understand it, for the degree. He called it Melvin, and he loved it, delighted in placing it unexpectedly around the house – perched on the loo seat, slumped on the couch with a remote control in its witchy fingers. I hated that damned thing. I found it creepy – all that chalky whiteness, the clatter of the bones when it was moved, simian arms dangling. I hated it more so when Nick revealed it wasn't artificial, as I had previously assumed. I could honestly barely even look at it then, and I asked him to keep it out of the room at night, or at least covered up. Most of the time he obliged, reluctantly, but he knew how much it bothered me.

One night we'd been out for a friend's birthday, just a small thing, drinks at a bar in Soho, but when the invitation came, I remembered how much I had missed things like that. Nick had done his usual nit-picking – I'd drunk too much, why did I leave him alone with so-and-so when I knew he couldn't stand her, who was the guy I was talking to by the bar, how many people in there had I slept with before him – but it was early days then, so this was relegated to small scraps, not the full-blown accusations they would later become. I thought we'd made up before we'd even left the bar. Back in his room, I'd wrapped my arms around his neck, kissed him on the mouth as I wobbled out of my heels and said I was sorry, that I honestly hadn't meant to upset him, why didn't we cancel brunch plans tomorrow morning, stay in bed all day, just the two of us. He always preferred it when it was just the two of us. He'd kissed me back, slipped his hands under the back of my T-shirt and pulled me into bed with him. All forgiven.

I had woken later, mouth bone dry and probably still a little drunk, wandered downstairs to the loo. His room in that house was small, the bed pushed against the wall to maximize space, and I always slept on the outside, my body wrapped in Nick's.

When I came back to bed, I lifted the duvet and slid my body underneath it, but as I did my flesh met with cold bone, not Nick's familiar warmth, and when I turned my head, my eyes met with the empty black sockets of Nick's skeleton.

I screamed, leapt from the bed, and seconds later he burst out of the wardrobe, doubled up with laughter. I shouted at him, reaching flailing arms out to push him away from me, my anger slowly subsiding as his took over, turning from good-humoured ribbing to 'It was just a fucking joke' to 'Get over yourself' to churlishly tossing the thing down the stairs.

We lay in bed, back to back, not talking, but then I felt the weight of the mattress shift, his body turn, an arm slowly reaching for me across the duvet.

'I'm sorry, Lil.'

Even then I knew he wasn't. I had seen the slick of pleasure in his eyes, as they had reflected the terror in my own. But I forgave him. As you always do. The thing is, though, little incidences like this get tamped down into the pattern of a relationship like squares of a mosaic, the light and shade making up a picture of a whole which is, somehow, sustainable. And then, over the years the shade spread over the light until there was almost no pattern left at all, until the night I looked at him across the floor in our poky galley kitchen, said, 'I can't do this any more.'

I'm sorry

Staring down at the message on my phone yet again, I watched my knuckles turn white.

What would it take, to free myself from his menace for good?

It was a Sunday, my day off, and Laurie had suggested – insisted, even – that I spend the day by myself.

The night before, I had pored over the local guidebooks in the library, and in the morning, Laurie pressed the keys of the car into my hands. 'They could use a day being bored,' she promised. 'And I'm sure you could use a day on your own. Besides –' she gave me a reassuring pat on the shoulder '– you've quite frankly exhausted them this week. They'll be delighted to sit and watch television all day.'

I took Laurie at her word, kissed the children good-bye and headed off to explore on my own.

It was a hot day, and I felt oddly peaceful, unused to having had a journey to myself without the requisite rounds of 'I Spy', 'Are we nearly there yet?' and 'William, stop kicking her'. I had stopped in Fowey first, a hand-some town on the mouth of the river, where a shopkeeper had recommended a coastal walk that passed through the setting of many of Du Maurier's books, and I had planned a village called Charlestown as the final stop on my way home.

The guidebooks promised a Grade II listed harbour and pastel fishermen's cottages, but when I got to Charlestown, I discovered that it had recently been used as a location for a BBC period drama and was now overrun with souvenir sellers touting themed liqueurs. A location tour was in full swing when I arrived, the cottages obscured by a double-decker coach.

I got an ice cream from a little hut at the top of the harbour, window-shopping the boutiques that held the same paraphernalia I had come to recognize from most Cornish tourist shops: driftwood signs with pithy quotes ('What if the hokey-cokey *is* what it's all about?'), ducks in wellington boots. In the inner harbour, a group of school kids were jumping off the pier, hurling their wet-suited bodies from the rounded pinnacle at the far end. I watched them, from a distance at first, but then came to a rest on the ledge behind them, drawn by their laughter, my phone in hand.

I had managed to preserve my ice cream, saving it from dribbling over the edges of the cone, and then I did something I hadn't done since I was a child: raised the cone above my mouth and crunched off the tip, sucking the remaining ice cream through it like a straw. The children were lining up, taking their turns, and I was drawn to the littlest one, her hair in a ragged plait down her back, hopping nervously from foot to foot. Occasionally, a little whimper escaped her lips. The boy in front of her – older, a brother maybe – kept looking back to admonish her – 'Stop being a baby . . . Go back to Mum and Dad if you're scared' – but when it came to his go, he turned around, took her by the hand, and said, 'Come on, Soph, let's go together. I'll look after you.'

As I watched them leap, I thought of Bess and William. Before she'd gone to bed the night before, Bess had handed me a picture she had drawn – a boy and girl surrounded by flowers and trees. 'It's Mary Lennox and Dickon –' we had been reading *The Secret Garden* '– but they reminded me of you and Joss. I thought you might like it for your room.' Earlier, tucking William into bed as I sang along to some silly song he'd made up about a one-armed penguin, he'd patted me on the head and declared, 'You're my favouritest nanny. Mummy and Daddy have been so much happier since you arrived.'

I thought of Joss, too.

A gentle flutter of a thought I wasn't quite sure I was ready to let in.

I was happy, I realized. Happier than I had been in a

long time. The peace suited me. And the space. The expanse of land and sea made my soul feel fresh. My employers had their idiosyncrasies, but they were warm, and they were kind, and generous, and in the day's light reflecting off the harbour walls, I felt so very far away from Brixton, and from Nick. I couldn't face losing it all. I had to do something, to secure it.

I unlocked the phone, and without allowing myself too much time to dwell upon my actions, navigated to his name. But this time, I went beyond that final note, reading back over every single message he'd written to me, even the nastiest, most bitter missives. I hadn't deleted any of them, not a single one. Perhaps, subconsciously, I had wanted a record, maybe for this exact moment, for me to be able to look back at them, see how far I'd come. I watched our relationship play out in two-tone speech bubbles, from the **See you tomorrow**, to the **Love you**, to the mundane **We need bread**, to the insults that slowly became more commonplace than not.

And then I flicked the service on, calling Nick's number and quickly pressing the phone to my ear as the ping of alerts made it vibrate, not wanting to acknowledge what they said or who they might be from. My throat was as dry as sand, even though it went straight to voicemail, as I knew it would, even though the sound of his voice on the recording alone was enough to make my skin crawl.

'*This is Nick. I'm probably off doing terribly important things. Leave a message after the tone, and if it's worth it, I'll get back to you.*'

'Nick,' I forced through the dryness. 'I know I haven't called you for a few weeks, but I needed space. I meant what I said when I left. We're over. Please, don't try to find me.' I hope you're OK.' I hesitated, but found the courage I needed, to add, 'And that you're looking after yourself. I couldn't forgive myself if something happened to you.'

I hung up, tapped airplane mode once more, before staring at his contact information on the screen. His profile still had a picture of the two of us – taken on Christmas Day at his parents' house last year. Things were bad, then. He'd given me a black eye the night before; I hadn't helped his mum out enough with the washing-up; and I'd spent the first half an hour of Christmas morning trying to cover it up. In the picture, I was sure I could still detect the shadow.

I didn't know if the message would be enough. But then I didn't know if anything would ever be enough, or if a tiny part of me would always be on edge, wondering.

I reached my thumb around to the side of the phone, pressed firmly, watching the screen fade to black. And then I stood, walked to the water's edge, and watched my fingers unfurl, the phone tipping from them, falling soundlessly into the sea.

The brother and sister came up to the pier again. They were soaking wet, and she was shivering lightly, but laughing. When they reached the edge, he held out his hand for her, but she pulled away. 'No, no, I want to do it on my own!'

I watched her for a moment, her head cresting to the surface of the water, as she called up to him, 'I did it! I did it!', before slipping my hands into my empty pockets, turning to go.

8

I embraced that second week with the children with a renewed zeal, finding ever more new and exciting reasons for us to leave the house for the day: an hour's drive to the Barbara Hepworth Museum, pressing our hands to the cool, alien-like structures; a matinee of *A Midsummer Night's Dream* at the outdoor Minack Theatre, the fairies donning see-through ponchos during the inevitable drizzle; wandering the battlements of Tintagel with Bess and William in my wake, stick 'swords' at the ready.

Some mornings Charles would join us for breakfast, lingering over a cup of coffee as I laid out the plans for the day, an itinerant sergeant major. I enjoyed his presence there, his easy manner making me feel less like a nanny and more like a family friend.

'You're certainly keeping them busy,' he remarked one morning as I packed them off to gather rain macs, wellies and beach towels for the inevitable Cornish cycle of sun and storm.

I twitched my shoulders, took their plates over to the sink.

'A regular Nanny McPhee,' he teased, referring to the snaggle-toothed heroine of William's current favourite film.

'Hey!' I slapped out with the dishcloth I had been holding, catching him playfully on the upper thigh.

'Only joking.' He caught the cloth from me, wound it through his fingers so that I found myself pulled towards him. 'She's much prettier than you.'

At that moment, William stormed into the room, citing a hole in his jacket, and I turned, distracted, wondering if my face looked as hot as it felt.

'Right, I'm off to work,' Charles coughed, handing me back the cloth. Without another word, he was gone.

Towards the end of the week, Laurie told me they would be hosting a dinner party.

'It's just a small thing,' she insisted, cornering me at the base of the stairs as I was about to pick the children up from their respective playdates. 'A few of the parents from school we're friendly with. It's a bit of a rolling tradition every couple of months or so. Only . . .' And here she paused, looked around as if for eavesdroppers, then bent her head towards me, conspiratorial. 'One of the couples in our group – the Maynards, parents of William's friend Benji? They got divorced six months ago.' I saw a light come into her eyes, evidently thrilled by the scandal of it. I vaguely recalled Benji, a perpetually worried-looking little boy, and his frenetic, long-limbed mother. 'We should have read the signs, really: he bought a Ferrari, started all this cockamamie hair-loss treatment. Next thing we knew it, he was moving in with his PA, saying he wanted to "recapture the passion for life he had felt fifteen years ago". Anyway.' She pressed her palms together at her breastbone, rested the tip of her chin on them in a gesture that primed me for a request in the making. 'Sandy's on her own now. She's the only one, and I don't want her to feel uncomfortable. About the odd number – you understand?'

Despite the relative calm I had felt since Charlestown, the thought of being around other people still made me nervous, and I wasn't sure I did understand, not really. But I gave her an encouraging smile that showed I was on her side, allowed her to continue.

'I would ask someone else, maybe a colleague of Charles's, but that's going to look so obvious. And I wouldn't want her to think I was trying to set her up on a date, that would be awful.' She made a face, fluttered her eyelids in a way that seemed a little too coquettish for Laurie. 'Would you . . . would you hate very much to join us? Unless you have plans, of course,' she added unnecessarily. Because where was I going to go?

'No, I have no plans,' I said carefully, found her reaching for my hand before I'd finished speaking.

'Oh, you are such a help.' Task achieved, she came alive with her usual Laurie energy, crossing past me on the stairs and talking directions at me as she made her way up. 'It's seven-thirty-for-eight, so you'll have time to get ready after the children are in bed. We meet in the drawing room for cocktails, and then on to dinner in the formal dining room. There's a lamb dish the chef at Sardo's has been working on that no one else has tried yet, hah-hah. And chocolate fondants for pudding; they're always a favourite. We'll pay you for the extra hours, naturally.'

I blushed inwardly. I had begun to notice that she had an unsettling way of doing that, Laurie: flipping between friend and employer from one moment to the next. I didn't mind coming along to the party – as I had said quite truthfully, I had nowhere better to be – but the thought of her paying for my presence seemed faintly sordid.

'Oh, oh no Laurie, don't worry about that. I'm happy to do it.'

Laurie paused on the top step, looked down at me.

'You really are a godsend, Lily. I don't know where we'd be without you. Well, in that case, you have to allow me to buy you something to wear. On that, I'm not taking "no" for an answer . . .'

Before I could respond, she disappeared down the hall.

The dress Laurie bought me was short – shorter than the dresses I'd borrowed from her in the past – an ivory broderie anglaise, with a high neckline that just about made up for the hemline, and capped sleeves that fitted neatly over my shoulders.

When I modelled it for her, wobbling slightly on her dressing-room carpet, in a pair of black patent heels she'd loaned me, I worried that it seemed a bit showy, skimming over my body in a way I wasn't entirely comfortable with. My hesitation seemed to annoy her.

'You're being ridiculous,' she huffed. 'Honestly, they do say that youth is wasted on the young don't they? Take it from me, you look perfect. And I'm not going to have a chance to order anything new before the party now so it'll have to do.'

Her snappiness put me on edge, and I realized I was

sounding ungrateful, turning up my nose at something she had obviously taken time and care to select.

'I'm sorry, you're right,' I appeased, eager to make things up. 'I'm just not used to fancy dinner parties like this.'

The tightness in her lips relaxed. She put a hand on my shoulder. 'Then you'll just have to believe me. You know you can trust me, don't you?'

The night of the party, I jumped into the shower the second the children were down and then raced to get dressed.

As I was doing up my buttons, I noticed movement outside my door, glanced up to see Laurie hovering, still in a dressing gown, her hair in curlers. 'Just wanted to see how you're getting on. I thought you might want to borrow this.' Her fingers unfurled to reveal a lipstick in her palm, a sleek black bullet. 'It would really suit you.' She came fully into the room, handing me the canister.

'Oh, thank you.' I uncapped it, revealing a shiny, deep red that I would never normally wear – certainly not in front of Nick, who was prone to referring to women with full faces of make-up as 'slags'.

'Go on,' she urged, 'for me.'

I turned to the dressing table, slicked it across my lips; watched my features enhance and change.

'See,' she crowed, coming up behind me. 'But I think hair up, though.'

Before I could answer, she was pulling my hair away from my face, fixing it into a tight ponytail with a flick of a wrist. Looking at my reflection, I saw that she was right, saw how the high neckline sharpened the angles of my face, made me seem older, more sophisticated.

I couldn't help but feel a prickle of pleasure running down my back. It had been such a long time since I had had cause to dress up like this, to take unashamed pride in the way I looked. I felt sexy. It felt good.

'There we go.' She observed me, and in the mirror's reflection I could see the satisfaction blooming across her features. 'I told you that you could trust me, didn't I?'

I made my way to the drawing room, treading lightly in the heels to soften their clack against the Great Hall's marble floors. Pushing open the heavy oak doors, I expected to find at least one of the other guests already inside, but it was empty apart from Charles, standing over the gilt-edged cocktail trolley, a drink already in hand. He was wearing a linen jacket the colour of a cloudless sky, and the blue brought out the swarthiness of his features, his dark curls. My dress suddenly felt much shorter than I had thought it, and I reached a surreptitious hand to tug it down.

'Ah, Lily.' He looked up as I hovered in the door frame. I wondered if he'd say something about my dressing up, but he regarded me with the same casualness he did every day. 'Laurie mentioned that she'd cajoled you into joining us. Thank you for humouring her. Drink?'

Despite having shared a drink with Charles and Laurie multiple times now, the formality of the situation made me feel awkward, and I hesitated before taking a step towards him, smoothing my hands over my hips.

'I don't know . . . what are you having?' I became all

too conscious of my arms, with no handbag or purse to hide them behind; crossed them, immediately felt rude and uncrossed them, clasped my fingers behind my back before giving up, letting them fall limply by my sides.

'A Martini. Dirty.' Charles, oblivious to my acrobatics, took a sip from an etched, conical-shaped glass. 'Want one? How do you take them?'

I tried to recall the last time I'd drunk a Martini. I was pretty sure it wouldn't have been with Nick – towards the end we so rarely went out. Which means it would have been with girlfriends, celebrating Finals, maybe. I had a vague memory of Pornstar Martinis, viscous, sweet, passionfruit liqueur with a shot of Prosecco on the side – nothing like the simple sophistication of Charles's clear swirl of liquid. I grimaced.

'To be honest, I'm not sure I could tell you. I don't think I even know there was a difference between a Dirty Martini and any other kind.'

'Oh, well in that case, this is just the moment to teach you.' He beckoned me, began busying himself with the trolley in front of him, hands deftly plucking bottles, tonging ice into a glass cocktail jug and stirring gently with a long metal spoon. 'Gin or vodka, wet or dry, olive or a twist.' It was fun, watching him at work. As I had got to know Charles, I had begun to recognize how animated he became when he was explaining something, how he seemed to delight in imparting knowledge. He clearly liked to play teacher, and I, used to thinking of myself as lacking knowledge, was happy to play pupil. 'Let's try you on this one and see how you like it.' He plucked a glass from a rack on the side of the trolley, twiddled his fingers to right it on the bar top. 'I know dirty may sound obscene, but it just means a dash of brine from the olives.' With a flick of the wrist, he demonstrated. '*Et voilà.*' He skewered an olive with a pick, lay it in the glass and handed it to me. 'Vodka, by the way. Gin tends to make me melancholy.'

I reached for the glass, took a careful sip, conscious of the wide rim, and rolled the liquid around my tongue. It had a savouriness to it, as one would have assumed from the olive and brine, but it wasn't unpleasant.

'It's almost isotonic,' I concluded, swallowing, and Charles nodded, looked pleased.

'Clever girl. That's the brine. The salt levelling out the sugars in the vermouth. I prefer it a little too much on the wet side if I'm honest – that just means leaving the vermouth in, by the way, rather than just rinsing the glass with it. Ah, and here's my wife.' He tilted his head towards the door, his face carving into a smile as Laurie appeared, and began to mix again. 'She prefers it melancholy,' he said with a wink, 'and dry as a bone.'

She looked stunning, resplendent in a dark-green chiffon dress that accentuated her auburn hair and slender limbs, and yet I recognized a tightness in her expression that I had come to associate with her being stressed – her mouth thin, a slight clenching of her jaw, a tendency to worry at the corner of her lip. In fact, now that I thought about it, she had been tense all day, snapping at the children for making the sofa cushions sag, moving through the house with a frenetic energy as she adjusted and rearranged. I had seen Laurie entertain several times now, and I had never seen her this nervy before . . . I wondered what it was about this particular group of people that set her on edge.

'Charles, if you've got nothing better to do than make jokes, you can go to the kitchen and tell the caterers to start preparing the canapés.' She took the drink and almost drained it in one sip. Her right wrist was stacked with thin gold bangles that jingled together as she tipped the glass, as though wind chimes had been set off in the room. When she set it down, she looked at me as though she had just realized I was in the room, her tension evaporating into a smile.

'Lily, darling, don't you look fabulous!' She held me by the fingers and stepped back, taking me in fully as if she hadn't seen me only a moment before. 'That dress looks as though it were made to measure. Charles,' she called over her shoulder to her husband, who was doing as commanded, and was halfway to the door, 'did you tell Lily how pretty she looks?'

'I haven't had a chance to yet, my dearest.' He stopped, glanced over me like a schoolchild being made to look at a whiteboard. 'Lily, you look very pretty.'

I blushed, noting the deliberate robotics in his voice, but Laurie seemed satisfied.

'Well, get on with it then.'

When he had returned and Laurie was busying herself around the room, adjusting the lighting and tweaking books, I felt Charles's hand on my shoulder.

'You do, by the way,' he said quietly, and I looked back to find him not quite meeting my eyes. 'Look pretty, I mean. I just don't like being told what to say.'

The couples started arriving, seven in total – eight,

if you counted Sandy Maynard and me – spilling into the library and giving Charles their drinks orders. Like Laurie and Charles, they were all of a similar type: early-to-middling middle age, well-coiffed and good-looking; the women in soft summer dresses, the men in pastel-hued shirts and tailored trousers. They were all, overwhelmingly, white – it was the first time since leaving London I had been in such a large gathering, and I was struck at once by the lack of diversity – and all palpably wealthy. Even without the tip-off of the stacked eternity rings and diamond tennis bracelets weighing down the wives' hands, it was evident in the way they held themselves, in their tinkling voices and turns of phrase.

'Blini?' Amidst the exclamatory greetings and easy small talk, I quickly found myself alone, so, not wanting to look like a complete sore thumb, I took one of the silver-plated canapé trays that had been resting on the grand piano by the window and began to circulate the room.

'You're the new nanny.'

It was a statement, not a question. A woman with a triple-stringed pearl choker took a blini from the tray, and I blinked up at her, trying to remember how we had met. I had taken William and Bess to the odd playdate, but I couldn't picture her, or which children belonged to her.

'Meredith Baker.' Her hand shot out. 'We met at the PTA meeting.' And then, sotto voce, 'The one with the terrible salmon.'

I remembered her now as the woman who had been

pretending to get a glass of water at one of Laurie's events. Something about the way she acted then had made me uneasy, and I didn't like what she was doing now, trying to goad me into disloyalty.

'Yes. Lily.' I shook her hand, ignoring the comment about the salmon. 'Lovely to meet you properly.'

I made a move as if to go, but her hand reached over to the platter to reach for another blini.

'English?'

Took a bite, observed me.

I nodded.

'Hmm.' She popped the rest into her mouth, pressed her fingertips to her lips as she swallowed. 'She does go for the pretty ones, doesn't she?' I felt her eyes skimming my body, shifted my body weight uncomfortably under her gaze. 'The other one was, too. Slightly . . . grubbier . . . though.' She wrinkled her nose. 'And a complete nightmare, as I understand it. No wonder Laurie traded up.'

The comment caught me off guard. Was this the other nanny? Nina, the one the children had spoken of? She must have done something pretty dreadful, to have made her persona non grata. I wanted to ask more, but before I could think of an appropriate question, she motored on. 'My son, Samuel, is in Bess's class. And Laurie and I are on the Parents' Association together. I'm the chairman. Laurie's the vice-chair.' She said this pointedly, with a soupçon of pleasure, and then gave me a conspiratorial look. 'They're wonderful people, Charles and Laurie, aren't they? My family have known the Rowes for generations. They thought it was so funny, him marrying an American. Especially one with no family to speak of.'

'I've been very lucky. They're very kind.' I said measuredly. The way she was looking at me, eyebrow arched, made me uncomfortable, and I scanned the room for an exit strategy.

'The golden couple.' She underscored the title with a courtly flourish of her wrist. 'Almost makes you wonder where they bury the bodies.'

She laughed then, riotously, but before I had to engage any further, I felt Laurie's arm around my shoulder and turned gratefully towards her.

'Lily, dear, why are you doing that? That's the caterer's job.'

'Oh.' I looked at the tray in my hand. 'I don't mind. Someone had left it on the piano.'

'That's sweet, but it's not your job. Just put it back where you found it.'

'Honestly, it's no bother, I—'

'Just pop it back on the piano and people can help themselves.' Her tone was neutral but her expression was a little too fixed. 'You're off duty.'

She followed me as I obliged; once I had set down the tray, she turned me back to face the room, linking her hand into the crook of my elbow. Meredith had melted into the crowd.

'I'm sorry for abandoning you. Let me introduce you to everyone properly. I want to show you off.'

As I followed her, Meredith's comment stuck in my head. I thought of Laurie's particularness, how hard she was to please. What could Nina have done, to leave her position on such dire terms? I couldn't help wondering what she was like, picturing her in the house, in my role. Had she slept in my room? Did she get on with Bess and William, with Charles? But perhaps I was making more of it than necessary: it was evident that Meredith was a gossip, and that she seemed to delight in any small pitfaz Laurie's. Perhaps calling her a 'nightmare' was just down to Meredith's propensity for embellishment.

The thought flitted away from me as I observed Laurie working the room. She seemed to have relaxed since the guests had arrived, greeting each one with increasingly incandescent hoots of delight, although I couldn't help but notice that she had quickly helped herself to a second Martini, drinking it thirstily as she circulated the room. Dutifully, I followed her, answering the same questions over and over as painlessly as I could – 'Bath – History – London' – without sounding like an utter neophyte. No one seemed surprised, when Laurie introduced me, that I was crashing their soirée, and yet to each one (or to the women at least) she added, sotto voce, 'To even up the numbers,' with a hasty look at Sandy. I got the impression that divorce wasn't a common occurrence amongst this set of Cornish elites.

When asked, by a man with slicked-back dark hair introduced to me as 'Jonesy', why I had decided to come all the way to Cornwall from London, I froze, caught off guard.

The image of Nick's face as I watched him from the bedroom door. The smell of the dank hostel room. The whispered thought, *Get far away, far away, far away.*

'... I liked the idea of being by the sea?' I replied weakly, taking a swig of my drink to lubricate my throat.

'Wouldn't Torquay have been a bit closer to home?' he guffawed. I started to formulate a response but he'd already turned away, started talking to another man about cricket.

'Don't mind Jonesy.' Laurie slid beside me, looped her arm into mine. 'He thinks Cornwall should be reserved for the Cornish. I think he'd sever the whole region from the UK if he could, turn the damned place into an island.'

She rested her empty Martini glass on the mantelpiece behind her – her third by then, I realized – and clapped her hands together, addressing the room.

'Well, ladies and gentlemen, could I ask that you make your way into the dining room? Supper will be served shortly.'

There was a clattering of glass as people downed their drinks, made their way back out into the Great Hall and towards the dining room. I surveyed the debris – crumpled napkins and discarded cocktail sticks dotted the bookshelves and occasional tables, surfaces slick from spilled drinks – and began a hasty attempt at tidying up, but no sooner had I gathered together a handful of glasses than an unfamiliar girl in a navy apron scurried inside the room, bearing one of those large grey plastic catering trays they use to clear up school lunches.

'Lily.' Laurie appeared in the doorway, back resting against the frame. 'Don't make me tell you again, you're off duty.'

'I . . .'

The girl came towards me, proffering the tray. 'Please. I do.' She couldn't be much older than me, her accent Eastern European.

'Thank you.'

I relinquished the glasses, setting them as noiselessly as I could in the base of the tray. Laurie remained watching me until I had followed her out.

I hadn't yet eaten in the formal dining room, the large room which took up the main chunk of the eastern ground floor. Sundays, when the Rowes traditionally dined in there for lunch, were nominally my day off, and, unusually for Laurie, she had so far neglected to extend an invitation to me. I had passed its open double doors many times though, marvelling at the jade-green walls, the flocks of tiny birds in flight that had been hand-painted across them, the gilt-framed ancestral portraits – men in livery, women with their hair pomaded skywards. I had gazed up at the impossibly large crystal chandelier that hung over the dining table, imagined, without too much difficulty, what it would sound like if it came crashing down.

Now, however, the room had burst into life. Vases of wildflowers spilled across the dining table, were crowded into corners and heaped onto occasional tables; a cacophony of deep pinks, vivid blues, and pops of yellow, the powdery-sweet scent thickening the air. Candles lined every surface: long tapered ones in antique brass holders threaded through the centre of the table; they flickered from sconces on the walls; thick pillars in variegated heights lined the mantelpiece, bouncing light off the gilt-framed mirrors and casting the room in a buttery-yellow glow. Somewhere, unseen, speakers played out soft female vocals at just the right level to round out the small talk in the room. Laurie had hit this with the full force of her artistic flair.

'Do you think it looks OK?' She came up behind me now, her breath hot against my neck.

'Laurie . . .' I took in the small crowd of guests, standing, heads together in conversation. The scene looked as though it had been staged for a fashion magazine. 'It looks perfect.'

'I know.' She squeezed my shoulder. 'Not bad, for an American.' As she walked away, I noticed an almost imperceptible stumble, the wobble of her glass as she righted herself, liquid sloshing over the rim and dribbling down the crevice of her thumb and forefinger. Four Martinis now. 'OK, everyone.' She held her hands above her head, clinked her ring finger against the side of her glass, exuberant. 'Places, please!'

The guests turned their attention to the dining table, shuffling past one another to find their names propped in front of the green-and-gold-rimmed charger plates. I located my seat, reached for the cream place card that bore my name in gold calligraphed letters. Beside it, a sketch of a flower – a lily – petals curled and stamen proud. I imagined Laurie's pleasure as she completed it.

Playing to tradition, we were seated almost perfectly boy–girl, single Sandy Maynard cleverly subsumed into the middle of the room, Laurie at the head with me beside her, smoothing away the unevenness. To my right, a man I hadn't yet spoken to, with a shock of white-blond hair and a ruddy blush to his cheeks and nose, turned to face me.

'Frederick,' he announced, with a rhotacized 'r', sticking a hand across my charger.

'Lily.' I held mine out in response and he gave it a hearty shake.

'The au pair?'

'Nanny.'

'Is there a difference?' he responded, lightly enough that I had to assume his flippancy wasn't deliberate.

Before I could reply, Laurie, whose seat had been left empty, stepped back into the room with the maid from earlier at her heels, each of them holding a tray.

'Now, before you lot start scoffing supper,' she declared from the doorway, her American accent more prominent wrapped around this English phrase, 'I want to take the opportunity to announce a little—' She broke off as a groan rose from near the middle of the table, tipped her chin to roll her eyes at the perpetrator. 'You don't even know what I'm going to say yet, Jonesy.' She cleared her throat dramatically. 'To announce a little game: Wink Murder.'

At that, the whole table erupted into good-natured grumbles, to which she gave a little mince of her shoulders, protested, 'You guys!' in such a manner that I assumed this was all part of an act; a general spirit of teasing and frivolity that seemed to hang over the room.

'We always play a game at the Rowes',' Frederick leaned across me, confirmed my theory. 'Laurie always wins.'

'Does everyone know how to play?' Laurie continued, when she had the room's attention once more.

'I'm sure you'll remind us!' Frederick bellowed from down our end of the table, hands cupped around his mouth. He had already helped himself to, and drunk, a full glass of red wine from the decanter in front of us.

I was sure I caught a rising flush in her cheeks at this, a flash of irritation as she watched him set the decanter down before her expression smoothed and she continued.

'So, if everyone would be so kind as to remove their chargers, you will all find a piece of folded paper underneath.' The sound of fifteen china plates being tipped up. I removed the square of paper from mine, let it rest in the palm of my hand. In truth I was grateful to Frederick, dim recollections of detectives and murderers doing little to fuel my knowledge of the game. 'You can all look inside your papers, but don't show them to anyone else. You'll find either a V, a D or an M. D is for detective. M is for murderer. V is for villager –' she lowered her voice conspiratorially '– or victim. Now, the murderer has the rest of the evening to "kill" as many people as possible – by winking at them – and the detective must guess who they are before the end of the night . . . or everyone dies.'

'Ooh, I'm the detective!' Charles, three seats down from me, held his unfolded paper aloft.

'Cha-arles.' Laurie stamped her foot. 'I didn't say you could start yet.'

'But I would have had to announce it in a second

anyway. I'm just speeding things along. I'm hungry.' He gave a semi-petulant whine.

'Fine.' She huffed, but signalled for the girl to start handing out the plates along one side of the table, as she proceeded down the other. 'So, Charles is the detective, but no one else tell anyone what's on your paper. Now, enjoy your starter: it's burrata with peaches and toasted walnuts. The peaches were grown in our very own greenhouse. And remember: die with style.'

I carefully unfolded my paper in my lap, felt an unwarranted thump in my chest when I saw the black M scrawled across its centre. Somehow, I wasn't surprised: I had a feeling that Laurie would want to take full advantage of my 'helping out' to ensure that the game would play out with adequate enthusiasm.

I crumpled the paper up tightly and squeezed it under the rim of my plate just as Laurie took her seat beside me.

'I think you've got an unfair advantage here, Laur.' Frederick stretched across me to pour Laurie a glass of wine, with only a momentary hesitation before he filled mine too. 'You could know who the murderer is.'

'Maybe I do, maybe I don't.' She raised the glass to her lips, gave him a wink.

As Frederick stabbed a fork into his cheese, I sensed Laurie's eyes on me, convincing me that she knew exactly who had received the letter M.

The noise in the room rose to a comfortable chatter as cutlery found plates and neighbours their conversation. Frederick, one step away from actually repositioning his chair, turned almost entirely to the woman on his right, a soft-faced blonde I remembered from one of Bess's playdates. To my left, Laurie began a conversation about an exhibition at the National Gallery with the man beside her, who I gleaned to be Meredith's husband. I tried to follow along, feigning interest with well-spaced head nods, but I found my mind wandering, my participation in the debate hardly adding much, and so I sat back to observe the room, wondering how to play my first move.

I did think it seemed a little unreasonable of Laurie, giving me this role when I was the only outsider in the party, and as I looked around the group, I couldn't help but feel a sense of absurdity at the idea of randomly winking at one of them. 'Don't kill me first,' she had whispered, as I tried to wink at her under the guise of passing the breadbasket, 'it'll be too obvious.' Instead, I found myself catching Jonesy's eye, down the other end of the table, as he reached for the white wine. As his fingers caught the bottle and his focus thrust forward, I tossed my hair, just enough to cause movement, and, as he looked up, I winked.

It took him a breath to realize what was going on, but then he cocked his head, winked back.

'Gaaaargh,' he moaned, giving it the full Amateur Dramatics Society effect. 'Help me, I'm dying.' He raised a hand to his temple and writhed in his chair, before slumping against the seatback, announcing, after a few more coughs, 'I am now dead,' shutting his eyes and lolling his head against his chest.

The room was silent for a moment, before bursting into a round of applause.

'Bravo, bravo, Jonesy.' Charles rose from his chair and

Jonesy unslumped, reached for his wine glass and took a deep drink. 'An excellent death. And a very interesting one.' He surveyed the room, fingers to his chin, plotting potential eyelines with his finger. It was silly, but I couldn't help holding my breath, at the thought of being 'discovered' so soon. 'For argument's sake, I'm going to take a first punt: Laurie, my love, is it you?'

Mock gasps abounded as Laurie stood.

'How dare you accuse your darling wife of such a thing?' She held her piece of paper aloft, showcasing the black V on it. She was in her element now, jovial with attention. It was quite clear in her typical, Laurie-ish way that she enjoyed the orchestration of it all. 'I protest, I am innocent. You'll be lucky to get pudding, with a betrayal such as that.'

The theatrics complete, the couple took their seats and the conversation resumed.

'Fun, right?' Laurie gave my wrist a squeeze. Her eyes were bright.

'Yes!' I answered, enthusiastically enough. And it was, if not a little odd. Although by that point I had grown used to my ridiculous new dwelling, to the quirks and whims of my eccentric hosts, this was the first time I had been so fully immersed in their lifestyle. Did posh people really still live like this? Throw elaborate dinner parties and host parlour games? I vaguely recalled my parents having friends over for dinner, in that window when I was both old enough to remember, and young enough that they were both in my life. But they tended to revolve around one of mum's one pots – lasagne or a casserole – a couple or two crowded round the kitchen table, probably one of the supermarket's better wines.

Starters morphed into main courses, and I managed to wink my way through three more murders without being detected. Frederick deigned to talk to me (even if it were only to draw me into a lengthy dictation about river fishing), and as my glass was filled and filled again, I felt a soporific warmth envelop me, softening the edges of the evening and melting away the last of my apprehensions. I was drunk, I knew. But not as drunk as the hostess beside me, who seemed to be filling her glass as quickly as she could drink it.

When the main courses were cleared, Laurie announced a shuffle to the seating plan, asking all the men to stand and move one place to their left.

'It's very traditional,' she slurred at me, over the scraping of chairs, 'and, in that respect, unusually feminist, gives women a bit of respite if they've been landed with someone dull. Do I look like a man to you?' She broke off, suddenly hostile, to stare Frederick full in the face as he hovered behind her chair, expecting her to move. 'I'm the hostess, I'm staying put.'

She poured herself another glass of wine, offered me the decanter as my new dinner companion took his seat. It was Charles.

I felt relieved to see him, at the opportunity to extricate myself from the conversational doldrums. But there was something else there, too. An odd feeling that had lingered since the drawing room. Perhaps longer.

'Well, hello there.' He squeezed into the seat beside me, lifting the decanter from Laurie's hands and tipping it into his own glass. 'Long time, no see. How are you enjoying the evening's festivities?'

In the flickering candlelight he looked undeniably handsome; even more so now that he was ever so slightly drink-dishevelled, top shirt buttons undone, hair curling at the temples.

I gave myself a mental shake. I had often observed Laurie and Charles together, remarked to myself what a good-looking couple they were. But it seemed totally inappropriate to think that of Charles in isolation.

'It's fun,' I answered hurriedly, so that a question curled itself around 'fun', made the pitch just high enough not to ring true. I saw Charles's mouth twitch, looked down at my chocolate fondant, embarrassed.

He glanced across at Laurie, now held captive to Frederick on her left, before leaning in.

'I find the whole thing a fucking bore, to be honest.' He left a pause for me to interject, but I didn't know what I was supposed to say, so he carried on. 'It's the same thing, every time: jaded rich people going on about their jaded lives. And with this lot, it's even worse; they already know all the stories, all that's left is one-upmanship. "We're going skiing at Christmas," "Us too, must dust off the custom-made skis," "Yes, yes, need to remember to call the housekeeper, get the heating sorted in the chalet."' He shook his head, took a drink from his glass, and I heard the liquid swill around his mouth. 'Sorry, I'm being grumpy because Laurie sat me next to Anna Gladsby, who she knows particularly rubs me up the wrong way. You're a welcome replacement. Go on: how are you, really?'

I felt a deep pressure, suddenly, to say something interesting. With Laurie, I found myself skirting her moods, trying to avoid doing anything that might anger or upset her, but with Charles it was different: I actively sought out ways to please him. It had started the day in the library when we had talked about *Jamaica Inn*. I'd finished it quickly, moved on, on his recommendation, to *My Cousin Rachel*. When I told him I'd enjoyed it, even more so than the first, he'd given a little hum of pleasure, 'Hmm, I'm glad – I thought you might.' After that it was small things: making sure his favourite coffee mug was always in the right place; collecting a particular shell, when he mentioned offhand that they were his favourite as a child; engaging Bess and William in an afternoon's baking because he mentioned, that morning, that he really 'fancied something sweet'. I didn't do it consciously; certainly, I didn't act with any sort of ulterior motive, but it was just *so nice* to feel appreciated. It had been so long since it had been that easy to brighten someone's day, and I found myself enjoying the results this elicited – the 'Gosh, you shouldn't have', the 'Well isn't that lovely' – too much to stop.

'Well,' I said then, feeling an illicit surge of endorphins as I angled myself away from Laurie, knowing, unfairly, that I was about to betray her. 'If you really want me to be honest . . . I'm finding it really fucking boring too.'

He laughed at this, a real tip-of-the-head, open-mouthed guffaw that caught Laurie's attention, made her turn her head and watch us, eager to get in on the joke. As she turned, I became aware of how close Charles and I had been sitting, his knee brushing my upper thigh, where the fabric of my dress had risen up to expose flesh. I shifted, breaking the contact.

'What?' She looked into our faces, trying to read the answer on them.

But Charles shook his head. 'Nothing, darling. Lily just said something funny.'

Turning to face her, I found myself staring directly at her, saw her smile dip down. It was only a momentary inflection though, because then she was heaving it back, patting my arm affectionately.

'She's a funny girl, our Lily.'

I grinned at her, over warm. 'I'm glad you think so.' Clumsily trying to emphasize my allegiance to her.

The spell was gone, though, and Charles's attention drifted away from me. Jemima, the woman on his right with an impossibly long neck and impossibly deep voice, asked him to pass her the wine, and in doing so drew him into a conversation about politics. Laurie circled me back in with Frederick, but every now and then she would stop, tilt her head to me and widen her eyes suggestively. I couldn't work out what was going on until the third time, when, leaning into me so that I could smell, deeply, the alcohol on her breath, she hissed, 'The game, Lily, the game.'

'Right,' I breathed, blinked swiftly at her, once.

'Ooooh,' she began to groan, quietly, a hand to her temple. And then again, a little louder, 'Ooooh, I've been poisoned.' The people nearest her quieted down, watching her show with interest, but Charles, deep in conversation, had his body turned completely away from her, waving his arms passionately. 'Ooooh!' she roared, as slowly the rest of the diners paused their conversations. When this still had no effect on him she sat bolt upright, spat in his direction, 'For fuck's sake, Charles, you're the only one.'

'What?' With a pout in his voice he looked round at her as she revived her performance, writhing in her chair, and quite visibly rolled his eyes. 'God, are we really still playing?' She threw him a look, and in response he stood, cleared his throat, 'There appears to have been a murder: whoever could it be?' His voice was deliberately flat, no attempt at hamming.

'Get on with it, Charles, or we'll be staying for breakfast!' a voice called across the table.

'Fine, whatever, let's get on with it.' His voice was short, making his irritation palpable, and next to me I felt Laurie stiffen. He flung a hand in the direction of the woman opposite him. 'Annabelle.' But she shook her head. 'OK then, Meredith.'

'I'm already dead,' came the response.

'Oh, Jesus fucking Christ.' Charles jigged on his feet, scanning the room like a reluctant child.

'I said I was poisoned, Charles, surely that gives you a clue?' Laurie spoke evenly, but I saw the flex of her fingers as they curled around the stem of her glass.

He brought a hand to his head, scratched furiously at the hair near his temple. 'Right then, Frederick.'

'Errr.' Frederick thrust a thumb down, made a sound like a gameshow buzzer.

'OK, all right then, I give up.' Charles flung his hands in the air. 'Just tell me who it is and let's be done with it.'

'Why are you doing this?' I noted the edge of hysteria

creeping into her voice, saw, to my surprise, tears smarting the corners of her eyes. I wondered if she cared that everyone could hear.

He thrust himself towards her, body loose like a petulant toddler

'Because it's a stupid game, Laur. No one asked to play it.'

Gritting her teeth against the tears, Laurie jerked her head up at him. 'Then finish it, and they can all go home.'

'No.' He flung himself into his seat. 'I'm done.'

Laurie exhaled deeply, propelling the air from her chest.

'Fine,' she spat. 'Fine. It's Lily. Are you satisfied? It's fucking Lily, all right? It was so goddam obvious, you must have known it, you were just purposely ruining the game to upset me.'

Feeling increasingly awkward sitting between them, knowing any attempt to move would only make me more obvious, I had resolved instead to just keep staring at the same spot on the tablecloth, but at the sound of my name I felt the eyes of the entire dinner party on me, wished with a desperate fervour that I could disappear underneath it.

'Are you listening to yourself?' Charles, oblivious, raised his voice. Around me, I saw the other guests shift uncomfortably, not quite knowing where to look. 'It's just a game, Laurie. I'm not trying to sabotage it. It's a stupid children's game. I don't care. Just get over it. No one cares.'

'*I* care, Charles,' she hissed back. 'Did you ever think

about that? I—' But whatever she was about to say faltered, because as she spoke she slammed her fists against the table, and knocked the corner of the glass so that it crashed onto the corner of my plate, breaking cleanly in two. I watched, frozen, as wine dripped off the edge of the table and a deep cherry-coloured bloom began to spread across my lap. 'Oh . . .' Her fervour silenced, she pressed a hand to her mouth. 'Oh, Lily, I'm so, so sorry, I . . .'

'Laurie, it's all right,' I murmured as she began to dab at me with the napkin. 'Please, don't worry about it, I . . . I'll go and change, honestly, don't stress.'

I was already moving, up out of my chair before she had a chance to protest.

The moment I was free from the room I pressed my back against the wall of the corridor, breathing in the fresh, candle-free air. A headache threatened my temples, and I hadn't realized until now I was shaking.

It seemed such a silly thing for Laurie to get so worked up about, and yet I couldn't understand why Charles had goaded her like that. Why couldn't he just play along, if it were so important to her? And why did I feel like I was involved?

In the quiet of my bedroom, I unzipped the dress and dug out a pair of jeans and a jumper. I would look odd, I knew, but there seemed little point in dressing up again now. Besides, after the exposure of the game, not to mention the dress, I found myself craving comfort.

I left the dress in a heap on my bed, resolving to tackle it in the morning.

By the time I returned to the group, it was clear that

the party was over. One of the couples had already left and several others were pulling on their coats, spilling out into the Great Hall. The dining table had been abandoned, but I could see Charles over by the fireplace, talking to Jonesy, his wife hovering just out of earshot.

'Thank you, Laurie, for tonight. It was as exquisite as always.' As I came down the stairs, I spotted Meredith hovering by the door, wrapping a cashmere shawl over her shoulders. She lowered her voice as I stepped into the hallway, but I heard, all the same, 'Call me, won't you, if you ever need to talk?'

Laurie pressed a gentle but persuasive hand to Meredith's shoulder as she opened the door fully.

'Thank you, darling. Everything's fine. I just got a little . . . overemotional.' She spied me then, perched on the bottom step, gave me a small nod of acknowledgement. 'I'll see you at the committee meeting next week. Drive safely.' She turned to me fully, leaving Meredith to make her own way into the drive, and eyed my clothes. 'Probably more comfortable, at least?' And then, before I had time to answer, 'Lily, I know I did say you were a guest this evening, but would you mind ever so much blowing out the candles in the dining room? The maid should have finished clearing everything by now.'

'Of course.'

I was relieved that Laurie's anger seemed to have diffused, or at least that she had, and made my way to the dining room, announcing my duty to Charles and the remaining guests, who soon got Laurie's hint and left the room.

I hadn't quite made it around the second half of the dining table when I heard the front door slam shut, the echo of wood reverberating on the hinges. Seconds later, the sound of voices, raised. When I looked out into the hall they were in a stand-off, facing one another at the base of the stairs. Someone had turned off the hall-way lights, but the thin light of the full moon outside glowed through the sash windows, illuminating them.

'I hope you're happy. You made an absolute fool of yourself tonight,' Charles was saying. 'You shouldn't have drunk so much. You know the effect it has. Why do you feel the need to do this to yourself?'

With just the slightest bit of guilt, I abandoned my post and crept to the doorway, tucking myself behind one of the double doors so that I could spy without being detected.

'Don't patronize me, Charles, for God's sake.' Laurie came into view, swaying on the bottom step, rolling her weight from her heels to the balls of her feet. I watched as she overbalanced, reached for the banister to right herself. 'I don't need a psychiatric evaluation from *you*.'

'You should go to bed.' He crossed his arms with a sigh.

'Don't tell me what to do. I'm not a child.'

'I'm not telling you . . .'

He took a step towards her, but she batted him away, her arms flailing.

'I said don't fucking tell me what to do.' Laurie's voice became a shriek, so sudden and so high-pitched it made me flinch.

'Stop it, Laurie. You'll wake the children.' His voice was even, low, his body still. The hard rock to Laurie's messy fluidity.

'Laurie, you'll wake the children.' She danced on the bottom step, sprite-like, mimicking his English accent. Her face was pressed so close to his that in another situation they might have kissed.

I knew I shouldn't be listening, but at the same time, I couldn't force myself to turn away. So much about Charles and Laurie's relationship fascinated me; the idea of seeing them alone, completely unfettered, was too compelling to resist.

'Go to *bed*, woman.' He turned his head, presenting her with his cheek, I heard it then, the rising anger in him. The low growl underpinning his words. When he looked back, he took a step towards her, hand pressing into the banister just centimetres from her own.

'No.'

'Please, just go to bed, Laurie.'

'Make me.' She took a step towards him, defiant. 'You know you want to.'

The sound he made was guttural, ripped from somewhere between his chest and throat. And then, without warning, he lunged at her, grabbed her by the waist, pulled her to him. She yelped out in pain, beating his back with balled fists as she tried to rip herself free, but he was much stronger than her, easily holding her in place, and out of instinct I shut my eyes, not wanting to watch as Charles half carried, half dragged her up the staircase.

They reached the entrance to their wing, where they

were half-hidden in the shadow of the corridor, and he finally set her to her feet. Taking a risk, I left my post and crept into the hallway, concealing myself under the base so that I could watch undetected. Charles's back was to me, but in the dim light I could still make out the tension in his shoulders, his back taut, fists clenched. It was undeniably menacing; but rather than retreat, I watched as Laurie's body shifted, her shoulders melted as she leaned against Charles, arms reaching for his neck as she began to sob. In response, he unclenched his fists, brought her to him. They moved towards their wing as one, Laurie's arms wrapped around his torso, and the last thing I saw of them before they disappeared was Charles's hand reaching for the back of Laurie's head, stroking the length of her hair as tenderly as he would a child.

I stood in the hallway for a long time, trying to process what I had witnessed, the events of the evening as they had unfolded before me. Had Laurie designed from the start to get herself so drunk? And if so, what for? Her behaviour seemed completely self-destructive, as though she had been on a mission to take herself down from the get-go.

The house was quiet now, bar the usual creaks and groans, and I heard nothing more from Laurie, or, thankfully, the children. I felt entirely shaken up by the episode, though, the depths of my stomach twisting against all the rich food and drink. I knew I wouldn't be able to sleep. Instead, I blew out the rest of the candles and made my way into the kitchen – left spotless by Laurie's serving girl, who seemed to have slipped out unawares – took a mug down from the cupboard and made myself a chamomile tea.

I pulled out one of the bar stools and sat down at the kitchen counter, swirling the teabag round by its tag as I inhaled the sweet, herbaceous scent. Nan used to make me chamomile tea when I was upset. She was a big believer in all that – lavender for sleep, peppermint to invigorate you. I've never known if it's the tea itself or just the memory of Nan administering it, stroking my hair as she held the steaming mug before me, but I've always found it helps. I didn't bother to turn on the lights, instead I allowed myself to enjoy the lack of stimulus, the darkness and the quiet an antidote to the kinetic evening.

As I bent my head to take a sip, I heard movement behind me, turned to see Charles in the open doorway. There was a moment, a brief pause before he realized I was there, and in that moment I saw him raise his fists in the air, squeezing his fingers so tightly I saw his knuckles tremble, before he slackened, his arms dropping to his sides.

His fingers found the light switch and I flinched, covering my face as the room was plunged into brightness. 'Oh!' I looked up as he momentarily shrank back, relaxing when he realized it was only me. 'Lily, I didn't see you there. Why were you sitting in the dark?'

He dimmed the lights to a more comfortable level, stepped fully into the room.

'I didn't think to turn them on. And then it was quite nice. Peaceful.' My voice caught in my throat. It felt like it had been a while since I had last spoken out loud. I cleared it, gestured to my mug. 'I was just having some tea, but I can take it upstairs, give you some space.'

'No, stay.' He held an arm out towards me, pausing me as I started to raise myself from the chair. 'I'd like the company . . . if you don't mind?'

I sat.

He moved smoothly through the room, taking a rocks glass down from a shelf. I hadn't noticed until he crossed past me that he had been holding a bottle in his hand, one of the cut-glass decanters from the drawing room. He uncapped it, poured himself a good measure, came to sit beside me.

'My father was a big whisky drinker. It was the one outlier, for someone as puritanical as he purported to be.' He rolled the glass around in the palm of his hand, took a drink. 'Used to get cases of the stuff sent down from Scotland. Every night without fail, he'd pour himself a glass and sit in the library, drinking and working on those ships in glass bottles – you might have noticed them, they're still there on the top shelves?' I bobbed my head, not wanting to interject. 'In my second year at school I was sent home for drinking. Me and another boy paid one of the B-blockers to buy us a bottle of vodka. We got pissed and killed our house mistress's cat. Silly thing: we were larking about and obviously one of us kicked the bugger too hard. When I got home, my father sat me down in the library – at that same desk where he made his impossible bottles – and made me drink an entire decanter of whisky. Wouldn't let me leave until I did. I was sick about halfway through but even that didn't stop him. He said if I thought I was such a man, I should drink like one.' He raised the glass to his lips, drained it. 'It was years until I could touch the stuff again.'

I tried to think of something to say – 'That's awful', 'I'm so sorry' – but nothing seemed quite appropriate. Eventually he set the glass down, shifted his body weight so that he was facing me.

'I'm very sorry about what happened tonight, Lily.' His tone was formal, but his eyes were soft, almost pleading.

'Really, it's fine, I . . .'

'No, honestly. It wasn't fair on you, to witness that. Laurie . . .' He looked down at the glass as if he'd forgotten he'd finished it. 'Laurie can be . . .' He struggled, seemingly unsure how to finish the thought, but then he rested his elbows on the marble counter, leaned over them so that his face was inches from my own. 'She's always been . . . what I suppose people call "complex".'

'How do you mean?'

'She didn't have a happy childhood. It was one of the things we first bonded over, actually.' He sighed. 'Now, it's like she's making up for that, trying to form this vision of a perfect life, herself as the perfect person, and if something or someone doesn't live up to that ideal, it's as though she holds herself personally accountable. She agonizes over every little detail. She needs everything in her life to be just so. You could call her the ultimate perfectionist.'

I recalled everything I had learned about Laurie over the last few weeks, her niggles here and there, her displeasure in disorder, the light coercion around how I dressed, acted, that I had come to explain as commonplace. I could see how behind each incident lay a tautness, a mania for control that must have given way to the release I had witnessed that evening.

'She . . . she hurts herself.' Charles spoke into the pause in conversation, letting the moment land. 'When she was a young woman, she was institutionalized. Her wrists.' This he said opaquely, but it didn't take much imagination to guess what he was insinuating. I thought of Laurie's kimonos, tried to picture the slender curve of her wrists as they held a paintbrush aloft. Would I have guessed, if I'd thought to notice?

'I . . . I'm so sorry.'

He shook his head.

'From how I understand it, there was a lot of disruption at home. Parents who couldn't stand each other, but didn't believe in divorce. Catholics. They blamed her for their unhappiness . . . and in return, she blamed herself. They framed her as "wilful". She spent a stint in something called a Wilderness Camp – awful place, a sort of religious boot camp for troubled teens where they did wicked things to her: verbal abuse, starvation, whipping. It wasn't long after she was released from there that she . . .' He looked down, fingers circling the rim of his empty glass.

Whipping.

With a shudder, I recalled the scars on her back. Now I knew their source. How could anyone do that to a young girl?

'They diagnosed her with "borderline personality

disorder" or some other psychobabble horseshit. Her family was very wealthy, and got her the best treatment money could buy, more like a private boarding school than an institution, but she was in there for two years before I . . . well, that was how we met.'

My mind staggered, crawling over what Laurie had told me the day I had arrived.

'But didn't she . . . I thought you met her when she was an art student . . . ?'

He gave me a sad smile, just the faintest breeze of it blowing across his face. 'That was always the easiest way of explaining it. It was part of a programme I volunteered for, a series of lectures they did at places like she was in.' He must have seen the look on my face, because he added, 'I did say it was a particularly privileged environment.' His hand went to the glass again, and he hesitated, before moving it purposefully away. 'When I first met her, you wouldn't believe she had any of that darkness lurking beneath the surface. You've seen her yourself – her energy, her exuberance.' He smoothed a hand through his hair, fingers catching in the curls. 'Lily, I'm only telling you this because I want you to understand why Laurie behaves the way she does. She would hate it if she knew that you knew. You'll . . . you'll look out for her, won't you? Take her little foibles with a pinch of salt, understand that they come from a very complicated place.' He looked very tired then, all of a sudden, lines creasing down the centre of his brow. I thought of Laurie's yo-yoing moods, the erratic highs and lows that I had found myself trying to second-guess.

It must be a lot to live with, isolated out here in this big old house.

Instinctively I reached across the marble, placed a hand on top of his. 'Of course.'

'She was so young, when we got married.' His voice was hoarse, and when I looked at him, he seemed so sad. 'We both were, really. If not in age, in wisdom. I didn't know . . . I didn't fully appreciate . . .' He sighed. 'Sometimes this life feels like a prison.'

I hadn't noticed, until then, how the distance between us had collapsed, how over the course of the conversation our bodies had angled into one another so that our knees were almost touching. In my sluggish, wine-racked mind, in the snug warmth and dim light of the kitchen, I realized a second too late what was about to happen, didn't anticipate the way my knees had moved, my upper thigh brushing his. But then, before I fully knew what was happening, he was leaning forward, his face moving towards me. As I felt his lips touch mine, I could taste the whisky still burning on his breath, feel the warmth of his hands as they found the back of my head, fingers enmeshing with the hairs escaping from the nape of my neck, and it was the corporeality of this that snapped me into life.

'Oh. Oh God.' I pulled my mouth from his, my body away, slid from the stool; in one movement, like a loose thread dragged from a hem. 'I'm so sorry. I didn't mean – that shouldn't – I need to go.'

I expected some reaction – words, reasoning – but he barely even moved, sat on that stool as passively as though I had never been beside him, and so, as though uttering another word would give credence to this reality, I left.

In the bathroom I removed my make-up, untied my hair, trying to put my thoughts in order, to make some sense of the discombobulating night.

What had I done?

I was attracted to Charles. I couldn't deny that any longer; couldn't deny the effect he had on me, the way my lips still burned at the thought of his mouth on mine. It wasn't just his looks; there was something enigmatic in his personality, too. Up until then it hadn't been something I had consciously acknowledged, but rather a pleasant underscore to my life at Kewney Manor, much like the soft cotton sheets I slept on, or the lime-and-basil scent that Laurie's favourite candles perfumed throughout the house.

Clearly, I had done something to implicate my attraction, even if my awareness of it was a half-formed thing.

But acting on it, what had just happened . . . this, this was *wrong* . . .

It was Nick, as always, who inserted himself in my thoughts. He had constantly accused me of inviting unwarranted attention. He cited my 'desperate need to be liked by everyone', the clothes I wore, the way I did my hair, my make-up – even the way I stood – as evidence that my behaviour was deliberate. 'What do you take me for, a cuck?' he'd accuse, wrenching me away from whatever man I happened to be near or, God forbid, talking to. 'Why don't you just get your fucking tits out and be done with it?'

But I hadn't been that person. And I didn't want to

be, now. And yet here I was, fulfilling every cliché Nick had accused me of.

And lord, what about *Laurie*? How could I have done this to her, after all the kindness she had shown me? After all that she had given me – without her even realizing the magnitude of it – by offering me my escape?

I brushed my teeth, hard, but I was sure I could still taste the lingering smoke of whisky on my breath.

Tonight was a mistake. A drunken misunderstanding. I was sure that Charles would feel the same. If we were lucky, neither of us would ever have to mention it again.

I would wash away every trace of that cringe-inducing moment. And in the morning light I would start afresh. I had let myself be drawn in by Charles and Laurie's kindness, to their insistence I was more than an employee. And in doing so, I had forgotten myself, and all that I could stand to lose. I needed to keep my head down and focus on what I had nominally come here to do: my job.

Back in the corridor I saw all the house lights were off, the kitchen door closed. There was no sign of Charles. I made it to my room undetected.

I undressed quickly, in the dark. The dress was still where I had left it, sprawled across the bed, a torqued body marred with red. My thoughts turned again to Laurie, the heat of her that evening, and I swiftly rolled the lace into a ball, stuffed it into the far recesses of the wardrobe.

Sleep came, eventually, but as I tossed and turned, the image of the dress remained: the ugly red, violent against the white lace; a scarlet letter whose stain I wasn't sure would wash away.

9

The next morning I woke early, my body eager to rid itself of a rotten sleep, never so grateful for a Sunday. I blindly threw on the first clothes I could find and crept into the Great Hall, relieved to see that the adjacent rooms were empty. I couldn't bear the thought of facing them yet. Either of them. So, although the day was still pale, I forced myself into the car and drove, ignoring the hungover throb at my temples, following signs on autopilot until I reached Truro, and spent the day trying to forget myself.

It was still early afternoon by the time I made myself return home. There had been a shower earlier, but now the sky was an opaque blue, the sun high in the air. The jasmine had been baked in the clear heat, and the pungency of it cloyed as I shut the car door, trod towards the house.

'Lily, is that you?'

Laurie's voice called for me as soon as I passed the threshold, from all the way over in the parlour. Almost as though she had been waiting for me.

I shut the front door behind me, the sound reverberating around the high ceilings and wide corridors. The world of Kewney closed around me once more.

'Lily?' she called again, her voice insistent and, did I detect it, angry?

Although it was clear from the gleaming hallways that a team of cleaners had been in to expunge the remnants of the party, a smell still lingered – champagne and fried food and the cloying, thick scent of the floral arrangements – renewing the hangover I thought had been forgotten; my stomach curdled with a wave of nausea.

So much had passed in the relatively short time since I had last seen her, wild and rambling on the stairs. As I took a step in the direction of the parlour, a thought struck me: did she know I had seen them fighting? I cringed at the thought. If so, it must have looked awful to her this morning, to discover that I had just taken off without a word.

And then another thought hit me, far worse: *what if she knows?*

Drunk as she was, what if she had slipped down the stairs on another one of her nightly wanderings, spied us in the kitchen?

'*Liii-ly*,' she called again, and the paranoia that had settled in me since Nick began to rise. I had watched them argue, seen how upset she was, and then how did I repay her? By kissing her husband. 'Are you there?' My stomach tightened. 'Can I have a word?'

I recalled the incident in the kitchen, not long after I had first arrived. Her coldness as she tipped the chicken carcass into the bin. And that was over nothing. A trifle.

What would she do now? Fire me?

And, if she fired me, where would I go? How could I leave, and risk exposing myself?

Pressure swelled inside my temples as I reached the

parlour, a sense memory of that final night in London rising in my nostrils: the smell of the flat, acrid and biting. Nick's sleeping form affording him a gentleness that *almost* made me hesitate.

Would I ever be free of him, or would I forever be looking over my shoulder?

No.

I steeled myself.

I couldn't afford to leave Kewney Manor. Not when I was finally starting to feel safe. Whatever I faced on the other side of that door, I had to do everything in my power to stay.

I wrapped my fingertip around the scrolled door handle. Turned. Pushed.

'Laurie?'

But as I looked around the room, she wasn't waiting for me at all. She was painting. Wrapped in a deep-blue robe that made her hair appear richer, a more vibrant red. Sunlight streamed through the French doors, bathing the room in warmth. A scented candle was burning on the mantelpiece. She was even humming.

I breathed in the candle's clean citrus scent and the fear began to dissipate. Maybe I had got it all wrong? She didn't know anything about what happened last night. Perhaps she didn't even know I had witnessed the argument.

As I breathed out, I felt light.

I was safe.

'Hi,' she said simply, her back still turned.

It was a new canvas, I saw, much smaller than the last, depicting a bay – presumably ours – in the soft evening light. Also unlike the last one, this had an aura of calm about it, the tide low, barely a wrinkle of a wave, the canvas washed in muted tones: peach, rose and periwinkle blue melding with the soft gold sand. In the right-hand corner, the outline of two figures could be seen, holding hands.

'William and Bess,' she clarified when she saw me looking. 'This one isn't to sell, it's just for me.'

'It's beautiful.' And then, tentatively. 'Where are they?'

'With Charles. He's taken them paddle-boarding. There's a good surf over at Polkerris beach today.'

Her tone was even, but my morning's absence lingered in the air, the unsaidness of it, of the night before, weighing on me.

'I'm sorry for not telling you I was going out.' I looked down at my feet.

'No need to apologize,' she breezed. 'Sunday is your day off. The children did ask if you'd want to come, but when I saw the car was gone, I assumed the answer was "no".'

I marvelled at this, her ability to make me feel reproach even when she was allegedly placating me.

'I was up early,' I stammered. 'So I thought I'd give you some space. I thought, perhaps, after last night . . .' I stopped myself. I had managed to escape Laurie bringing up the party; why would I go and bring it up myself? 'Anyway, I'm glad you're not cross I wasn't here. If there was nothing else you needed, I think I'll go and take a quick shower before they get back, if that's OK? I was at the beach near St Agnes today and I've got salt spray all over my—'

'Lily?'

'Yes?'

She placed the paintbrush she had been holding on the corner of the easel and walked around the back of sofa so that she was facing me.

I felt a wave of light-headedness.

'I wanted to talk to you about what happened last night. With Charles.'

There it was.

It was as though the floor had given way. I found myself reaching out for a chair back, steadying myself as my vision lurched.

'Laurie – I – we—'

'That behaviour was clearly unacceptable.' I bowed my head, chastened, prepared for the blow. 'It's not something you ever should have witnessed.' She sighed deeply as I held my breath. 'I shouldn't drink like that. It doesn't mix well with me. And I'm sorry.'

'*Oh.*' I looked up, my mind in a jumble. It wasn't *my* behaviour she was talking about, but hers. My breathing eased. 'No, no, Laurie, please. There's nothing for you to be sorry about. It was a party, it was just . . . part of the fun.'

My voice come out flat, and I could tell that we both knew it.

She gave me a long look.

'Did Charles . . . did he say anything to you, about me? The way I acted?'

I pictured the two of us, huddled in the kitchen. *She hurts herself.* I glanced at her wrists, at the naked space in between her hand and the kimono fabric, quickly looked away.

'No . . . nothing. Why?'

Out of the corner of my eye, I saw her twitch the sleeves, adjust the robe.

'He's a good man, Charles. When he wants to be.' Her voice curled. 'Wouldn't you agree?'

Now I wished the floor had given way. That it had swallowed me up. 'I'm sure he is. But I wouldn't say I knew him that well.'

She gave a throaty little laugh. I tried to force myself to look up, make myself part of the in-joke.

'My husband likes to think he knows me better than anyone else. But I know him, too.' She leaned against the back of the sofa, draping her arms over it. 'When you get married, Lily, you are agreeing to take on the whole person: the good, and the bad. "In sickness and in health," as they say. It's up to you to make the good shine brighter than the bad. It's all about trust. And understanding. We have both been shaped by our pasts. The things that happened there that we'd rather forget. Neither of us are perfect.' Her features darkened momentarily. 'But although we may have our faults, we are partners: two halves of a whole. And we do whatever it takes to make our marriage work.'

Her words were a riddle.

We do whatever it takes.

Did she know? Was she . . . could she possibly be condoning it?

'You're both very lucky,' I spoke carefully, 'to have

found one another. I could only hope to have a relationship like that one day: true equals.'

She was silent for a moment, taking me in. I felt her parsing my features, tried not to squirm under her keen gaze. And then she beamed at me, as bright and clear as I had ever known her.

'You're a smart girl, Lily. Smarter than I think I appreciated.' And then she sprung into movement, stalking back over to her easel and picking up her paintbrush, demonstrably bringing the conversation to a close. 'Anyway. I'm sure you don't want me lecturing you about marriage. Thank you. For accepting my apology. I hope that this has cleared the air, and we can move on?'

I thought of Charles. There was nothing I wanted more than to move on from last night, to pretend it had never happened. I couldn't believe that I would be leaving the parlour with both my job and my dignity intact. Now all I could think about was leaving the parlour as quickly as possible before I ran the risk of exposing the cracks.

'Yes, Laurie, of course—' I opened my mouth to excuse myself, but she interrupted me.

'In that case, you'll join us for dinner tonight?'

'Oh . . .' I hesitated. The request caught me off guard. I hadn't seen Charles since our kiss. How could I sit through an entire dinner with him, with his *wife*, pretending that nothing had happened? 'Are you sure you don't . . . want some space?'

'Of course not.' Her face softened. 'Your company is just the tonic we need.'

In my fluster I couldn't think of another excuse to offer up, and when I didn't answer straight away, she stood, breaking the moment and suddenly business-like.

'So, it's settled. Dinner at eight.' She turned back to her canvas. 'You should run off and have that shower now. Before the children get back.'

I twitched, was about to move when she called out. 'Oh, I nearly forgot: I have something for you.'

'Oh?'

She pointed offhandedly to the Chinese screen that stood behind a pair of antique cane chairs by the window. 'Hanging off the screen, there.'

When she didn't move, I stepped over to the screen, pulled down what I saw was a garment bag hanging off it.

'Oh Laurie,' I started, 'honestly, another dress, I . . .'

'Open it.'

Slowly I unzipped the garment bag, revealing the spill of white lace beneath it. The dress from the party, miraculously resurrected. Or, rather, reproduced, as the brand-new labels indicated.

'. . . I don't understand?'

'I found the old one in your wardrobe. I knew the dry cleaner wouldn't be able to fix it, so I couriered you over a new one.'

'Oh.'

I felt an odd little jolt at the thought of her in my room, and she must have read it in my face, because she held her hands up in submission. 'I was instructing a new cleaning girl. The agency sends them to us on rotation.'

She did me the courtesy of turning then, stepped

towards the dress to snap the tags as I faltered, 'Laurie . . . you honestly didn't have to . . .'

'I know.' She rested a hand on my shoulder. 'But I did it anyway.' She had painted her nails, I noticed, buffed them into smooth rounds. Yesterday, they had been a soft pastel pink. Today they were a deep, vermillion red. 'I do hate seeing things stained.' She gave a little shudder. 'And it was so easy. To fix the problem.'

I nodded dumbly. I wasn't sure I'd ever want to wear the dress again. Certainly not in Laurie's presence.

'Besides, I wanted to show you how much I care about you, how much I value your position in this house.' She took the dress fully out of the bag, shook it lightly so that it hung straight. 'You're so much more than an employee here, Lily. You're my friend.'

'Thank you,' I answered weakly. 'That's a kind thing to say.'

She shifted, and I thought perhaps she would finally allow me to go, but then she paused, curled her head to one side, pure feline.

'You'd tell me, wouldn't you, if there was anything you were unhappy about here?'

I felt her waiting for an answer. Swallowed hard. 'Yes, of course.'

'Good.' A smile slicked itself across her mouth. 'I hope you think that you can trust me, the way that I trust you?'

For the first time I fully noticed the smell of paint and turpentine on her clothes, making my eyes sting. 'I trust you, Laurie.'

'Wonderful.' And then she lay the dress across the back of one of the cane chairs, turned to her painting.

'Take that up now, won't you? You remember how I hate to see things lying around.'

Wordlessly, I moved through the room, picked the garment bag up by the hanger.

'Laurie?' I spoke softly, but not so softly that she couldn't have heard. I watched her for a moment, the way her brush glided over the canvas, taking charge of the painting as she had done with our conversation.

When she didn't turn, I left.

10

I offered to put the children to bed that night. Laurie tried to protest, *No, no, don't be silly, it's your day off,* but I resisted. If anything, it would buy me time before I had to face Charles.

As I listened to them chatter about their day, their happy burble about which one of them had lasted longer on the waves without falling off and who'd chosen the better ice-cream flavour, I found myself replaying my conversation with Laurie in my head, sifting through the gap between the words in search of a deeper meaning to our odd interaction. I found her such an enigma; at once both alarmingly candid and frustratingly obscure. Despite saying nothing to indicate it, I still couldn't shake the feeling that she knew about what had happened with Charles. Her half-revelation about their marriage gave off a whiff of knowing more than she was alluding to. And what had she meant about their pasts? Charles had already painted a picture of Laurie's childhood, of his own strict upbringing. How *had* it shaped him?

The longer I stayed here, the more my list of questions grew, none of them answered.

'Lily? Are you coming?'

Bess's voice called to me in the corridor as I closed the door to William's room, pulling me out of myself.

'Coming, love.'

She was waiting for me, punctilious eldest child that she was, ready to begin our nightly ritual, where we took it in turns to read a page from whatever book we were currently working our way through. So far, we had visited chocolate factories, and midnight gardens, and met talking spiders, but that night, she held up an ageing yellow hardback illustrated with what looked like twin girls in matching bathrobes, peeking through a doorway.

'Can we try this one?'

I fingered the cover – *The Twins at St. Clair's*, an Enid Blyton book I didn't recall having read myself. I was surprised – the book was old, one I hadn't seen before, and I questioned her on it.

'I found it in the attic when William and I were playing hide-and-seek. It says it's "a school story for girls".' She traced a finger over the subtitle. 'Please can we read it?'

She looked up at me, her brown eyes wide, tugging easily at my affections, and I gave her shoulders a squeeze.

'Yes, of course we can.'

I took the book in my hands, leafing through the pages to find the start. As I did, I noticed a scrawl of handwriting in the top right-hand corner of the title page: Christine Anne Rowe, September 1959.

The handwriting was childish: bulbous, perfectly formed letters spaced neatly apart; a skill being practised. I pointed to it.

'Who's Christine?'

She looked for a moment and then shrugged, bored of thinking.

'Dunno. Can we start, please?'

'Sure.' I cleared my throat to elicit my best 'reading voice', but as I slipped into the easy rhythm of the narrative, my mind wandered, the name and date nagging at me. Charles would have been born around 1963. There was therefore no way the book could have belonged to his mother; she would have been a grown woman by 1959. So who was Christine?

I thought of Charles's sister – the older one Joss had mentioned. Could it be her? Joss had said that there were rumours, that people thought she was really Charles's mother, but he never said what had become of her. Charles never mentioned her, so I had assumed she had passed away. But how was it that Bess didn't recognize the name of her own aunt?

'Lily.' Bess jerked the book in my direction, snapping me back to attention. 'It's your go.'

'Sorry, yes, where are we?' I turned back to the book, forcing the thought away from me.

When I had finally negotiated a last page and pretended not to notice the glow of Bess's bedside light coming on as I shut the bedroom door, I made my way downstairs and into the kitchen to find Laurie standing over the range, washed and dressed in a pretty floral-print dress that skimmed the ankles of her bare feet. The smell of cooking hung in the air: fried onions and the smoky saltiness of bacon that she was browning in a heavy Le Creuset pan. On the counter beside her was a net of what looked like clams.

'You're here!' she chimed, handing me a champagne flute. 'Perfect timing. So you'll join us, then? Do say yes?'

She gave me a wistful look, as though the request from earlier had been an invitation, rather than the command it had been so clearly intended as.

'Thank you, Laurie.' As I took the glass, I glanced at the intricate leather bracelet that was wrapped around her wrist. On the other, a watch with a thick gold strap. After our encounter earlier I realized that this was why I'd never happened upon any scars on her wrists; she was too adept at hiding them. I pressed the rim to my mouth, steeling myself to address the other figure in the room. 'Yes, I would love to join you . . . if that's OK with you, Charles?'

His name crackled on my lips like the champagne bubbles as I turned to face him. He was hunched over a sheaf of papers on the island counter, mere inches away from where we had been sitting last night, and the duality of it made my vision momentarily blur.

In addressing him, I thought I was taking control, erasing what had happened. But seeing him again now threw everything into relief.

'Certainly,' he drawled, turning to face me. How could he appear so calm? 'I could think of nothing nicer.' And then he looked towards the empty stool beside him, the stool I had been sitting on when his lips touched mine. 'Pull up a pew.'

I froze, seeing the corner of his lip curl in a tease. 'I . . . I think . . .'

'The fishmonger had these lovely clams in today,' Laurie, buoyant, talked over me, patted the net beside her.

'For some reason they got me thinking about home – my childhood home, Boston – and so I really felt like making a clam chowder. Does that sound good to you?'

'Delicious,' I said weakly, glad for the distraction. I wasn't sure I'd ever eaten clams before, let alone chowder, but the name conjured up vague notions of a sort of creamy soup, and the thought of that, combined with the heat of the room – the steam from the stove clouding above Laurie's head – and the proximity of the three of us, triangled around the island unit, heightened my dizziness, made me reach out for the marble surface, pressing my hand into its coolness. I took a deep gulp of my drink, and then, thinking again, finished it.

'Why don't you two go and set up the table outside. It's still nice out, so I thought we should take advantage. We can always move inside if it rains.' She moved rhythmically, oblivious to any discomfort; snipping through the netting and tipping the clams forcefully into the pot so they hit the bottom in a toneless clatter. 'This'll only take a few minutes longer.'

I looked from her to Charles. Was this some sort of test?

But Charles was already pushing his papers away.

'Great idea, Laur. Come, Lily, let's go.'

'Yes.' I followed blindly. 'Yes, of course.'

Together we took the necessary accessories – cutlery, napkins, side plates, wine glasses – out on to the flagstone terrace, setting up on the oak table where Laurie and I had eaten lunch that first day. We moved around each other in a silent, choreographed dance, retreating to the house to fetch wine bottles, water jugs, a basket of hot, sliced baguette. The sun had dipped down beyond the cliffs, bleeding deep pinks and oranges into the clouds, and despite the warmth of the day I could feel the impending chill, the scent of jasmine subsiding with the heat. In the distance, the unceasing push and pull of the waves underscored our silence. The thought of the icy water made me colder still, and a shiver rippled through me. I wondered if I should fetch a jacket.

Charles struck a match, the sound of it searing through the silence, and leaned over to light the two pillar candles set in the middle of the table. As he did, the angle of his body brought him towards me, and his bare wrist grazed my forearm, causing the hairs to stand on end, even beneath my jumper.

'Hi,' he said, stopping to turn, to look.

'Hi.' It came out thickly, the word clinging to a web of mucus in the back of my throat. I felt his eyes probing my face, urging me to look back.

'Okay, let's eat.'

The sight of Laurie stalking cheerily through the French doors, a wicker tray in her hands, made me spring back, sever whatever connection there was between the two of us.

She moved around us, setting down the chowder and a large green salad at the top of the table, and took up position at the head, Charles, and me on either side.

'What are you two standing around for? Sit!'

Pupil-like, we obeyed.

The clatter of bowls and plates being passed obscured the silence, but once we were settled, eating, the air hummed with the lack of conversation.

'So, Laurie,' I proffered, filling the void, 'you were saying you used to eat this a lot growing up?'

I watched her surreptitiously, unsure of the protocol for dispatching the clams from their shells, following suit as she held a shell with her fingertips, scraped out the flesh and tossed the empty shell into a china bowl she had set in between us. The soup was surprisingly light, with a pleasant smokiness from the bacon and little bursts of texture from the clams, diced potato and the occasional sliver of chive, and I dipped my spoon into it hungrily. Anxiety had dulled my appetite all day, and now I found myself ravenous.

'Not a lot.' She clacked an empty clam shell into the china bowl. 'But it's one of those homegrown dishes people have a lot of affinity for. It was my grandfather's favourite thing to eat. When I was a little girl he used to look after me on the weekends, and there was this place we'd go to, I think it was a bit of an institution. He'd always have the same thing: clam chowder followed by apple cobbler. I was a bit of a disappointment as a kid: I always chickened out and got the grilled cheese. But after he died, I went back there a few times and had it. It made me think of him.'

'What was it like, growing up in Boston?' I asked neutrally, dipping a corner of baguette into the broth. I could do this. Make small talk. Get through the evening. Ignore the sly glances Charles was giving me over the rim of his bowl, the way they somehow, despite my best intentions, seemed to make my throat go dry.

'Boston? Oh . . .' She shifted in her chair, took a swig from her wine glass. 'I couldn't say I miss it. Spending the odd weekend with a seventy-year-old in a seafood joint was about as good as it got.'

'I'm so sorry, Laurie.'

I had said barely anything to Charles all evening, and yet I sensed his presence keenly. The soft curl of his fingers around the stem of his wine glass. The pout of his lips as he brought a napkin to them. The smoothness of his just-shaven cheeks, which I knew, having pressed against them, would smell of cedar and spice.

I knew from the subtle glances he kept giving me that he felt mine, too.

The invisible thread that had pulled us together last night was somehow still taut.

'What about you, Charles?' I tried to make a pretence at casualness, looking boldly across the table at him, the first time I had properly faced him all evening. I watched him rearrange his features in the flickering candlelight, his eyes widening with surprise at my sudden directness.

A light breeze had picked up now, rustling through the expanse of orchard in front of us, and pulled at the sleeves of my jumper. I regretted not fetching the jacket.

'Me?'

'Yes.' I felt myself growing in confidence. I took a long sip of my wine, replaced the glass. 'Were you close to your family?'

The image of Bess's book came back to me, the name scrawled inside. *Christine Anne Rowe*. Perhaps, inadvertently, I had stumbled upon a way to find out what had happened to her?

He drank from his own glass, mirroring me. Placed it

back on the table, but kept his hand on the base, his middle fingertip making small circles as he framed his reply.

'Nothing out of the ordinary. My parents were strict, quite old-fashioned. I spent a lot of time on my own to be honest, out in the fields or the sea.'

'But you . . .' Here I trod carefully, holding his gaze, but trying to not to alert him that I was trying to pry. '. . . You have a sister, don't you? I think you mentioned her, once?'

Even in the gloaming light, I saw the change in his body, the way his shoulders stiffened and shortened, his jaw became set.

'Had a sister.' He spoke with a gruffness I wasn't used to, his fingers tensing and untensing around the glass stem.

'Oh, I'm so sorry, did she . . . ?'

He turned his face away, breaking eye contact, focusing on some middle point on the tablecloth in front of him. 'She . . . she had an accident a long time ago.' I saw it then, the immense sadness that took over his whole features, pulling at something deep in me, and I had to resist the urge to reach out to him. 'She was older.' He cleared his throat, and the look was gone, his tone becoming short, dismissive. I felt him pulling back from the conversation. 'Much older. Actually . . . Laurie?'

He touched a hand to her wrist – intimate, marital – and instantly she sprang into action.

'Has everyone finished their soup?' Without waiting for an answer, she began to gather plates and spoons. 'Lily, sweetie, would you mind helping me bring everything inside? I've made dessert too: Eton Mess; *not* Bostonian, but the berries are from the garden so I couldn't resist.'

She spoke purposefully, without leaving a gap for conversation, and before I could say another word, she had bustled me inside, the French doors banging shut behind us.

'Charles doesn't like talking about his sister.' She spoke once we were out of earshot. 'It was a complicated relationship and one I think he'd rather forget.'

I could hear the agitation in her voice, wavering somewhere between anger and distress. Her movements were frenetic, scrubbing at the plates in hurried, twitching movements and thrusting them into the dishwasher with a loud clatter.

It was disorienting, the sudden change of tone. I hadn't realized my question would sour the evening so abruptly.

'Of course, I understand. I'm sorry for bringing it up.' I stepped in to help, righting a bottle of washing-up liquid that she'd knocked over with the jerk of an elbow.

But I didn't understand, not really. Was it true, the rumour Joss had told me? Was Charles's sister really his biological mother? Was this what Laurie had alluded to? I opened my mouth, on the brink of daring myself to ask, but then she handed me a bowl, our fingers touching on the rim.

'That's OK, you weren't to know.' And then she paused, sighed. 'She had a terrible accident when Charles was young – I think he was only ten or eleven at the time.' She watched me carefully, looked towards the door as if checking whether Charles could overhear, and then leaned in closer. 'I mean, to be completely truthful, it wasn't quite an "accident". She hanged herself. Here at Kewney, in her room.'

'Oh . . . my *God*.' I pressed a hand to my mouth, the chill I had felt outside reawakening despite having moved indoors.

Laurie nodded. 'It was awful –' her voice lowered to a near whisper '– Charles was the one who found her.'

This must have been the past that Laurie was alluding to. I turned my head towards the French doors, picturing Charles out there alone.

'Poor Charles. I can't begin to imagine . . .' I said, echoing my own thoughts. Despite the mess of what had happened with us, Charles had been a friend to me, an ally. I should never have brought it up – Laurie had said herself the past was something they'd rather forget. It was clumsy of me. Crass. And to think, all I had been trying to do was make peace.

'Yes. Her parents found it very difficult. You can imagine, especially at the time – the stigma of mental health, the shame of it.'

'How old was she?' I asked, curiosity getting the better of me. This could be my only chance to bring her up. Perhaps Laurie would set the rumour to rest.

'Mid-twenties.' She shook her head sadly. 'They were very close. Poor Charles has never truly gotten over it. Witnessing it. He was only a boy.'

I thought of all that Charles had said of his childhood, his draconian parents, and couldn't stop my heart reaching for him.

'It must have been terrible to see something like that, so young.'

Laurie ran a glass under the tap, absentmindedly watching the soap suds disappear.

'I'm sure it was.' She spoke slowly, and, I thought, deliberately, curling her mouth around each word. 'Although from what I know of Charles, he wasn't without his own issues.' I felt as though she was being cryptic again, compelling me to pry. But I didn't know what she was leading me to ask, and when I said nothing, she sighed, placed the glass on the side. Continued. 'Anyway, Charles's way of dealing with things is to not talk about them. He doesn't bring it up. So, you can understand, can't you, that I'd rather this was the last conversation you and I had about it?'

'Absolutely. Only . . .' I hesitated, certain that I knew the answer to my question but needing to hear it from her. '. . . Was her name Christine?'

'Yes.' Her features faltered. 'Why?'

'No reason. Bess found a book in the attic and it had that name inside it. I had been wondering who that might have been.'

Laurie's features creased into a scowl, her tone harsh.

'Why did you let her play in the attic? She shouldn't be up there. The flooring isn't safe.'

I held my hands up, surprised by her vehemence. 'I'm so sorry, Laurie. I didn't know she'd gone up there, she only told me this evening. I'll have a word with her tomorrow.' Chastened by her silence, I continued. 'Honestly, Laurie, it won't happen again. And I won't say another word about Charles's sister, I promise.'

Laurie turned off the tap. Swivelled to face me, her back pressed into the ceramic lip of the butler's sink.

'I'm sorry, Lily.' She exhaled deeply, and for the first time I noticed the shadows under her eyes, the waxy sheen to her normally bright skin. It had been a long weekend. And her antics last night must have taken their toll. 'You must think I'm a crazy person. I just really wanted this to be a nice evening, but your mentioning Christine rattled me. Of course you weren't to know – about her, or the attic. Can we start over again, please?'

She looked at me so beseechingly that I couldn't help but want to please her. And I was tired, too. Tired of trying to keep up with all the secrets and levels of deceit that seemed to swirl around us.

Laurie was a woman who dealt with surfaces: keeping the superficial things in her life perfect was her way of coping with the stresses that ran deeper. I thought of Nick, of everything I had run away from; the lies I had told, to bring me here.

In a way, we were really no different.

I took the last bowl from the sink, placed it in the dishwasher and turned to Laurie, fixing a broad smile on my face.

'So, what do we need for dessert?'

Whatever mood had threatened to settle before Laurie's and my departure seemed to have been dissipated by it, and by the time we had finished dessert – cream and meringue swirled with the sweet-sour burst of strawberries Laurie had been so proud of – it was as though we had returned to those first few days of my employment, with easy conversation and spirits high. Perhaps moving quite deliberately away from their childhood, Charles and Laurie told me stories of the early days of their marriage – before the children, they had travelled practically everywhere and painted me fantastical pictures of rice paddies in Ubud, rock-cut churches in Ethiopia, snorkelling the Great Barrier Reef.

The spectre of Nick still lingered in my recent past. I didn't know what to tell them in return, when the biggest incident of my life threatened to topple me, focusing instead on my early university days – the late-night scramble to finish essays, the drunken eighties-themed club nights, those manic girls' trips to Magaluf and Mykonos.

The friends I had had, before Nick drove them all away.

I still felt a lingering guilt, for upsetting Charles. Setting aside what had passed between us, I enjoyed his company. As Laurie herself had said, I wanted to start again: to put the weekend behind us and get back to the people we were before. And so I laughed enthusiastically at his jokes; asked the right questions; showing, subtly and without saying anything directly, that things between us were OK.

It would be a lie to say I didn't feel it though. That thing between us. The thread, pulling tighter. His eyes finding mine as the light dimmed, the curl of his lip, when he thought Laurie was looking away. But I squashed it down, trying to ignore it. Hoping, if I did, that it would disappear.

And when it was time to retire, it was Laurie who I

thanked. Laurie who I hugged, profusely. Laurie, my friend, and confidant, who I had wronged. And whose forgiveness, real or imagined, I desired.

Hoped that Charles would get my hints. And let this thing between us lie.

I hadn't quite fallen asleep when the light of the motion sensors flickered on in the gap of the curtains, startled me into consciousness.

I rose, loosing myself from the sheets, went over to the window in time to see Laurie's form striking across the lawn.

Behind me, a sound in the darkness. The fumble of a doorknob twisting. I turned, my breath shallow, watching as it creaked open, widened fully to reveal a figure in the frame, silhouetted by the dim light in the hallway.

'Charles?' I quavered. Although really, when I searched myself, I wasn't surprised to see him.

He didn't answer. Tilted his chin to look beyond me, to the edge of the curtains where my fingers still held fast.

'Where does she go?' I tried, following his sight.

'Walking.' His voice was gruff.

'Why?'

'Does it matter?'

'Charles—'

'You were asking a lot of questions tonight, weren't you?' His voice reverberated in the darkness.

My throat went dry.

'Charles, what are you doing here?'

He took a step towards me.

'You know what.'

I shook my head. Loosed my fingers from the curtains to face him squarely. 'You shouldn't be here. What happened last night . . .' I hated giving a voice to it. Hated myself for making it real. 'Shouldn't have. It was a mistake. We were drunk. And you were upset, about Laurie. We shouldn't . . . we can't . . .'

'Why did you ask about Christine tonight?'

He shut the door behind him, snuffing out the last of the light. In the darkness, my senses heightened. I could make out his cologne, the wood and cinnamon asserting itself on the space, reminding me of our kiss.

'Because I wanted to know about her.' My voice was hoarse. 'Because I wanted to know about you.'

I was fully awake now, nerve endings tingling, electric with the corporeality of him, the rounding of his shoulders, the jut of his head. I heard every clench of his throat as he swallowed, could smell, now, the subtle notes of whisky that dispersed into the room as he exhaled, moving soundlessly towards me, his bare feet silent on the thick carpet.

'Why do you want to know about me?'

He came to a stop a foot from me, and I became aware of my lack of underwear, of the loose, oversized T-shirt that did little to conceal the points of my body, that, even now, slipped off my shoulder as I twitched to pull it back.

'I don't know. I find you interesting.'

I lifted my chin, followed him with my eyes as he stepped closer, my body alive with the closeness of him. Wanting and not wanting.

He reached out a hand, stroked the exposed skin on my clavicle.

A shiver shot up my spine.

'Wait, Charles—'

'I have nothing to tell you apart from facts.' His fingertips fluttered across the outline of my body, running down the peak of my breasts, the curve of my waist, fingering the edge of my T-shirt so that his skin brushed my upper thigh, making the core of me molten hot. 'My name is Charles Thomas Alexander Rowe: fact. I have lived at Kewney Manor for almost the entirety of my life: fact. I have a bachelor's degree in Economics, and an MBA from INSEAD, even though I don't actually give a bloody toss about business, or money: fact, fact, fact.' He spoke smoothly, the rhythm of his voice moving with the steady pace of a wave against the shoreline. 'I find myself unbearably attracted to one Miss Lily Stern, as of late also residing at Kewney Manor, Roseland, Cornwall. Also a fact.'

'Charles.' I pleaded, once more, even as his lips found mine, as my body slackened against his, limbs curling into his, drenched in him, drowning in him.

And I said nothing more. Nothing as he pulled me towards the bed, the mattress heaving and sighing with the change of weight, as he peeled the T-shirt from me, discarding it on the bedroom floor like a snakeskin. Nothing as he palmed the top of my thigh, kneading the flesh into the heel of his hands, or as he placed himself on top of me, murmuring into my neck, *Lily, Lily, Lily.*

I should have said something.

Something to justify it, one way or the other. If I had

said yes, or no, or *anything* to the contrary, then the line between permitting and encouraging would be clearer cut. But in that moment, I truly didn't know if I wanted it, or if my lack of resistance was because it seemed inevitable; a conclusion that was fated to be borne out.

I stirred once, in the night, his back curled against mine. To my sleep-drugged ears, it sounded as though he was crying.

When I woke up fully, daylight was streaming through the open curtains, and he was gone.

11

I showered quickly that morning. Stepped, blinking, into the brightness of the bathroom, unable to believe it remained the same when everything had changed. Allowed the stream of hot water to both purify and punish me. But it turned out that fate – or something less ethereal – had other ways of chastising me.

I was hurrying Bess and William out of the kitchen, eager to avoid an encounter with either of their parents so soon, when I felt a sudden clenching in the depths of my stomach, my insides squeezing together with such force that I was compelled to stop, bent double, one hand reaching to grip the kitchen countertop until it passed.

It was the first day back after half term, and I was grateful for the merciful freneticism this required. I buried my thoughts in the final dash to complete homework, in uncovering sports socks from the laundry, retrieving art projects left to dry and a forgotten object for Show and Tell. But no sooner had I waved the school bus goodbye, was I sucker-punched once more, fists pressed to my stomach as I rasped, breathless with cramps.

I made it to the bathroom – just – hoping that the ferocity with which my stomach emptied itself indicated that whatever plagued my insides was 'out', but from there my symptoms deteriorated rapidly so that by midday I had confined myself to my room, the sun too bright, my limbs too shaky and dehydrated to do little more than lie in bed. On one of my multiple trips to the bathroom, I eased myself into the corridor to find Laurie waiting for me, her face pinched with concern.

'My goodness, are you all right?'

'I . . . I don't know,' I answered honestly, pressing my hand to mouth, knowing I smelled stale. The thought of seeing her like this, after what had happened, made me want to crawl deep inside myself.

'Let me help you to your room.'

Waves of humiliation cascaded through me as she led me gently down the corridor, the irony of her kindness compounding with an awareness of the carnal nature of my sickness, my body as rancid now as it had been in betraying her. But this petty degradation was eclipsed as she took me to my bed, pulled down the covers, and I was hit with flashbacks from the night before, the shadow of her husband's body beside me, his arms on my bare limbs. Was his scent on my pillows? Could she smell the sex tangled in the sheets? Was there some sixth sense only a wife could have, that could alert her to Charles's illicit imprint on my bed?

'I'm fine, honestly Laurie.' I waved her away as she helped me into bed, willing her to leave. Hating myself utterly in her presence. 'I think I just need to wait it out.'

'Don't be silly.' She fetched a glass of water from the bedside table, held it to my hands for me to drink. 'I have nothing better to do. I wonder if I should call the doctor. Could it be something you picked up from the children, do you think? Or something you ate or . . . Oh, lord . . .' She clamped both hands to the side of her face. 'Oh, honey, I hope it wasn't the clams. Both Charles and I seem fine, though. I did check them before they went in the pot. You didn't . . . You don't remember if you ate any that were closed? Sometimes if they're still closed after cooking, that means they're bad.'

I tried to recall the dinner, the clack of clam shell against spoon. A spasm rippled through my stomach and I clenched my teeth, waiting for it to pass.

'I don't know,' I whimpered, despite myself. 'I've never eaten clams before. I wouldn't have thought about whether they were closed or not.'

'Ah. I assumed you would have known.'

But before I could answer my stomach clenched again. I sat up, wild with panic, as I watched her stalk across the room, pass me the bin from the corner.

When I stopped retching, she touched the heel of her palm to her neck, thinking. 'Well, that probably rules out a bug. The bad news is, you can't really take anything for food poisoning, you just have to let it pass. I'll fetch you some water, and do you think you could eat something? I'll bring you up a piece of toast – it'll help line your stomach at least.' She placed her hand on my forehead. 'No temperature, at least. You just rest up here, and I'll be back in a few minutes.' In the doorway she paused. 'Poor you, Lily. I'm afraid the next couple of days aren't going to be much fun.' And then she wrinkled her nose, gave me a pitying grimace. 'I'll fetch a candle. For the smell.'

When she was gone, I lay in the silence of my room,

contemplating my predicament. If I had been a religious person, I would have considered this the hand of God, a divine intervention to punish my sinful act. I could barely remember what the inside of a church looked like, but it certainly felt like some form of karmic retribution, nothing short of a sign.

Lying in bed, I became uncomfortably aware of the sheets, sullied from the night before, was forced to recall with the hazy soft focus of seventies pornography the feel of Charles's palms against my naked flesh, his kisses grazing the underside of my breasts.

What had I done? Worse: *why had I liked it, when it was so clearly wrong?*

Charles was the first man I had been with since Nick. Towards the end of our relationship, I couldn't imagine how I could ever have enjoyed sex; couldn't imagine a world in which I would be able to open myself up to a man again. In the five years we were together, it had turned from something powerful – the lynchpin of our relationship – to something I began to loathe, even dread. How easily, I thought, he could turn his mind from whatever venomous mood he had been in that evening, and reach for me beneath the covers like it would all be OK. And I had let him, numbing myself to it, because I didn't want to know the consequences my refusal would bring.

And yet suddenly, here was Charles: a man I felt such a strong connection to, who seemed to understand me. Who wanted me. Caressed me. Unlocked in me feelings I had long forgotten. Made me feel alive.

It was wrong. It was so, so wrong.

And yet.

Another cramp seized me, and I hobbled to the bathroom, dry heaving into the toilet bowl until I brought up whatever thin bile was left inside me. My mouth tasted rotten; even after I brushed my teeth the taste didn't go away, as though it were emanating from somewhere deeper within me. I managed to get back to my room where I hauled myself into the bed, but pulling the sheets over myself was like drawing sandpaper across me, my skin flushing hot and cold. Thirst made my temples throb and I felt blindly for the bedside table, waiting for my fingers to connect with glass, but when I felt nothing, looked, I remembered that Laurie had taken it away.

Where was Laurie?

A thought began to tap with insistent fingers at the corners of my mind. Laurie's bright mood at the dinner table last night. Her omission to tell me about the shells. The subtle note of smugness in her voice when she realized I was sick.

Her concern had *seemed* genuine.

But what if it wasn't?

What if this was her punishment, for finding out what had happened with Charles and me?

Would it really have been so difficult? To select the offending shells; to ensure, with undetected sleight of hand, that they would reach my bowl?

No, this was madness. My fears about Nick were messing with my mind, making me question everything. Why would she be trying to poison me? If she knew, she would have just come out and said it, turfed me out at the first opportunity.

And yet.

Why did I feel that Laurie wanted this to happen? That she had, in some way, orchestrated it?

I thought back over my time at Kewney. To the dinners. The dresses. The dinner party placement and carefully manipulated game. The way she was always showing me off to him. Singing my praises and asking him to admire me.

The words from the parlour came back to me. *Whatever it takes.*

If Laurie wanted me to be with Charles, what was this: some sort of test?

My stomach clenched as if in response.

I pressed a hand to it, let out an involuntary moan.

None of these things made sense to me. Laurie's hot and cold behaviour. Charles's silence about his sister. Their reticence to speak about the nanny who came before me. Was there something I was missing – some way they were all connected?

I thought Cornwall was an escape. What if I'd just swapped one form of chaos for another?

I fell into a fitful half-sleep, dreaming of spools of rope falling from beams, of a faceless woman trapped in a room of cupboard doors, of him and of her, and when a hand rousing my shoulder woke me, for a moment their features blurred into one, his dark eyes and her pale skin, red hair flowing.

'Lily?' they said, their form eventually focusing into one: Laurie, standing at the bedside, a tray in her hands. 'I'm so sorry I've been such a long time. I got a phone call, and then there were two deliveries back to back, and then I remembered I needed to file some urgent paperwork, and then the kids came home . . .'

Her voice trailed off, but I raised myself up, startled, looked across to the open curtains to see the sky mellowing with late-afternoon light.

'Bess and William are home already? Laurie, gosh, I didn't mean to sleep so long, I'll go down now and . . .'

'Shush shush shush shush.' I tried to shift myself from the bed, but she pressed a hand on my shoulder, keeping me back. 'They're downstairs doing their homework, and I've already put a mac and cheese in the oven. I don't want you going anywhere until you're 100 per cent better. We'll be absolutely fine for the night.'

'Are you sure, I don't want to . . .'

'I don't want to hear another word about it.' She set the tray down beside me. There was a glass and flagon of water, a plate of scrambled eggs and toast, and, as an added touch, a couple of magazines. 'It's what my mom used to give me when I was sick,' she said, pointing to the eggs. 'Try to have a little if you can face it.'

Before she could leave, I reached out across the bed for her, caught the fingers of her right hand in my own.

'Thank you. For being so good to me.'

She took her hand back, and I watched as she clenched and unclenched her fist, as though she had a cramp. When she looked back, her expression was unreadable.

'I'm good to the people who are good to me.'

When she was gone, I scooped a scrap of egg onto a fork, put it tentatively to my lips. It was cold. Not just cool, but stone cold, as though it had been sitting in a fridge for hours. I tried to recall if I had heard the sound of the house phone, the doorbell signalling not one but two deliveries.

When I couldn't, I ate the eggs anyway, every last bite.

12

It took me another full day and night before I felt anything remotely considered recovered. Laurie was attentive the next day, bringing me a cup of tea with lemon first thing, and when, in the early afternoon, I felt well enough to venture downstairs, she welcomed me into the parlour where I sat making small talk with her as she worked, the mellowing light through the French doors the only indication that any great deal of time had passed.

There was no sign of Charles.

Laurie's kindness made me contrite, all suspicion of her behaviour written off. What cause would she have for treating me badly, when she had never shown me anything but good will – had in fact gone above and beyond to welcome me in my position?

I had been sick. My mind confused. Laurie knew nothing. And just as well: it didn't matter what I felt about Charles, I had to put a stop to things, before I was too far down the rabbit hole to get back out.

And then there he was in the kitchen, the morning of my recovery, sitting at the island unit with the children. Unchanged.

I stepped into the room, overcome, after the solitude of illness, with how bright everything was, how loud. Steeled myself.

'Well, if it isn't our favourite plague victim!' he said brightly, as every organ inside me squirmed.

'Good morning, Mr Rowe.'

Then, his tone gentler, 'The house hasn't been the same without you.'

I felt the colour flush to my sick-bay-pallid cheeks.

'I'm sorry if I'm late.' I looked down at my feet. I was all too aware of the presence of the children, their eager little faces looking up at me, no idea how I had betrayed them. Looked up, spied toast crumbs on the marble counter, busied myself with fetching kitchen towel, wiping them away. 'We aren't normally down for breakfast until seven forty-five.'

'Nothing to be sorry about.' I listened to the tip of his spoon scrape the base of the cereal bowl, the cereal breaking down between his back molars, crunch, crunch. 'The kids were up early, so I thought we'd hang out. *Relax*. No one's in trouble. Why don't you sit down, join us for breakfast? There's a seat here.'

He nodded at the stool beside him, then held my gaze, daring me to look away.

'Thank you,' I breathed, 'but I'm not feeling quite up to eating yet.'

'We missed you, Lily,' Bess lisped at me, holding her hand out for me as I gratefully took the distraction. 'I'm sooooo happy you're better. Mummy doesn't do all the voices in the books like you do.'

'Did you get our card?' William spoke over her, spooning a heap of cereal into his mouth and getting half of it down his chin. 'I did all the stickers.'

The card, a folded piece of purple recycled paper

featuring flowers, dinosaur stickers and Bess's meticulously written 'Get Well Soon, Lily!', had appeared under my door the night before to a chorus of giggles.

'I did!' I ruffled William's hair, so pleased I hadn't had to face this reunion with Charles alone. 'I think it must have been laced with healing potion. I've felt better and better since I got it.'

'Well, we're all very glad to have you back with us,' Charles tried again. 'Some of us more than others.'

'I certainly missed these two, that's for sure.' I answered plainly, refusing to take the bait.

'Mummy said you had a tummy bug and were puking.' William set his glass of orange juice down on an angle so the whole thing tipped and spilled. I rushed to pick it up, never more grateful for the distraction.

'No, not a tummy bug, she said she must have "a weak constitution", because she and Daddy were fine,' Bess corrected, but before I could feel the whole hit of this slight, she shrieked, 'William, you've got my socks all wet. I'm going to have to change them.'

'I hate puking,' he continued, ignoring her, as I swooped to staunch the flow of juice. 'One time, when I was really sick, I puked so hard, it came out of my nose.'

He giggled, began to demonstrate, mocking the sound of throwing up and making me feel queasy as Bess pressed her hands to her ears, jumped down from the stool, knocking it to the floor with a loud clatter.

'Stop it, William, stop it, you know I can't hear it, or I'll throw up too.'

He leapt down to chase her, and I let myself get swept

away with the normality of it, righting the chair, clearing the spill.

Charles's eyes were on me still though. Watching. Waiting.

The pressure was suffocating.

When it was clear to him that I wasn't going to rise to it, he stood, silently. Left without a word.

It seemed like an age since I had been in the house on my own. Laurie had mentioned, when she came to check on me the night before, that she would be out of the house most of the day, at a planning session for the school summer fête, and with Charles and the children definitively departed, I found myself alone with my thoughts.

My interaction with Charles had unsettled me. And now the manor felt stifling. I could see that there was a drizzle in the air, the sky a dank grey, which made the outside world less than inviting, but once I had roamed the empty corridors, finding my mind too restless to read or watch TV, I borrowed a waterproof jacket and some wellies I unearthed in the boot room and resolved to get myself some fresh air, to clear my mind.

With the hood of the jacket over me I was quite content to roam. I was familiar with the gardens, but as a Londoner I'd naturally been drawn to the exoticism of the beach. Now, though, the thought of the dank sea and damp sand repelled me, and so I turned in the direction of the perimeter path, letting the winding route take me further and further from the shadow of Kewney Manor. I found the greenhouses, the air thick with humidity, dared myself to pluck a handful of tomatoes straight from the vine. I passed the old stables, empty now even though the smell of hay and horse seemed embedded, and a small walled Victorian garden whose flowers had largely withered away.

At the foot of the garden, shading the south wall, a small apple tree had bloomed and shed, carpeting the surrounding ground with shrivelled leaves and bloated apple corpses. I thought I noticed odd patches in the trunk, came closer to take a further look. It was a series of names tattooed into the bark, each one distinct in size, script, direction. There must have been ten or so in total, the majority unfamiliar – Algernon, Miles, Grace – but amongst them, the letters neat and capitalized, was Charles. Pulling my hood closer against the rain, I traced the letters with my fingers, the wood rough and wet beneath, his name stark and biting out there in the open. Beside him, up and to the right, I noticed a patch of wood the size of my palm had been scraped away, scythed off, most probably with a penknife or small switch blade. In the remaining grain I could just make out the imprint of the letters the bark had once held, C – H – R . . .

'Hey!'

An angry voice made me jump, and I whirled around to find Joss standing at the entrance, his arms full of cut branches.

I let the hood fall to my shoulders, revealing my face in full.

'Oh,' he said, as sanguine as ever. 'It's you.'

He disappeared from view for a moment, and I thought that was it, but then he returned, arms empty, pulling at the fingers of the thick gardening gloves that covered his hands.

Three decades might as well have passed since the last time I saw him. I felt like another person entirely.

He stepped fully into the garden and I saw that he had had his hair cut, the flaxen strands that escaped his ponytail touching just above his chin.

'Where have you been, then?' he asked, arms folded.

'It's Wednesday. You don't normally come on a Wednesday?' I deflected his question with a question.

'I didn't know you kept such a close watch on my comings and goings,' he teased, sweeping a hand across his forehead to wipe the moisture from it. The rain had intensified, the rhythmic patter of droplets hitting leaves bathing the air around us. I pulled my jacket tighter at the chin but left the hood loose, blushing inwardly. Whatever badinage Joss and I had previously entertained now felt simultaneously welcome and weird. I was all at once confronted by the things that had happened since the day on the beach, things I didn't think I would ever be able to explain to him. When I didn't rise to his retort, he stuck his hands in his pockets and shrugged. 'The weather's making the plants go haywire; the roses don't know if they're coming or going. I told Mrs Rowe they really needed to hire a second gardener, but they didn't want to take someone on, so I agreed I'd do Wednesdays over the summer as well.'

'Oh.' I waded through my thoughts, each one thick as glue. 'I was just—'

'Is everything—'

We spoke in unison. Stopped, sighed, met eyes.

He frowned. 'I was going to ask if everything is all right? You seem . . . I don't know . . .'

'Yes, I'm fine.' I said with false brightness. And then, catching myself in the lie and realizing the better, more valid excuse. 'Actually, I've been sick. Nothing too serious. Food poisoning.' I grimaced. 'Clams.'

'Oh.' I saw him relax a little, his shoulders release. 'That's good. Well, not good,' he stuttered, scuffing his toe against a clump of fallen leaves, 'but I'm glad that's all. I thought maybe . . . well, I hadn't seen you and . . . I thought maybe I'd said something or – I don't know. I was worried. Are you better now?'

I was about to answer him when there was a great crack overhead, a whip of thunder across the sky that sent a deluge of rain in its wake.

'Quick!' He grabbed my hand so instinctively I didn't think about the intimacy of it, hurried to follow him out of the walled garden and across the lawns to the old stables, huddling together in the entrance of the empty structure as we watched the water come down in sheets.

'There goes my day for the foreseeable,' he raked his hand through his wet hair, letting mine drop as casually as he'd taken it. Looked up at the heavy sky. 'What about you? What are you up to?'

I flexed the fingers on my empty hand. 'I don't have any plans. This was kind of it, until the children come home from school.'

'Does it ever get boring?' He relaxed against the door frame, holding himself up by the midpoint of his shoulder blades. 'Hanging about here all day on your own?'

I thought about it for a moment, the absurdity of being bored in the last three days.

'I haven't really had a chance to be bored,' I said obliquely. The storm was passing through. I could hear the plink of rain easing off on the stable roof. And then, thinking more roundly about my time there, 'Everything was so new, at first, and then it was half term, then I was sick, so . . .' I shrugged. 'Anyway, sometimes it's nice, to be on my own. Where I was living before . . .' An image of Nick's face flashed in my mind's eye and I pushed it away. 'I just didn't have much free time.'

If he picked up on any subtext, he didn't rise to it. 'And is she ever in, Mrs Rowe? I've often wondered, if she doesn't work, why the nannies?'

'Now who's gossiping?' I raised an eyebrow, but his last comment pulled at me, the chance to uncover at least one of Kewney's mysteries. 'Wait . . . you knew the last one, didn't you? Nina?'

He poked his head outside, distracted by the subsiding downpour. 'Not that well.' He stuck his palm out into the fresh air, assessing the droplets.

'Well, what was she like?' I remembered what that woman Meredith had said at the dinner party. That she was pretty. I wondered if Joss thought she was.

He fiddled with the zip on his waterproof, toggling it up and down.

'I really didn't spend much time with her. We tended to keep to ourselves. I think she said she was from Durham, from memory. Somewhere like that. She really wasn't here all that long.'

'Why did she leave?'

'I don't know.' His shoulders jerked, edging on petulant.

'Where did she go?'

He pulled a face, but I couldn't tell if his patience was drawing to a close or if he was being deliberately cagey. 'Lord, how should I know? Got a different job? Moved back home? Were you planning on being here for ever?'

His question floored me.

'I . . . I don't know.'

The morning after the party, when I was certain that Laurie knew about me and Charles, I could think of nothing except how I would be able to convince her to let me stay. But then I had been concerned with the immediate present, with keeping intact the hermetic seal I had so carefully placed around what had happened with Nick. Thinking beyond that was like looking into the abyss.

Of course Joss was right: I couldn't stay at Kewney for ever. I wasn't delusional enough to think I had a proper future with Charles. But would I ever feel confident enough to stand still somewhere, or was I fated to be forever running from my past?

'Is everything OK?'

'Y-yes.' I gave myself a shake. 'Sorry. I should get back to the house.' It suddenly felt too close in that stable, the air stale and dank. 'It's stopped raining.'

'Oh.' Joss turned back to face me. 'Yeah, sure.'

'Sorry, I just didn't mean to have stayed out this long. Laurie might be wondering where I am.' I knew that he sensed the abruptness of it, that I had risked offending his implied offer of company. 'Maybe . . . maybe I could come find you tomorrow if the weather's nice?' I gave him a coaxing smile. 'I could bring you that cup of tea you've missed?'

'Sure, that would nice. Or . . .' He looked away, pinning his sight on the corner of the barn door. 'Or, if you find yourself at a loose end, we could go out somewhere? There's this cove I think you'd like, right at the tip of the Lizard Peninsula.' He shifted his feet. 'Only if you're not busy.'

It surprised me just how much I liked the sound of it.

'No, I'm not busy. How about next Friday? If you're not working?' Laurie tended to be out on Fridays, a regime of yoga classes, manicures and hair appointments to prep her for the weekend. And the thought of getting away from Kewney was particularly appealing.

'I'm not working next Friday.' He paused, as though he was giving me the chance to back out. 'I could pick you up after breakfast, around nine-ish?'

'Sure. Nine-ish sounds good.' I mimicked his casualness. Pulled on my hood, sheltering from the droplets of rain that still clung to the trees, and stepped out into the open. 'It'll be fun.'

I returned to the house, my resolve restored. The monumental walls of the manor tended to have a myopic effect on me; seeing Joss reminded me that there was a world outside it.

Laurie noticed. 'You seem better?' she remarked, popping in to see Bess and William having dinner.

'I am, thank you. Much better.' I touched her arm,

feeling the warmth stirring between us. 'Thank you, for taking such good care of me.'

When she asked, nonchalantly, 'Will you join me for dinner? Charles is working late,' I acquiesced, my new-found conviction forming a shield around me.

I ate heartily, my appetite returning with force after my period of convalescence; drank moderately, listening to Laurie's comfortable burble about the new perform-ing arts centre at the children's school, a black-tie fundraising event they had coming up to support it.

After dinner, I helped Laurie wash up, chiming in as she sang along to Kate Bush warbling through the speak-ers. Before heading up to bed, I stopped by the library, running my fingers along the shelves in search of my next read.

I didn't hear the library door open, but the sound of it clicking shut made me turn, take a step back as I saw Charles standing before it.

'Hello.' His voice was low, mellifluous. It made my breath shorten.

'Hi.' And then, stumbling to fill the empty air between us. 'I was just looking for something to read – I was thinking perhaps of an Iris Murdoch; I've never read anything by her.'

'Why were you acting like that this morning?'

He seemed to cross the distance without moving, appearing steps away from me almost as though no time had passed.

'I don't know what you mean.'

'You do.' He took another step, reaching to stroke a

strand of hair at my neck. 'Cold. Indifferent. Like the other night never happened.'

I looked over to the library door, certain his voice would travel. 'Charles . . .'

'What were you trying to do, get a rise out of me?'

'No, *no*!' My face felt hot. That hadn't been my intention at all. How had I got it so wrong? I felt his hands on my shoulders, turning me around. 'Charles, what we did—'

'Because that's exactly what you did,' he continued over me. 'I couldn't stop thinking about you. All day, all I could think about was this moment, seeing you.'

'Charles, *please*.'

'I'm being serious.' His hands rubbed rhythmically up and down the outside of my arms. 'Every second I was outside this house, I was thinking about you. You're intoxicating, Lily. Has anyone ever told you that?'

I closed my eyes. 'Please, Charles, stop.'

He touched a finger to my cheek. 'I don't want to stop.'

I turned my head away. 'Don't.'

It was as though last night had pulled the stopper out of him, allowed him a flow of candidness I found overwhelming.

'Come here.' He brought an arm around my waist and I felt the wide flat of his palm pressing into my lower back, pulling me towards him.

'Charles, don't.'

I brought the heel of my hand to his chest, pushing him away, but he held strong, his other hand finding the back of my head, pulling my mouth towards his.

'Charles, please, *stop it*.'

I wrenched myself out of his grasp, torquing my body to escape from under his arms.

'Excuse me?'

I had backed away, putting the chaise longue between us, and now he stood, facing me, his face knitted in annoyance.

'I can't . . . we can't do this any more.' I sucked air into my lungs, propelling myself on. 'We need to stop. What we did wasn't right. It shouldn't have happened. And I'm sorry if I did anything to make you think . . . to suggest that I was in any way . . . but it's not . . . I'm not . . . I don't . . .'

I tried to form coherent sentences, but I was watching Charles, his muscles taut, jaw set. I thought of Joss, his lopsided smile when I had agreed to go with him on Friday, how he made me feel safe. And I thought of Nick, and how he hadn't. Where on this scale did Charles fit?

He didn't answer immediately, let me stutter myself out in the silent room. Elsewhere, a grandfather clock struck the hour. We both turned towards the sound, waited the chimes out. When he spoke, his voice was flat, calm.

'Don't pretend this isn't what you wanted.'

I worried my head. 'What do you mean?'

'I know you're attracted to me, Lily.' His lip curled. 'You felt it, that night of the party. Before that, even. This thing between us. You must know the effect you have on me. The effect we have on each other. I see the way you move about this house. How you behave when we're alone. That night, the way you twisted your body towards me. And now you're going to take it all back? Deny it? It's a good act, Lily, but not quite good enough.'

'It's not an act,' I breathed.

'So you're saying you're not attracted to me? You never have been?' I didn't answer. 'Go on.' His voice turned round and coaxing as he took the point of his finger to the underside of my arm, running it from wrist to elbow. I quivered involuntarily. 'Look me in the eyes right now and say that you want this to stop.'

'I . . .'

'Say it. Say I've got it all wrong, and I'll leave you alone.'

I couldn't deny it. Despite my best intentions, despite how wrong I knew it was, it was true. I was attracted to him. It had started with an itch, a mere tickle in the depths of me, but over time it had grown more powerful, scored my insides whenever he walked into a room.

I hadn't meant for any of this. What had happened in London had been pure action, not thought. Then, my only concern had been getting away, gaining distance, making sure I wouldn't be found.

And Nick had made me feel so worthless. Useless. Unlovable. It was easy to believe that I could become invisible.

And now here was Charles. Seeing me. And I wasn't sure I was strong enough to resist.

I shook my head.

He smirked, triumphant.

'You make such a pretence of trying to follow the rules, don't you, Lily?' He took a seat on the chaise longue, the cushions sighing underneath him, crossed his legs at the ankles. 'You always want people to think of you as doing the right thing. Being the right kind of person. I could see it in you the minute I met you: you're desperate for people to like you.'

'Is that such a bad thing?' My voice was hoarse.

'It's not about "good" or "bad". You need to stop living your life by some sort of faux moral compass, and for once ask yourself, "What do I want?"' He left the sentence lingering in the air, waiting for me to answer it. And then, softly, 'Admit it. This is what you want.'

The truth was, until the moment I left Nick, I had never thought much about what I wanted. After Mum died, I had always been so conscious of the burden the very fact of my being was. Getting good grades, keeping out of trouble at school, passing my driving test, getting a degree: they were all checkpoints; attempts to seek validation, to try to prove to everyone that I was worth their time and attention. And then, later: always the friend holding another's hair up when she was being sick; the one who remembered birthdays, sorting out the whip-round for presents when everyone else seemed to forget; the one who put in the extra fiver on the bill because the numbers didn't quite add up. And I had always, always bended to Nick's will.

But what had happened with Nick wasn't nice, was it? So what good was behaving, now?

'I can see you wrestling with it,' he said with a tease in his voice. 'It's quite the seismic shift to go from thinking about pleasing other people to thinking about pleasing yourself. But all this goody-two-shoes behaviour . . . it's just a mask, isn't it? It's not how you really feel, is it? Deep down. Deep down, you know the truth.'

'How do you know how I feel?' I asked softly.

He took my fingers in the palm of his hand, running his thumb over the sensitive tips.

'I see it, Lily. How you brighten when we're alone together. I feel it too. We've gone this far.' He pulled me towards him so that I was tipped forward, off balance, and had to reach for his shoulders to right myself. 'Don't take it back now.'

I felt his breath against my neck. The tingle of his fingers against the bottom of my ribcage as he found the corner of my T-shirt, pulled it over my head. And then his lips were on my collarbone, kisses working their way up my neck. A moan escaped me as I felt my body soften under his touch.

'See,' he murmured into me. 'I think I read it in your face the first time I saw you: even though you try to hide it, you have a taste for danger. You like our little tête-à-têtes. You've enjoyed the illicit thrill of what we have. When you came into the drawing room that night of the party you knew exactly what you looked like, and the reaction it would have on me, pursing your lips . . . you liked it.'

He bit my bottom lip – right on the fleshy part – a vampiric nip that tingled through me.

He was right, wasn't he? I could have said no. Could have asked Laurie if I could wear something else. Could have done something more to stop him.

But I hadn't.

I had liked the way I looked. The same way that I liked the way it felt, being with him. And deep, deep down, I knew it.

'What about Laurie?' Her name caught in my throat as an image came to me unbidden: the two of us in the kitchen earlier that very night, spatulas in hand, singing into them like two old friends at karaoke night. How could I betray her?

His fingers found my bra straps, freeing them from my shoulders, exposing my breasts to the cold library air.

'What *about* Laurie?' he contradicted.

I thought her name would impede him; give him pause for thought as it had done for me; but he was all motion, finding the clasp of my bra, pulsing it open.

'She's your wife . . .' I attempted as his lips pressed against my collarbone.

'The thing about marriage, Lily,' he mused into my neck, 'is that it operates in a different realm from the rest of your life.' His fingers found his buttons and he tugged his shirt loose. 'Laurie and I love one another greatly. Don't underestimate that. When you have been married a long time, that love takes on a different meaning. Do you understand me?'

'I . . . I think so?'

His hands ran down the sides of my torso, the pads of his fingers teasing the hem of my skirt. My skin was on fire. I had to marvel at the effect he had on me, the way he knew exactly which buttons of mine to push.

'Marriage is all a careful balance, like placing pieces on a chessboard. Laurie likes everything to be in harmony, everything to run smoothly. The chessboard is balanced when I am happy. It's symbiotic. I'm happy – so Laurie is happy. And, right now, being with you is making me happy. So, if you were to go ahead and tip up that chessboard . . . well, Laurie wouldn't be very pleased then, would she?'

I felt his hands on the points of my hips, the press of his fingertips on the waistband of my underwear.

'No.'

'So, as long as I'm happy, everything will be all right. You see?'

His fingers dipped inside me, clouded my brain. 'Yes.'

I was losing all sense of where I ended and he began. It was as though I was nothing but feeling, nerves pulsing, limbs slackening. And as we tangled into one another, flesh against flesh, I no longer thought of Laurie, or Joss, or even Nick. I no longer thought of myself, or what I was doing, or if it was right. I thought of nothing but that moment.

In that moment, I convinced myself I was free.

13

I think that was when I let myself fall for him. That moment, that second of letting go; it was as if something had been unleashed in me, and then I couldn't put the genie back in the bottle.

My days were top and tailed by him. Smiling at me in the kitchen at breakfast, sharing a secret, special look over the children's heads. The sound of his footsteps as he returned each night, his voice echoing in the hall. The way his face erupted into pure joy when he saw me descending the stairs. We were careful, always careful. He avoided the house in the day, when Laurie or an errant housekeeper could be lurking. At dinner we were friendly, courteous. Picking up the thread of Laurie's convivial banter as if we weren't both thinking about what would come after the plates were cleared. There was nothing in our manner in front of her or the children to suggest we were anything other than professional.

And then he would come to me, late, late, our bodies aching for each other after a day spent apart. Feelings intensified by our constant proximity, time condensing in that strange way it does with repetition, like when you're on holiday and two weeks feels like two months.

I worried, often, about Laurie. The terror of being caught – worse, being thrown out – nibbled at the edges of my thoughts, always. What did she do at night, and how was it we avoided detection? When I woke, found myself alone, the sheets besides me cold, I had to assume he timed it. But if I asked him about it, he was vague, angry even, saying to me once quite fiercely, 'How I handle my marriage is my business.' And so I refrained. They had both spoken in couched terms to me of their relationship; I told myself I had no right to question it.

I hated myself for abusing Laurie's trust, the friendship she seemed to hold so dear, but on the contrary her mood seemed buoyant. When I dared to venture in the parlour, stopped by to watch her work, I saw her paintings were light: soft clouds and limpid blue sea, the sky at dawn, tinged pink.

Perhaps Charles was right, and whatever we were doing had balanced the chessboard, brought harmony to strange discord of Kewney.

And those nights, alone with Charles in the sanctuary of my room, I gave myself over to that harmony. I was incredibly flattered that someone like him – older, and cleverer, and funnier – could be interested in someone like me. I drank it all in, listening and learning and hanging on his every word. I was drunk on him. Didn't see my self-destructive tendencies repeating themselves.

Tangled in my bedsheets, he would wrap his arms around me, tell me stories – of his youth, of his travels, of the people he had met and seen. He brought me books, books that he had read, that he knew I would love, and sometimes, curled into each other, he would read passages from his favourite chapters as I drifted into a doze, sleep affording me the dignity of not seeing him depart.

I know how awful this seems. I know how awful I

sound. How naive it was for me to behave this way, how blind I was to everything, everyone, I was potentially destroying. All I can say is that I fell. I fell hard and deep. It was as though I were two people: Lily-of-the-day, who was polite and eager and good with the children, and Lily-of-the-night, who belonged to Charles. My ego had been bashed and bruised by Nick. What had happened with him had nearly destroyed me. But with Charles, I began to forget. In my desire to be free, I allowed myself to believe he had saved me.

And then time propelled forward, and it was morning of the trip to Lizard Point.

I had considered cancelling. When I had chanced upon Joss in the grounds the day before, remembered, our plans with a jolt, I didn't know how I could make a pretence that everything was as it had been – everything seemed so topsy-turvy, so out of sync with the girl I had been when I agreed to see him.

But Joss had seemed so excited, and despite the wildness of my nights with Charles, I couldn't help finding the days long and lonely, and so I matched his enthusiasm, told him I couldn't wait.

My feelings for Joss were complicated. I liked him. As a friend. Once, I had half entertained the thought it could be something more. But with everything that had happened with Charles, I knew I had to put Joss firmly out of my mind. I wasn't worthy of someone like him. And he was far too good for someone like me.

Even still, the thought of spending the day alone with him made something within me flutter, something that made me keep our plans secret from the rest of the family, Charles in particular; and so when Laurie asked me offhand, breezing out of the door to some committee meeting, if I had any plans, I answered, 'Oh, I hadn't thought . . . I'll probably go down to the sea,' with a vagueness that exculpated me from any outright lie.

Those days, I felt as though I were keeping secrets on top of secrets, hoping one wouldn't topple the other, make them all come crashing down.

Joss didn't come to the door. Not that he should have done; it wasn't my house, and we had said nothing to suggest that this was a date. But still there was something vaguely awkward about seeing him waiting patiently for me in his van – a spotlessly clean Citroen Berlingo that nonetheless looked like the engine might fall out of it – at exactly nine o'clock.

'Morning!' I called through the open window, waving to get his attention as I made my way towards the passenger door and pulled at the handle, only to find it locked.

'Sorry.' He jumped to attention. As he leaned across the driver's side to open the door and I clambered up, I thought I saw his face pinken. 'I probably should have come around to help you in or something.'

'Don't be silly,' I brushed him off, deliberately chummy. 'I'm fine.'

It wasn't a date.

We backed out of the driveway in silence and as we passed through Kewney's great iron gates I became aware that this was the first time we had been alone together outside of the manor. He was wearing different clothes, for one thing. A pair of navy shorts and a freshly washed red T-shirt to replace his work tracksuit and jersey. I wondered if it had been a conscious decision, or purely coincidence. And he smelled clean. Not that he ever smelled dirty, but Joss for me was always inextricably bound with the scent of freshly raked soil, and now he smelled of other things: laundry detergent and deodorant and a slick of sun cream. I had seen him just the day before, but being on the Rowes' land I felt bound to my secret life with Charles, unable to escape the knowledge of it and therefore unable to be entirely myself around Joss. Now, as those gates gave way to new surroundings, I felt my shoulders relax, the hold of that place release its grip on my core.

'Here –' I reached into my tote bag, placed a tinfoil square onto the dashboard '– I brought snacks for the road. Bess's blue-ribbon-winning flapjacks no less.'

He sniffed at it suspiciously over the top of the steering wheel. 'They don't have raisins in it, do they? My mum brought me round some flapjacks last week, but she snuck raisins in them. I think she was trying to make sure I ate something that was at least once upon a time a fruit.'

'Well, I can reassure you that these are about 90 per cent butter and golden syrup.' I unwrapped the parcel, broke half of a flapjack off and handed a piece to him. 'Nothing with even a passing resemblance to a fruit.'

He took it, put the whole thing in his mouth, chewed thoughtfully.

'Hmm, you're right,' he mumbled through the crumbs. 'Pure sugar. Much more my style.'

'Do you live close to your parents then?' I asked, trying to get more of a picture of this 'out of hours' Joss.

'Oh, you bet.' He paused as we merged from a narrow country lane onto an A-road, watching the steady stream of traffic before making his move. Same road. They're number 3, I'm number 8. And there aren't that many houses in Kewney village. My mum still does my laundry once a week.'

I looked again at his sharply ironed polo shirt and had to laugh. 'I bet she does. Does she cook and clean for you as well?'

'Hey!' He was focused on the road, but I saw the corners of his mouth crease into a smile. 'I'm the last one left she can mollycoddle. I'm doing her a favour.' He nudged an elbow in the direction of the passenger's seat. 'Don't tell me you wouldn't be delighted to have your mum doing your washing?'

'Well, my mum's dead, so I think I'd be surprised more than anything else.' It came out without thinking, a reflexive trigger I was so used to pulling, but I instantly regretted it, the shade it cast over our morning.

'Oh, Jesus.' I heard it, the shift in his tone, the awkward condolence sitting heavily on the car's recycled air. 'I'm so sorry, Lily. You never said . . .'

'No, please . . . it was ages ago, I shouldn't have . . . I don't know why I said it like that.' I wanted desperately to go back in time, to erase that moment. I had been so enjoying the pleasant ordinariness of it all, every kilometre we journeyed together taking me both mentally and physically away from Kewney. With one poorly worded retort I had jarred the atmosphere as successfully as though I had jammed a stick into the gear box. 'Tell me about your family.' I grasped any lever I could think of, pulled. 'Your brothers and sisters . . . what are they like? Are you close?'

Benevolently, he pressed no further, soon falling into an easy monologue detailing his four older siblings, their spouses and various offspring, so that by the time we reached the Lizard's untamed coast, we had fallen into a steady rhythm, leaving the last of the uncomfortable atmosphere back towards Kewney.

It struck me, and I couldn't help comparing: all the hours I had spent with Charles, every inch of his body that mine had touched, he never willingly volunteered any information about his family. I still knew no more about his sister and what had happened to her than I had heard from Laurie. Maybe I had read his nonchalance wrong, and Charles was as wary of our misbehaviour as I was. Maybe this was his way of keeping his two worlds apart.

Finally, we pulled into a car park that was already three-quarters full, Joss manoeuvring the van surprisingly effortlessly into a narrow space in the corner. As the engine wheezed to a stop, he jutted his head over the gear box to look down at my sandaled toes, huffed.

'Are those all you've got? It's a bit of a walk.'

I crossed my ankles, looking at them. 'I didn't think. That was stupid.'

'It's all right. It's a fairly easy one, you'd just be better off with something that covers your toes.' He turned to open his door, jumping down and disappearing momentarily to unlatch the back ones. When he reappeared, on my side, he was holding a pair of walking boots aloft. He opened the passenger door, offered them to me. 'I thought these were in here somewhere. 'Fraid I've only got a pair of my gym socks though – but you're lucky, they're clean.'

I took them from him, kicked my sandals off in the footwell, then swung myself round sideways to use the frame of the door to hinge my feet into the boots as he busied around the van, changing into boots of his own and procuring a small backpack from the depths of the van that he filled with two water bottles, a baseball cap and jumper.

I was beginning to feel sillier by the minute in my frayed denim shorts and tank top, imagining the outline of my hardback book knocking against me through the tote. The boots were a woman's, I noted, looping the laces, old and caked in mud. I wondered who they belonged to. Felt an odd twinge in my core.

'They seem to fit you pretty well,' he observed, offering a hand to help me down. 'You must have the same size feet as Ann.'

Ann. His youngest sister. I had learned that on the drive. The twinge eased.

'Yes, they're perfect.' I rolled my ankles in them, dispersing the thoughts of relief. He wasn't mine to claim. What did it matter, whose shoes they were?

We turned out of the car park and onto a narrow lane, following a signpost marked for Caerthillian and Kynance Coves. Joss picked his way through the path with ease, leading me along a hedge and then through the meadows beyond. He seemed at home here – more so than amongst Kewney's manicured hedgerows – stopping to point out the bright yellow celandine flowers, the pretty lilac shrubs that blanketed the fields, declaring animatedly that this was one of the finest examples of Cornish heath in the country.

His enthusiasm was catching, and, as I shadowed his journey, I felt it: the fresh earth and herbal flowers; the dappled sunlight warming us as warblers chattered overhead; that particular Cornish mysticism that had drawn me to the coast in the first place. Here, I could forget the dark things I was mixed up in, the missteps I had somehow taken. As I inhaled the fresh coastal air, I felt a weightlessness I couldn't remember experiencing for the longest time.

Part of me wanted to tell him. Like the odd root or rock that jarred my path, I found myself stumbling over flashes of memory – Charles's hand on my bare wrist, the graze of his stubble on my smooth cheek – and wanting to blurt it out, if nothing else to confide in him, make sense of some of the madness of my inner mind. And then Joss would flash me a grin over his shoulder, stoop to recover a robin's egg, the blue shell fragile in his upturned palm, and all thoughts of telling him vanished. I had no right to drag him into it all.

And then we reached Kynance Cove.

The sea had banded us as our journey wove around the coastal path, clearer and bluer than the deep teal below Kewney, but still nothing prepared me for what greeted us as we dipped down towards the cove, threaded the shallow rock face and finally sank our feet into the sand. The water here was pure turquoise, as mesmerizing as you'd see on the cover of any Caribbean guidebook, the colour amplified by the soft white sand that sat beneath it. It glittered in the late-morning sun, bouncing light off the gentle cresting waves, light that was then absorbed by the imposing charcoal-coloured rock formations that rose from the cove's centre.

'They've all got funny names,' Joss spoke quietly, at my shoulder, after giving me a moment just to take it in. 'The Lion, The Bishop, Sugarloaf.' He stretched out an arm towards each in turn. 'Out there there's Asparagus Island – that one actually makes sense; asparagus grows on it. You can walk to it in low tide, but I didn't think you'd fancy getting here for three in the morning.' He shrugged. 'Oh – and you can sometimes see dolphins or seals passing by from the cliffs. I never have, but my mate Greg swears he does every time.' He sank into the sand and began untying his shoelaces. 'Anyway, I thought you'd like it.'

'Joss, it's beautiful.' I remained standing for a moment, taking it in. It was heaving already – group of friends sunbathing or relaxing with cool boxes on the rocks, couples sheltering in windbreakers, sharing a newspaper or drinking takeaway coffee from the cafe up the hill, children splashing in the shallows, whilst further out figures slick in black wetsuits were attempting to bodyboard – but somehow this only added to the charm of the place, their cheerful voices mingling with the pleasant shush of the waves, all delighted to have made it to this oasis.

I sat beside him and released my feet, taking pleasure in the grit of sand underneath them and for a moment we were silent, observing.

'Sometimes I wonder what I'm still doing here, in this tiny corner of England.' When Joss spoke, he was cautious, feeling his way around the words as though he were voicing them for the first time. 'I had these grand plans when I finished school: travel everywhere, "see the world": but something always held me back. But on a day like this, I think, who needs it?' He scooped a handful of wet sand from the ground between his feet, let it drip through his fingers like an hourglass. 'Why did you come here?'

The question took me by surprise, and I straightened my spine. 'What do you mean?'

'To Cornwall. What made you come here?'

The question came at me with no warning, allowed the memory to break through, catch me by surprise.

Nick's hands on my wrists. My pleading. His promises, which soon morphed into threats. The final fight where I didn't know if I'd make it to morning, or if he'd finally follow through with what he said. The minutes ticking by as I lay beside him, willing him to sleep. The moment I made my choice.

Forget Charles, if Joss knew why I had left London, what would he think of me?

'I . . . I don't know, really.' I felt winded, tried to breathe the memory out, focusing on the cool sand beneath my feet, the glint of sun on the waves. 'I wanted to go somewhere different, I guess.' I felt my nerves steady. If Joss had noticed any hint of my alarm, he didn't express it. 'To "get away from it all", if that doesn't sound ridiculously clichéd. I mean, why does anyone go anywhere?'

'Who knows?' His shoulders jerked, once. 'Like I said, I've never been anywhere but here.'

We fell silent again, both alone with our thoughts.

'Do you like it enough to stay?' he asked, eventually.

'Stay?'

'If you didn't have the Rowes . . . if Bess and William grew out of needing a nanny, or you didn't like it there any more . . .' He swallowed. 'If you had another reason, maybe . . . do you think you'd stay?'

Enigmatic as they were, something in the riddle of his words pulled at me. Maybe I had got it all wrong. Maybe he saw something in me that was different to how I saw myself. With the sunlight beating down on me, in this cove at the tip of the country, I felt so far away from Kewney that I let myself get swept away by the day. In that moment, I so wanted to be the sort of girl he thought I was. I so wanted the simple, uncomplicated solution he was presenting. I didn't want to think of the men who shadowed my past, and my present. The part of me that must exist, to be drawn to their sort of darkness.

I turned my cheek to face him, only to meet his gaze head on. He looked swiftly away, focusing intently on the zips of the backpack at his feet.

I placed a hand on the rock between us, not touching but near.

'Yes,' I said softly. 'I'd stay.'

We stayed at the cove for an hour before wending our way back, completing the circular walk to the car park through bridle lanes thick with foliage. At Lizard Point itself we stopped for lunch, sharing fish and chips on one of the cafe's small wooden tables overlooking the sea. I wouldn't say the atmosphere between us had seismically shifted, but since that moment at Kynance Cove an unsaid something seemed to soften our surrounding air. We were more cautious, with our words, pausing on a sentence to consider one another, as though 'checking in' that we were aligned. Gone was the teasing, the broad jokes that had been commonplace, and in their place was something more mellow, sweeter.

But although I wanted myself to be carried away on this fantasy, could almost taste the future a life with Joss would offer – a place by the sea, a little fisherman's cottage, perhaps, a garden blooming with wildflowers; children, barefoot and shrieking at the pull of waves against the shore – somehow, I couldn't quite make myself believe it.

With each movement closer to the car park, it was as though I was getting closer to that other me, the night-time me that sunshine and distance had let me forget. I could hear Charles's voice in my head. That night in the library, he said he had seen the real me. 'A taste for danger,' he'd said. What if this day with Joss was just another attempt at pleasing people, at trying to hide from the me I knew I was inside?

After all, Charles was right, wasn't he? All those years with Nick, why didn't I just leave? There was nothing holding me to him: no children, no property to sell, no marriage to unpick. So maybe part of me relished seeing how far I could push him. Maybe all of those times I had spoken to another man at a bar, pressed myself too close, in Nick's full view, I had known exactly what I was doing, what the fall-out would be. So why would I keep on doing it unless part of me enjoyed it?

I knew deep down that I had no future with Charles, but discovering this about myself made whatever it was I had with him feel more tangible than a happy-ever-after with Joss.

By the time we reached the van I felt myself pulling away almost completely, such that when we were inside, bubbled within the van's hermetic seal, I felt Joss's hand creeping towards my own and I stiffened. He continued, and I watched it happening as though in slow motion: the shifting of his weight in the seat, the torquing of his body across the gear box, face looming over mine until the moment our lips touched. From then, it was as though time tripled in speed. A flurry of movement. Me pulling away. Hands raised. His face, cycling through confusion, hurt, embarrassment.

'I'm sorry.' I found the words somewhere in the guilt churning inside me. My face felt hot, my arms quivering with unspent adrenaline. He let the words fall heavily, no response. 'You don't want to do this.' I worried my hands in my lap. He was staring straight ahead, his expression now blank, unreadable. His silence made me verbose. 'I'm not who you think I am, Joss. I'm not who you want. It's complicated.' I searched for the words to explain what I didn't quite understand myself. '*I'm* complicated. Please. It's nothing to do with you but it's better this way. It's better. If we don't.'

He let my words peter out into nothing, and then he turned the key in the ignition. Before we backed out of the car park, he turned the radio on. Better the crackle and static of bad signal than the clarity of my rejection.

We were an hour from home when the van revolted. First a high-pitched whistling noise coming from the depths of the vehicle, followed by a loud knocking. When steam started to rise from the bonnet, Joss turned his head to the dashboard and swore.

'*Fuck*,' he said again, the first word he had uttered since we left Lizard Point. He slammed his palms against the wheel, turned on his hazard lights and pulled the van off the road.

He switched off the engine, waiting for the van to still, then turned the key. The van wheezed, revved, fell silent.

'It's dead,' he said into the ether. 'I think it's the fan belt.'

I swallowed, doing the mental calculations. The children got back home from school at four. I had planned to be back by half three, to give myself a buffer. If we could be back on the road in less than half an hour, I would be fine.

'How long do the insurance normally take to send someone out?' Joss didn't answer. 'Joss?' I knew he was angry with me, but to completely ignore me for a simple question seemed out of character.

'I don't have insurance,' he said eventually.

'Excuse me?'

'I don't have insurance.' He allowed himself to turn to me, and when he did his face was grey.

'Isn't that illegal?' I didn't know much about cars, but I was sure that was true. When he didn't answer, I knew I was right. 'So, what do we do?'

'I'll need to find a local mechanic, get them to tow me there.' When he spoke, his voice was dry, as though all the moisture had been sucked out of his throat. 'I've just never needed insurance before – it's one of those things that seem like a scam to get you to keep paying money. If I get caught with no insurance, it's six points on my licence. And a fine. I can't work without my van.'

I felt he was speaking more to himself than to me, playing the various scenarios out in his head.

'It's going to be OK.' I longed to reach out, put a hand on his shoulder, but my recent rejection filled the air between us, and I hung back. 'No one is going to call the police. Let's just find a mechanic quickly and get you sorted.'

'Yes, OK. You're right.' Somehow, what I said seemed to enliven him, and he reached into his pocket to check his phone. 'There must be a mechanic nearby.' I watched as he tapped at the screen, then hammered a fist into the centre of the steering wheel. 'No signal,' he spat. 'What about you?'

I faltered, remembered my phone was somewhere at the bottom of the sea. 'Sorry. I don't have one.'

He gave me an odd look.

'I haven't really needed one since I've been here.'

He huffed, but then sort of pulled himself together, gave a decisive nod.

'There'll be a mechanic nearby. I'll just walk to the nearest village and ask. It can't be too far.' He turned to me. 'Do you mind staying here to look after the van? Just in case. If anyone asks any questions, say . . . just don't say anything about insurance.'

'Yes, of course, that's fine.' Although the thought of sitting there waiting for an unknown expanse of time was making me extremely nervous.

'Here, take my phone – just in case you manage to get some signal. I'll try and call, if I find somewhere.'

He tossed the phone into my lap. Opened his door to leave.

As soon as he was out of sight, I grabbed the phone, stretching myself into every corner of the van to try and find signal. I toggled the settings on and off, restarted it. Nothing worked. Frustrated, I threw it into the footwell. The gap was closing on my buffer.

I attempted to read my book but couldn't concentrate, glancing at my watch so many times I kept losing my place, so settled for staring out of the window, watching the passing cars.

At three o'clock, Joss was back, riding in the front seat of a tow truck. I jumped out and watched as they fixed a chain onto the underside of the van. We drove off, thankfully moving in the direction of home. If we could get things sorted out quickly, I might just make it as the kids arrived home. I'd still have time to sort their dinner. Or maybe I'd order pizza once we were en route, make a treat out of it.

'So how long is it going to take?' I asked the mechanic when we arrived back at the garage.

'It'll take at least an hour.'

'*What?*' I tried to hide my distress from Joss, but the word escaped me without meaning to as the mechanic stood back from the van to report the damage.

He shrugged his shoulders, turned himself very obviously to address Joss instead.

'You'll need to replace the fan belt, which shouldn't take too long, but it's in a difficult position. And there's some damage to the cooling system too. It might take less time than that, but it depends on whether we have the right parts. If not, we might need to ring up the other garages in the area. There's a caff down the road you can wait in –' he assessed whatever pained expression my face was making '– that you might find a little more comfortable.'

In the caff, I sipped Diet Coke from the can and stared glumly at Joss's phone. I'd managed to get signal by then, but there was no one at home when I'd called Kewney, and no answerphone, just a dial tone ringing out. I pictured the sound trilling through the manor's empty hallways. Joss had Laurie's mobile number saved too, so I'd texted her, but there was nothing to indicate she'd seen the message, and I'd barely ever seen her take her phone out. I obviously couldn't call Charles.

'I'm sorry,' Joss spoke into the silence, interrupting my flurry of thoughts.

'It's not your fault,' I said, although I couldn't project the truth of it into my voice. It wasn't his fault, of course. Whether he had insurance or not wouldn't have had a bearing on the van breaking down. But in the absence of anyone else a part of me couldn't help mentally putting the blame on him.

'I shouldn't have suggested this trip. It was stupid of me.'

'No, no,' I placated, trying to imbue my voice with as

much kindness as I could muster. 'I had a lovely time. Really wonderful.'

'Just not with me.'

'Joss.' I tried to make eye contact, but he turned away, balled the napkin he was holding into his fist.

'Is it someone else?'

'I told you: it's complicated,' I answered, figuring it was the best way to tie up the loose ends of this.

'Is it Mr Rowe?'

My whole body prickled.

'*What . . . ?*' I stuttered, for want of anything else.

He jerked his shoulders, began ripping the napkin into shreds.

'You always seem so interested in them – the two of them, their marriage. And I'm not blind, I've seen the man. He's good-looking – for an old guy.' This he added darkly, and I knew it was a deliberate dig. 'Anyway, you wouldn't be the first.' I frowned at his obscurity.

'What do you mean?'

'Nothing.' He huffed. 'It's just interesting how money can have such an influence on people. You didn't strike me as silly enough for all that, but obviously I was wrong.'

'*Joss.*' I felt my face redden, tears smarting the corners of my eyes. I didn't know where the day had taken such an awful wrong turn, when it had started out so wonderfully.

I thought about trying to explain, to retaliate with an equally low blow, but then the bell on the cafe door jangled, and the mechanic appeared and the conversation was snuffed out.

'All sorted. See –' he made a show of looking at his watch '– record time.'

It was four o'clock by the time we set off. I tried the house phone, but it rang out again. Laurie wasn't always home when the children got back, that's why there was me. Luckily the front door was never locked, so at least they'd be able to go inside. I felt sick, picturing them calling for me, Laurie coming home and asking where I was. Joss's phone roamed in and out of signal without me able to catch enough to call, and then it died. We spent the rest of the journey in silence.

It was just gone five o'clock when we pulled into the gates of Kewney Manor. As we approached the house, I saw the ground-floor lights were on, and Laurie's car was in the drive. My chest tightened.

'Thank you,' I said, when the van sighed to a stop. He gave a small jerk of his head, and I felt myself breaking, the tears threatening to fall. 'Joss, I don't know what to say, I . . .'

Motion made me glance up, and I saw the door to the manor heave open, Laurie striding out of it. Even through the windscreen, I could see the thunderous expression on her face.

'Where the hell have you been?'

A combination of her pulling at the door and me trying to open it made me collapse out of the van.

'Laurie, I'm so sorry, I tried to call but . . .'

I stumbled to right myself on the gravel, turned to snatch my things from the footwell. Inside I saw Joss watching us both, lips apart.

'I've only just got in. The children have been by

themselves for an *hour*. Bess burned herself trying to make toast. William has turned the living room upside down. You—' For the first time, she noticed Joss in the driver's seat. 'Is that . . .' She peered inside. 'Joss?'

He gave a blunt nod, stared straight ahead.

She turned from him to me, and I could see her features morph into a snarl.

'What is this? You're an hour late because you've been messing around with the gardener? Is this . . . are you sleeping with him?'

'God, Laurie, no!' As I said it, I saw Joss flinch, caught sight of Bess and William, peering out from the doorway. I was overwhelmed by the horror of it all. 'Laurie, please, let me explain.' My heart was pounding but I tried to calm myself down, to think clearly. 'We went out for the day – just on a trip, to visit Kynance Cove. Down the coast? I was supposed to be back by half past three, but we broke down. I did try to call you, but I couldn't get through, I texted . . . didn't you see?'

I reached a hand out to her, pleading, wanting this to be over, this whole day to be done and forgotten about. She waved me away.

'Do you think we pay you to go gallivanting around the coast? Do you assume you are here on some sort of *holiday*? I respect that whilst the children are in school there isn't much "duty" for you to perform, but this is *totally* irresponsible.' She breathed sharply, a flare through her nostrils, and a look passed over her face, one that looked strangely like terror. 'What happened today . . . the two of you . . . you mustn't tell Charles.'

The sound of his name stopped me short. I

understood that I had let her down, but her reaction seemed extreme. Why the threat about Charles? She looked from me to Joss, and an unpleasant thought nagged at me, the one from our conversation in the parlour: *did Laurie know?* Was this part of some sort of game between them, where I had been deliberately kept in the dark? But even as she said it, she must have seen my look of confusion because she began backtracking, regaining her control with a little shake of her head. 'You know what it's like with the Rowes – so much history, so many old-school ideas. You know how much we care about you, Lily. You're part of our family. The *gardener* . . . it's just . . . not appropriate.'

Beside me, I saw Joss stiffen. I felt a wave of disgust myself. Was that all the issue was after all? Propriety? As much as I wanted to defend him, I just wanted to put this spoiled day to bed. I was painfully aware of Bess and William standing on the doorstep, their bewildered looks. I couldn't stand the idea of how this must look to them.

'It's not like that, Laurie,' I promised, even though I knew it would make Joss hate me more. 'We're just friends. I didn't realize it would be such an issue. It won't happen again.'

She blinked, taking it in, but her eyes were distant, unfocused. 'The children were so confused. I've been frantic with worry.'

I hung my head.

'I'm truly sorry for upsetting you, Laurie. Honestly. I tried everything I could to get hold of you. Please, please forgive me. I'll go inside and clean everything up right now, sort the children's dinner and we can forget this ever happened.'

I motioned to go, and it seemed to snap her out of whatever state she was in, because she blinked, ran her fingers through her hair, setting a chorus of jewelled bracelets jangling.

'Yes. Yes, you're right.' She licked her lips, the jut of her tongue peeking through her wide mouth, set her hands on her hips. 'I'm sorry, I'm probably overreacting. I saw the car was still here. And then the children were inside, but you weren't. I thought . . . I thought something had happened to you.' She straightened herself up, turned to face the open door, the silhouette of the children. 'Bess, William, let's get back inside, you've got no shoes on.'

Looked back vaguely in our direction. '. . . I'll let you say your goodbyes.' Her eyes flicked towards Joss. 'I apologize . . . if I offended you. That wasn't my intent. I'm sure you understand the need for your discretion over this whole . . . incident. If you'd like the keep your position.'

Joss's expression remained passive. 'I understand, Mrs Rowe.'

My ears pricked up at the slight emphasis on 'Mrs'.

The door closed behind them, and I looked back into the van, tripping over myself to find the words to begin. 'Joss, I . . .' He was staring straight ahead, his hands resting on the sides of the steering wheel.

'I'll be off, then.' He didn't look at me, but he didn't need to, I could hear the extent of his feelings in his voice: resentment, hurt, humiliation.

'I didn't mean any of this to happen. I only wanted . . .'

'Is that how you see me? "The help"?' He mimicked Laurie's feminine, snobbish tone.

'No! God, Joss, *no*!'

'Don't worry, I'll be sure to keep my distance from you fine manor house people from now on.' He cut across my pathetic apology, deliberately exaggerating his West Country burr. 'I hope you'll show me the kindness of doing the same.'

It took all my restraint not to cry in front of him. I sniffed sharply. 'Please . . . don't be like this.'

'Like what, Lily?' His hands gripped the steering wheel tighter, and if the sky weren't darkening, I was sure I would see his knuckles were white. 'Excuse me if I'm not jumping for joy at the prospect of losing my job. Some of us can't rely on sleeping with the boss to get ahead.'

He waited a moment, seeing if I would counter. When I didn't, he reached across and pulled the passenger door shut, revved the engine, and put the van in reverse.

'Goodbye, Joss,' I murmured into the air, watching the van disappear before I moved towards the house, utterly drained.

Charles came to me that night, but I couldn't get Joss's expression out of my mind. The look on his face at Kynance Cove, when he realized the reason for my rejection. The hurt, as he drove off from Kewney.

'You're distracted?' Charles leaned on his elbow, trying to read my thoughts in the lamplight.

'Sorry. Long day.' I attempted to clear my mind, rearrange my expression.

'Oh? Doing what?'

That morning seemed so long ago, I had to search my memory to remember what I had told him. 'Nothing exciting. It must just be the heat.' I felt the lies tangling around me like the bedclothes at my feet.

A funny expression came over his face.

'What?'

He chuckled, low. 'Nothing . . . just something Laurie said.'

I froze. '. . . Oh?'

'Yes. About you . . . and the gardener?'

I stared intently at the point of his knee, propped up above the covers. Why would Laurie tell him, after the extent she had gone to ensure it should be forgotten? 'That was just a misunderstanding. We're just friends.' I swallowed. 'Not even.'

He stretched to kiss the area between my cheek and chin, let out an exaggerated yawn. 'Thought so. It sounded like Laurie's typical sort of gossip.' Crept a hand across the bed, fingers walking up my naked thigh. 'Still . . . I would hate the thought . . . of you betraying me like that.' Turned to look into my eyes. 'I wouldn't like that at all.'

Later, when he had been long gone and I was still lying on my side, staring into the dark, noises from downstairs roused me: footsteps, the deep *thunk* of the front door closing, followed by a shout. Seconds later, the dull light of the motion sensor illuminated the fabric of my curtains and I took to my feet to peer through them onto the gardens below.

Charles and Laurie were on the lawn, he in his bed-clothes, a grey cotton T-shirt and striped pyjama bottoms, she barefoot and bare-legged in the silk kimono I had seen her wearing the first night I had watched her on the beach. He had been fully clothed when he had entered my room, and it sickened me slightly, thinking of the time between him leaving my bed and entering theirs, the marital intimacy his clothing signified, how fluidly he had transitioned from one person to another.

I watched them through the gap in the curtains – she a few feet ahead, he stalking behind her, moving, I assumed, in the direction of the beach path, as I had seen her do before. But I had never seen Charles with her, and her actions seemed more urgent, frenzied, than they had in the past.

There was a gauzy white sheer between my window and the curtains, so, fearing detection, I pulled it tightly closed, leaving the smallest gap to press my face against. If I strained my ears and shallowed my breathing, I discovered I could make out almost all of what they were saying.

'Laurie, stop this.' He caught up to her, grabbing her by the wrist and pulling her back in the direction of the house. 'Come back to bed.'

'Let me go. Leave me be.' She thrashed against him, hair and robe coming loose as she bucked beneath his grasp.

And he, holding her tighter. 'Dammit, woman, you'll wake the whole house.'

She said something I couldn't quite catch, something that made him hold her closer to her, but then she kicked him, so hard in the stomach that he doubled over, fell to the ground. She momentarily freed herself, but then he snatched out at both her ankles and, to my horror, pulled hard on them both, dragging her backwards so that she fell face down onto the grass, landing awkwardly on her wrist.

The cry that emanated from her managed to pierce through the glass, and for a moment they stopped, both of them tilting their heads towards the house. I shrank back, afraid of discovery, but when I heard nothing more, I peeked out again.

On the grass, Charles was holding her by the injured wrist, pressing it back behind her head as she lay beneath him.

'You'll make yourself sick, doing this. Stop this foolishness. Come back inside.'

She said something again that was unintelligible, her words clenched in the grip of her teeth, but then, with a stab of clarity, I heard the name 'Nina'.

Charles stopped. Raised himself up. Enunciated, quite clearly, *'Don't. Don't you dare.'*

When she said nothing, he bent over her, pressed his face close to hers, and then slapped her across the face so forcefully that she curled into herself in pain.

I involuntarily winced, turned myself away, but when I looked back, I saw she was staring straight up at him, her body tensed. And I saw her nod.

The slap came again, on the same side, and then his hands were over her, crawling up her thighs and to the belt of her robe, untying it and exposing her body to the open air. He settled himself on top of her, and I realized too late what I was about to witness, shouldn't be witnessing, but couldn't look away from.

As his body jerked on top of her, his fingers curled around her neck. At first she did nothing to stop him, but as he pressed down harder I saw her struggling, reaching her hands to her face to pull him off her.

'No, no, Charles, stop. I take it back. I take it back. Charles, I can't breathe!'

Abruptly he stopped. Wrenched himself off her, coming to stand over her as she looked back up at him, both unspeaking.

'Don't do this to me, Laurie.'

He left her there on the lawn, like a wounded animal, and as he walked away, I saw her relax, her limbs uncurl, so that she was lying starfished, staring up at the stars. She didn't move, she didn't cry; if anything she looked almost peaceful; and I was compelled to watch her, trying to make head or tail of what I had witnessed, wondering if I would ever make sense of the Rowes, or the secrets that lay hidden in the heart of their marriage.

And then there was noise in the hall, the sound of footsteps on the stairs, and my heart leapt into my chest. I hurried to my bed, convinced that Charles would enter, would know, somehow, that I had seen them. My breathing was ragged, and when I pressed a palm to my mouth, terrified the sound of my hyperventilation would travel, I realized my whole body was drenched in sweat. The seconds ticked by, and the moment passed. I was alone, but the feeling didn't leave me.

The man I had witnessed out there was not the man I had let into my bed. The Charles I thought I knew was intelligent. And kind. Loving. And yet . . . if I was entirely honest with myself, what I had seen tonight hadn't seemed entirely out of character. If I was entirely honest, I had to admit that there were sides to Charles's nature that worried me. Sometimes even scared me.

I thought back to his behaviour the night of the dinner party. The way he had grabbed her by the wrists. Hauled her upstairs. I had assumed it was purely to take control of her. But then my mind went to the other odd things I had experienced in my time at Kewney: the broken bottle, Laurie's midnight walks, her erratic moods. The look in his eyes, when he warned me about Joss. When I put them all together; when I thought of Charles's hands on his wife's throat; they began to build up a picture I wasn't sure I wanted to see.

Laurie had said Nina's name – why? Why had it caused such a visceral reaction? What had been so dire about her departure that they practically denied her existence to me?

Nina. Christine. These wispy figures whose existence no one seemed to acknowledge, but whose presence seemed to settle like cobwebs in the corners of Kewney's history.

She told me that she'd married Charles 'in sickness and in health'.

But in agreeing to that, what choice had she made? What choice had I?

14

I was distracted at breakfast the next morning. Burning the toast. Tripping over the corner of one of the bar stools and knocking over William's orange juice in the process. I was sure that someone would notice, say something, but Charles was his usual casual self, and when Laurie breezed through in search of coffee, she barely paid me heed.

I watched them, though, quietly, unobtrusively. How they moved around the kitchen – and each other – with the fluidity of a ballet chorus. Made gentle conversation – the weather; a review in the paper of a film they had both loathed; the event they were going to that night; the school fundraiser for the new theatre. How was this couple and the couple I had witnessed the night before one and the same?

Laurie was wearing a high-necked blouse, I noticed, and occasionally she would let out a little cough, as though trying to clear her throat. Once, she absent-mindedly reached for the pot of coffee with her injured wrist, yelped, and Bess turned to ask, 'Are you OK, Mummy?' Charles took it steadily from her, poured – 'Let me do that, darling' – and replied, 'Mummy just tripped on the stairs, but she'll be fine.' How, how, did they perform with such assurance? I found it maddening.

But then, hadn't I played the game too, with Nick?

When they had all departed, and the house was still, I found myself wandering through the empty wings, neither my mind nor my body at rest. I couldn't – or didn't want to – reconcile the scene I had witnessed last night with the domestic equilibrium of the daylight. I had let myself fall for Charles, and everything I thought that he was. I thought I had escaped Nick . . . what if my fate was no better here?

I passed the open door to Bess's room and my eyes were drawn to the painted white bookshelf against the far wall, crammed with the paperbacks we had spent happy evenings poring over. I paused. The Enid Blyton book was still wedged on the shelf, but beside it I saw another I didn't recognize, the cracked spine and yellowing paper marking out its age. I stepped fully into the room and removed the book from the shelf. *Swallows and Amazons*. The cover art depicted a hand-drawn map which wrapped around the front and back. I had vague recollections of a film, one of the VHS tapes Nan kept on rotation in the front room. Resting the book on my open palm, I flicked through to the title page. There, in the top right-hand corner, was the same scrawl again: Christine Anne Rowe, September 1959.

'Bess.' I tutted, smelling the paper's must on my fingertips. She must have been poking around in the attic again without her mother's knowledge.

Before I closed the book, my fingers lingered on the title page, looping over the letters of Christine's name. What had happened to Christine to make her take her own life? And why had it made Charles forbid anyone speak her name within these walls?

I peeled the original book from the shelf, resolved to return both upstairs and have a quiet word with her before bedtime, before Laurie found out.

Paused, at the thought of the attic, Laurie's distress at Bess playing up there. Was it really just loose floorboards she was worried about?

Listening out once more for any disturbance in the house, I replaced the book on the shelf and retreated to the corridor, heading past my room to the furthest corner of the house, where I was sure I had once spotted a set of stairs.

The steps were steep here; a narrow corridor with rope for a banister, spiralling sharply round a corner and up to a plain white door at the top. There was no lock, and the door handle opened easily with a gentle twist. Inside, a long, narrow room stretched across what I assumed was the entire length of the house. The room was built into the eaves, the ceiling sloping to accommodate the beams, with two small windows angled into each side of the roof, throwing a slim shaft of light onto the attic floor. It might have been servants' quarters once upon a time, I mused, noting the small white sink in the corner of the room, and thinking gratefully of my bedroom downstairs. I knew the room was currently out of use, but there was something desolate about it I didn't like.

To my immediate left, I could see remnants of what I assumed were from the current Rowes: two sets of skis, a tiny violin case with Bess's name on it, old games and a baby bath filled with rubber bath toys. Further in, the debris got more extravagant: one of those classic Silver

Cross prams with the metal frame and huge white wheels, gilt-framed artworks that were probably worth thousands, fine wooden furniture covered with dust sheets. I moved from treasure to treasure, unsure of exactly what I was looking for but convinced I would know it when I saw it. I found the cardboard box of books Bess had unearthed: they were mostly pulp fiction, reeking of mildew, but here and there were a few more Enid Blytons along with a selection of other classic children's literature: *Charlotte's Web*, *The Little Princess*, several volumes of the Chronicles of Narnia. I wondered which had been Christine's favourite.

Along the far wall of the attic, reached by climbing over old steamer trunks, a box of tarnished silverware and twin embroidered armchairs with the stuffing coming out, a group of clear plastic storage tubs were stacked two high. As I got closer, I could see they were filled with exactly the sort of ephemera we hadn't known what to do with after Mum had died and I moved to my grandparents: reams of paperwork, loose photographs, the occasional birthday card pressed face up against the plastic. The sort of thing that had no immediate use, but that we were either too sentimental about to chuck or too worried it might one day become important. It was here, I was sure, I would find something useful, and I felt the blood rush to my ears as I reached for the first one, unclicked the lid and delved inside.

There seemed to be no rhyme or reason to the contents, but rather someone, or maybe more than one person, had chucked in whatever they could fit, and when I looked across the six huge tubs, I got the sinking feeling it was all just junk. Nevertheless, I persevered, rifling through old mail-order clothes catalogues, Post-it notes with long-forgotten reminders, smart correspondence cards and embossed invitations in formal script, 'Lord and Lady X request the pleasure of your company . . .' The latter, along with a couple of Yellow Pages from the seventies and a year planner from 1982, gave me hope that at least these were from Charles's generation. I flicked eagerly through the planner, hoping for some mention of him – he would have been nineteen, then, at university; possibly there would be some visit home, a planned reunion his parents had diarized. I was disappointed quite quickly to find that it had been barely used: a couple of timings for the hairdresser in January and February, 'P's Wedding' encircled on a Saturday in March, petering out to nothing by June. I threw it back in the box, closed the lid and went on to the next.

Despite the mundanity of the contents, I found there was something quite soothing about ploughing through these relics from the past, and I soon entered into a pleasant rhythm of sorting and replacing, almost forgetting the task in hand. It was quite like being a modern anthropologist, piecing together the scraps of this recent history to form a picture of life at Kewney Manor and the people who had lived it. A shopping list, probably intended for a cook or housekeeper, included a request for 'five pounds of the best butter available', 'aspic' and 'three veal tongues OR one veal and one ox'. There was a school report for Charles aged ten, a single sheet of paper with a list of subjects down the side and the grades beside them, all Bs and Cs, accompanied by the weary comment, 'It's hard to tell if Charles hasn't done the work, isn't interested, or both.'

The photographs were few and far between, but with them I could finally put faces to the names of the family he so rarely spoke of. His mother, perm-haired and never out of formal dresses, looked far older than the forty-odd years she would have been as she held a small Charles's hand, and never seemed to flash a smile for the camera. The father, rarely in shot, wore oversized glasses and a dour expression entirely in keeping with a man who would force his young son to drink a bottle of whisky as a punishment. Charles, for his part, was mer-curial: ebullient behind an elaborate birthday cake; turtle-necked and long-haired in that classic late sixties style; pulling faces on a beach; scowling and sullen as a teenager. But it was Christine who interested me most.

It had to be her, I deduced. Not just because she was the only other common thread that ran through the series of images. But because she looked exactly like Charles. It chilled me when I saw it first. The dark, whirlpool eyes that sucked you in, made you desperate to know what thoughts were behind them. The full lips that brought a softness to Charles, but on her appeared sultry, gave her a brooding sexuality evident even at a young age. It was clear to me then, as it must have been to the people who knew them, even if the politesse of society made them deny it out loud, that she was Charles's mother.

Poring over their expressions, I was quite sure that Charles didn't know it – at least not then, in the years captured on film – but that he adored her. It was there in the brightness of his eyes, the way his face was tipped towards hers in every mise en scene they were captured in. Whatever reserve existed in his relationship with their parents seemed vanquished by the way he looked at his pseudo sister. For her part, she seemed to indulge him – hands pressed to her face as he blew out candles, crouching beside him as he showcased a sandcastle on the shore – but I was certain I could detect a sadness too, a wistfulness that made her not quite return his smile. In one shot – perhaps the youngest picture I had found of Charles – he was sitting in her lap, playing with a lock of her hair, which was long, then, spilling over her shoulders and halfway down her arms. He must have been two or three, which put her in her late teens, and she was wearing a school uniform, a stiff tartan pinafore and high-buttoned shirt. Her arms were around his torso, but barely, as though she was only just resting them there, and her face was tilted away from him, eyes staring out in the distance, as though she'd rather be anywhere but in her present.

What must it have been like for her, all those years of keeping their real relationship a secret? And was it the revelation of this that had eventually made their relationship spoil? I didn't like the way it made me feel, that photograph. I replaced it where I'd found it, burying it deep in the middle of the others where I wouldn't have to look at it.

It was in the second-to-last box that I found it. This one seemed more ordered than the rest, I noticed; a selection of primary-coloured files and folders pertaining to house and family maintenance: utility bills, school fees, tax bills. The binder would have passed me by completely amidst the wash of mundanity if one phrase hadn't leapt out from the pages: brain injury.

I paused, hand shaking, and removed the binder fully from its folder. It was a brochure; a colourful presentation folder with pockets on both the inside covers, with a booklet on the left-hand side and forms and paperwork on the right. My breathing stilled as I flicked through it – glossy photographs of smiling patients and their nurses, spirited close-ups of flower-filled gardens, promises of love, community, care. And then I turned to the paperwork – a facsimile, really; thin yellow paper with the tracings of ink, a title on the top, 'Patient Assessment Form'. And there I saw it: her name, in full, under 'Name of patient': Christine Anne Rowe.

With a shaking hand, I tried to follow the words on the front cover with the tip of my finger: Meadow Lodge, residential and nursing care, specializing in the treatment and management of dementia, palliative care, neurodegenerative conditions and brain trauma.

I scanned the rest of the form, brain whirling with the complexity of the questions: 'Is there a history of challenging behaviour?', 'Has the patient suffered from any previous delirium?', 'Can the patient swallow their medications?'.

I tried to cast my mind back to what Laurie had told me, but there was no way I had misheard: she had told me in no uncertain terms that Christine had died.

Beneath the form, a letter, addressed from a GP in Truro, confirmed the fears that pressed at me:

To whom it may concern,

I am the family GP for the Rowe family and have been overseeing Christine Rowe's care since the time of her injury last June. Christine is a twenty-six-year-old woman who suffered hypoxic brain injury as a result of attempted suicide by hanging. She has no past medical history of note prior to this incident (bar mild childhood asthma). The suicide was entirely unpredicted, and she has not suffered with previous depression or psychosis, however the family have acknowledged that she was often prone to periods of sadness and introversion that seemed particularly exacerbated of late.

The oxygen deficit to her brain has left her mute, unable to engage in any meaningful communication and dependent for all her needs. It is possible that over time, and with the right medical attention and therapies, she will regain some of these faculties.

The family have another child at home and are unable to dedicate the quality of care and attention that she needs, which is why I am referring her to you for the full-time continuation of her care.

Her behaviour is not troublesome, and I don't anticipate she'll be difficult to manage. I have no other cause for concern.

Kind regards,
Dr James Thirsk

The letter was dated 3 July 1973. Nearly forty years to the day. This must have been the 'accident' Laurie had spoken of. The timings added up. Only . . . only Christine hadn't died. She'd survived. And they'd sent her away to this place. But why? And why the lies?

And if she had survived the accident . . . was she still alive now? I felt a sudden wrench of sadness for Christine. To be parcelled away from her family – her own son! For her life to have been so gravely curtailed when she was barely older than me. I thought of the wistful eyes of the girl in the photographs, the dour parents whose rule she had lived under. How dragged low must she have been, to try to take her own life?

As I replaced the folder, a single sheet of paper escaped it, hidden as it had been right at the back of the binder. Pinching it between thumb and forefinger, I saw immediately that it had been written in the same hand as the previous.

Dear Mrs Rowe,

I am writing to follow up on our previous conversation re. Charles and your concerns about his temperament.

As you know, at your behest, following the tragic incident with Christine last year, I have assessed Charles at length as to his character and condition, and it is my professional opinion that it is not necessary for you to pursue any further psychiatric evaluation.

Charles is a spirited young boy, and, yes, he does seem prone to violence, but I do not believe this to be highly out of character for a child who has suffered a traumatic event such as the one he witnessed.

We cannot undo this sad chain of events, so the best course of action for everyone should be to put it behind them. I do agree with your husband that a boarding school, combined with rigorous discipline, will be entirely beneficial to Charles and will afford him both mental and physical distance from what has happened. I would be happy to discuss these options with you, and to provide recommendations should I be of assistance.

Yours,
James Thirsk

My grasp loosened on the letter, and it fell with a flutter to the floor.

My hands flew to my neck, feeling with the tips of my fingers the liveliness of the blood pulsating beneath them. And as they did, a thought flashed before me, one that made my pulse quicken and thud against the pad of my thumb.

Charles's hands on Laurie's neck.

Her cough this morning, the guttural jarring, as she'd tried to clear her throat.

I had seen flashes of intensity in him before, but nothing like that, that rage.

I tried to reread the letter, but the words swam. The couched terms, the polite discourse infuriated me, but I wasn't sure I could face seeing them written more plainly.

Charles's mother had been concerned about his character. Why?

Laurie had said Charles never spoke of Christine. He had told Laurie she was dead. But what if the reason for his denial lay deeper? What if he had learned something – something fundamental about their lives, who they were to each other – that had triggered something deep within him? Something akin to the anger I had witnessed the other night.

What if Laurie knew?

The doctor seemed convinced that Christine had attempted suicide by hanging.

But what if it hadn't been that at all?

What if—

A noise from the depths of the house made me freeze, my ears prick up. A shiver seared down my spine.

'Lily?'

My throat constricted, and in a flurry, I shoved everything back inside the box, placed it on top of the pile where I found it.

'Lily?'

I stood, scanning the room feverishly to see if there was anything left out of place.

'Lily, are you in?'

The voice grew louder, travelling, no doubt, through the hallway and up the main staircase with its owner.

I gave a last, frantic glance around the room before shutting the door behind me, treading carefully but hurriedly down the attic steps, hoping to pass them and reach the landing before I was discovered.

Before I had a chance to finish my thought.

And Charles found out where I had been.

15

'Lily!' Charles's face carved into a smile as he emerged on the landing to my wing of the house, just as I made it to the entrance of my bedroom door.

'Hello, Charles.' I was surprised to discover I could make my mouth move, let alone words come out.

'I was beginning to think you weren't at home, but I saw the car in the driveway, so I hoped I'd find you here, somewhere.' He leaned his body against the wall, arms folded, nonchalant.

'Sorry, I was in my room, I had the door shut so I couldn't hear you calling. What are you doing home?' I deflected, hoping to shift the focus back on him so that I could catch my breath, still my whirring thoughts.

'No particular reason.' He flashed me the sort of easy grin I once would have softened at. 'I had an incident with a resident that made me laugh. I knew you'd find it funny, thought about telling it to you tonight, and then I remembered we were out at this blasted party and figured, no, sod working, what I'd really like to do is go home and see my Lily.'

Nausea washed over me at the possessive term.

'Great!' I chirped, falsely bright. 'Why don't we go downstairs; you can tell me about it now?'

But he was already moving towards me, hands on my

shoulders as he led me backwards towards the door of my room. I had to fight the urge to push him away from me, sure he would feel the staccato thump of my heart against his fingertips.

'Never mind that now,' he crowed. 'I think we can find something to do that's much more fun.'

'Oh, Charles, I don't know . . . .' I pressed a hand to his, trying to stop him. 'Laurie . . .'

'Laurie's at Meredith's, sorting out that blasted party tonight, I've just spoken to her.' He nuzzled into my neck, his stubble grazing my cheek. 'They're in a tizzy because they're a waiter down – she won't be back for hours.'

His hands fumbled at my back, finding my bra strap. The amount of times we had done this, that I had encouraged it, wanted it. Now, the thought of it made me sick.

'But the children . . . they'll be home soon . . .'

The clasp came loose and I felt his palms beneath my top, pressing against my naked skin.

'Nonsense, they won't be home for at least an hour. Please, Lily, I need you.' He pressed his hips into me. I reached for the door frame, steadying myself.

'I don't want to take up your time. Surely you have far more important things to do?'

'Lily—' But he stopped whatever he was about to say, held me at arm's length. 'What's that all over your clothes?'

My throat constricted as I looked down, saw the skid marks of dust across my chest and tops of my thighs. My thoughts travelled up to the attic door, and I must have instinctively twitched, inclined my head in that direction, because I saw his eyes tracking mine.

'I was looking through some of the first editions.' I spoke quickly, the thought coming to me almost before I had time to process it. 'The Brontë ones are all quite dusty.' And then, pulling him towards me, hating myself for it, I whispered into his ear, 'I should probably have a shower . . . after . . .'

And, although the thought of it made me ill, I managed to coax him into my room without him questioning me further, my mind working quickly, trying to think how I would get any answers to my many, many questions. I couldn't ask Laurie. Joss wouldn't even look at me. Who else was there who would offer me any insight into the Rowes?

And then it had struck me: Meredith.

The party she and Meredith were throwing was at Meredith's house; a black-tie fundraiser for the Parent Teacher Association, raising funds for a new performing arts centre. Laurie had been there all day, due back here with enough time to get changed, and then they were all leaving together. The kids were sleeping over.

From the few times I had met her, I already had a keen sense of what a gossip Meredith was; how she seemed to derive pleasure in dropping unsavoury hints about her supposed friend. She had told me that her family had known Charles's for a long time; maybe there was something more she could tell me, something that could shed light on what had happened to Christine, or what Charles might be capable of. If I could find a way to get to the dinner party, perhaps I could get her alone.

As we lay still in the bedroom, I bided my time, letting him stroke the small of my back with tip of his fingernail as I tried not to flinch, waiting for an opportunity.

'What do you do here in this big old house all day?' he asked languorously.

'Oh . . .' I tried to push away the memory of the attic, convinced that he would read my mind in the silence. 'Well, there's always stuff to organize for the children, or I read, or go down to the beach. There's lots to keep myself busy with, honestly.'

'Still, it must be lonely.' He tiptoed his fingers up my spine, towards the nape of my neck. The image of his hands at Laurie's throat flashed before me and I tried not to squirm away. 'I was thinking, maybe I'll work from my study a couple of days a week. Keep you company.' He snaked his arm across me, palmed my right breast, squeezed. 'I'm sure we could find some way to pass the time between calls.'

I trod carefully, not wanting to upset the equilibrium. 'We'd have to be careful of who else was in the house, of course. Laurie's always coming and going. Talking of which . . .' I raised myself up against the headboard, pulling the sheet up to cover myself as I seized the opportunity. 'You mentioned that Laurie was worried about staff for tonight . . . what if I stepped in? I'll just be rattling around here anyway.'

I turned.

'You're volunteering to be a waiter? Why would you do that?' He brushed the hair away from my neck, kissed the top of my collarbone, where sheet met skin. I tried not to shiver.

'I want to help.' I arranged my face into what I hoped was a lascivious expression. 'I thought you'd like the chance to spend more time with me?'

He moaned, low in his chest, and I knew that I had him.

'You in a uniform. Now that's not such a bad idea.' He rolled over, reached for his shirt. 'Well, if you're so keen to help out, why not?' Stood, pulling on his boxers, gave me a gentle slap on the bottom. 'I'll call Laurie . . . as soon as we've had that shower.'

Once Charles had safely retreated to his study, I threw myself into preparations for the evening, hoping to distract myself from the wild thoughts that were running through my head.

Charles didn't re-emerge, but Laurie flew in as I was giving the children a snack, came straight over to me, arms outstretched. She was yet to mention anything about our altercation after Kynance Cove, but when she saw me there, she came to a stop.

'You're angel to help out tonight,' she said carefully. 'Honestly, I don't know what we'd do without you.'

'Oh, it's nothing, really.' I blushed at her overenthusiasm. I think we both knew it rang false. 'I have nothing better to do.'

'Even still.' She came over to me, squeezed my hand. 'I so appreciate it.' And then, in an awkward sotto voce, looking pointedly towards the children. 'I really am sorry about yesterday. I flew off the handle. I was being an anxious parent and I let it get the better of me.'

'Please don't apologize.' I grabbed a handful of cucumber batons from the chopping board, reached to put them on the children's plates. 'I totally understand. And it won't happen again.'

'Well, good. OK then.' She straightened, looking slightly lost in the midst of the kitchen. Went over to Bess and William and kissed them both on the heads. 'OK, gorgeous ones?' They nodded, mid-chew. 'Remember, once you're dressed, nothing messy or it's straight to bed when we get there.' Looked around the kitchen as if searching for something to tidy or put away. 'I should start getting ready,' she said, more to herself than to us. Paused in the doorway before she was fully out of the room. 'Oh – Lily, the caterers have an apron for you, but I've got a beautiful white blouse you can borrow, and a Chanel skirt I've been meaning to give you. I'll leave them both on your door, OK?'

She was gone before I could respond.

Bess, William and I were present and correct in the entrance hall when Laurie and Charles descended together at six o'clock, Bess spinning on the toes of her ballet flats, watching the layers of netting under her party frock fizz around her, William begrudgingly sitting at the bottom of the staircase, reading a comic book after I'd told him off for messing around and spilling a glass of squash down his shirt.

I was restless, compounding not only my own nervous energy but that which Laurie had blown in with her, let out an almost audible sigh when I saw them emerge from their wing, looking as handsome as the first time I had seen them together.

Despite myself, I couldn't help but notice how Charles

looked in black tie – the epitome of dashing – face cleanly shaven, his hair washed and set neatly back with gel. In fact, I couldn't help but be swept away in the fantasy of the two them: paused at the top of the stairs, she leaning over to adjust his bow-tie, regal in deep-purple chiffon, a pearl necklace wound close to her throat.

What if I had got this all wrong?

He placed a kiss on her cheek, held out an arm to her. She stumbled, taking a step, giggled as she righted herself, pulled herself closer towards him. They looked every inch the loving couple. How could they keep up this pretence?

At the foot of the stairs, Charles caught my eye, dragged his gaze down my torso, to the buttons of the white blouse Laurie had loaned me.

Carefully, he winked.

There was a buzz on the doorbell, offering me a grateful distraction as I went to open it. A driver appeared, the same one who had collected me at the station my very first day, placed Bess and William's overnight bags into the boot before helping first Laurie, then me, into the back.

'I hope they do those lamb kofta things they had last time – they were good.' Charles craned his neck in our direction from the passenger seat as we sped through the iron gates. He seemed buoyed by our previous encounter, his mood convivial, bright. He'd found the mints, the ones that had been in the car on my very first journey to Kewney, and I heard the sound of them cracking between his teeth, experienced a weird sense of déjà vu for the time that had passed, all that had happened since I'd last seen them. 'Kids, you know the plan of attack, right? You need to take up a good position near the kitchen. Then you get first dibs of the food before the trays empty. Anything you don't like, give to me. And if it's the mini burgers, get me two.' He chuckled, pleased with himself. 'Only reason I come to these damned things is for the food.'

A few weeks ago, his easy banter would have washed over me. Sooner still, it may even have charmed me. Now, I felt a little flip in the pit of my stomach. He had been barely more than a child at the time of Christine's accident. I had got it wrong. Surely, I had got it wrong.

His hands at Laurie's neck.

'Charles's temperament.'

I stared out of the window, tuning him out, allowing myself instead to be lulled by Laurie's nervous whispering, practising the speech she had written out on the ruled cue cards she flipped through in her hands. William and Bess, squashed between us, got into a fight about who was taking up more space, and I was grateful for the distraction, grateful to have a reason to roll down the window, citing everyone's evident need for 'a bit of fresh air' as I breathed, let it fill my lungs.

Leave. I told myself. *Leave. Forget this whole thing. Pack your bags and get as far away from him as soon as possible.*

And what if he came after me?

And then I thought of Nick.

Who or what was waiting for me, even if he didn't?

We pulled onto a winding coastal road, passing a flat scrub of beach, a row of low-slung holiday cottages, a small pitch and putt course where a couple of families were making the most of the lingering summer light. We drove through a bay where the houses grew more populous, typical flat-fronted, vanilla-yellow beachside cottages that were nevertheless of an affluent size, a stretch of nothing, and then: Meredith's house.

The house was nothing like I had expected, having spent as much time as I had within the confines of the manor. Not that it wasn't grand – it may even have been larger than Kewney – but size was probably the only characteristic by which one could equate them. Where Kewney was old, Meredith's house was an ode to modern design. Where Kewney was light, with abalone-grey brickwork that reflected the sunlight onto the surrounding acres, Meredith's house was dark, an angular, corrugated black box, pock-marked with irregular, flat windows that blinked out at you like some sort of anthropomorphic computer. Where, at Kewney, it could feel as though the gardens might engulf the manor, nature reclaim it at any moment, here there was no doubt that Meredith's house dominated the natural world, jarring proudly with the sweep of surf behind it.

'Hugh is an award-winning architect,' Laurie sniffed as she stepped out of the car beside me, saw me looking up at the place. 'Goes to show that talent doesn't always mean taste.'

She walked off before I could answer.

I heard music as we approached the front door, and when a woman holding a tray of champagne flutes opened it, I saw a string quartet positioned next to the entrance, playing what I soon recognized to be an instrumental arrangement of Lady Gaga's 'Poker Face'. Inside, smartly dressed men and women milled about a space even more grandiose than the exterior. A living room, for want of a better word, sprawled across what must have been almost the entire footprint of the ground floor, marked by double-height ceilings and floor-to-ceiling windows across one full wall, affording uninterrupted views of the sea. Velvet sectional furniture in deep jewel tones clustered around a vast coffee table which seemed to have been formed out of driftwood, whilst behind them, back-lit black metal shelving displayed artfully arranged ephemera interspersed with colour-blocked coffee table books I was sure no one had ever opened. Charles and Laurie were already making conversation with a cluster of other parents, so I looked around for the children, but they had dispersed, too. Before I could feel too out of sync, there was a touch of a hand on my shoulder and I turned to see Meredith looking down at me from a pair of high-shine patent heels.

'You're a doll for helping out tonight, Libby.' Meredith's skin appeared to have taken on the same luminescent glow as her shoes, which I suspected to be the result of a recent chemical peel.

My real name tickled against my lips, but I held back the urge to correct her. I needed her on side tonight. 'My pleasure,' I conceded in reply. 'Just let me know what I can do.'

I followed her through the corridor, toying with what I could ask to elicit the right information.

'Your house is gorgeous,' I began. 'A work of art.'

'Thank you.' She demurred. ' We're very lucky.'

'Did you grow up nearby?'

'Fairly close.' She slowed her pace, the rhythm of her heels against the floor growing softer and less purposeful. 'I grew up in a similar house to Kewney. But I didn't inherit mine like Charles did. Primogeniture.' She rolled her eyes. 'It worked out OK though. And at least Hugh and I don't have to worry about roofs leaking, or the central heating costing more than our salaries.' She smirked. 'Charles and I were always complaining about the temperature in our houses when we were kids.'

'Oh yes, that's right . . .' I saw my opportunity, but tried to keep my voice casual, light. 'You knew Charles growing up didn't you?'

Meredith paused, a small smile flirting with her lips. 'Yes, since we were children. I'm probably one of his oldest friends.'

'That must be so nice, to have known each other for such a long time. He's lucky to have such a good old friend so close by.' I was getting a real sense of what made Meredith tick, had a feeling flattery would get me everywhere.

Her mouth twitched. 'Yes. For a time we were quite close.'

'What was he like growing up?'

'Charles?'

We had reached the end of the corridor, and I could see the open double doors of the kitchen beyond us. She paused, pressing a hand against the wall as she turned to face me. I nodded encouragingly. She sighed lightly. 'Always very intelligent. We played together quite a bit when we were little, especially before he went off to boarding school. He was always taking things apart and working out how to put them back together – watches, old tractor engines, that sort of thing. Once he caught a frog and took it out to one of the abandoned barns, found an old biology textbook in their library, and made me read out dissection instructions whilst he had a go at it with a Swiss Army knife.' My stomach squirmed. 'I made out that I was horrified, but actually I thought it rather fascinating.' She tilted her head coyly. 'He could be mean, too. The usual sort of thing, pushing me in the mud if I said the wrong thing, not liking it when I talked to other children. I used to kid myself that it was that old adage about boys being mean to you because they fancied you. Of course, it got worse –' I could hear the glee of scandal creeping into her voice '– after Christine . . .'

'Oh yes . . . his sister?' I tried to keep my voice steady, but internally I felt my synapses bursting into life. I had agonized over how I would be able to drag Christine onto the conversational path; I never imagined we would happen to stumble upon her so easily. 'I think Laurie may have mentioned something about her, once. An accident . . . ?'

'Mmm.' Her voice dipped, turned grave. 'It was a terrible to-do. There was some fuss about her leaving home. She wanted to join some group or band. Her parents refused, and from what I understood, it sent her over the edge, and she killed herself.' She shook her head. 'It nearly crushed poor Charles though. I don't think he was ever quite the same again. It wasn't long after that that he left for boarding school, so I saw less of him, but when I did, he seemed like a different person entirely – like the sun had gone out of him. It took years before he seemed to be himself again. There were rumours—'

But whatever she was about to say got cut off, as a woman in chef's whites strode out of the kitchen past her.

'Oh, Astrid –' Meredith caught her by the upper arm, our conversation forgotten '– this is Libby, the girl I mentioned. Can you show her the ropes?'

She waved me off, downing the rest of the champagne she had been holding before setting the flute on a ledge, striding away.

I followed Astrid into the kitchen where a flurry of workers were plating canapés and loading glasses onto trays as fast as their fumbling fingers could manage, and within minutes I had been thrust into an apron, all thoughts of Charles and Christine gone from my mind as I rushed about wherever I was called to. Most of my work was in the kitchen, but occasionally I was asked to go next door to retrieve empty glasses and gather up dirty napkins, and then I would steal a glance at Meredith, try and determine what else I could glean from her, and how.

A small stage had been set up at one end of the room, and about an hour after we had arrived, the lights were dimmed and I saw Meredith and Laurie ascending it, positioning themselves behind a microphone stand.

Meredith began, thanking the crowd, before signposting that she would be handing over to Laurie, to highlight the key pieces in the evening's silent auction.

She was a confident speaker, her voice clear and

controlled, but I noticed a certain twitchiness about Laurie beside her, the same nervous energy I had felt coming off her in waves in the car. She kept fluttering her fingers to her neck, checking on her choker, and I wondered how much time she had spent covering up the marks on her throat, how worried she was that they would show. When she took to the mic, it was too low, and it gave an electronic squeak as she tried to adjust it, throwing her voice in and out of audibility. She secured it, finally, made a joke about how she hadn't used a mic since her days in a Bangles tribute band that elicited a gentle hum of laughter, and I saw her relax. As the crowd resettled, she looked across it and I followed her eyeline to Charles, propped up against one of the poseur tables that had been set up at the back. He gave her a nod and I saw her relax, sink further into herself as she turned to address the room in full.

It was an intimate moment, one very much reserved for the knowledge and familiarity of a married couple, and it made me feel thick-headed. I gathered up a handful of glasses from a shelf and stumbled from the room, taking slow, deliberate breaths to relax the tightness in my chest.

I hadn't yet reached the kitchen when I heard footsteps behind me, weighted and even. I turned to find Charles standing in the centre of the corridor, a smirk threatening the corner of his mouth.

'I thought I saw you in there.'

'Yes, I was just . . .' I held the glasses up, a barrier between us.

'I'm enjoying seeing you in this uniform even more

than I imagined.' He took a step towards me, his eyes teasing. 'You'll have to start wearing this at home.'

'I should get back to the kitchen.' I spoke quickly, glancing behind me in case one of the other staff should come out, see us. 'They're so busy, and—'

'Don't leave me all alone.' His voice had a whine to it. 'It's so bloody boring out there. I'd much rather be with you.' He curled into me.

More footsteps. I looked up in horror to see Meredith rounding the corner, her heels clacking neatly on the polished floor.

'Oh.' She froze in her tracks, observing us.

'Meredith!' Charles drawled, smoothly removing his hand from the string of my apron. 'Lovely party. Lily was asking where the loo was. I was just coming back myself.'

'Oh?' She looked from me to my hands, to the glasses they were holding.

'Yes, that's right,' I replied meekly.

She observed me silently, turned back to Charles. 'Well, you should hurry up back inside, Charles. Your wife's about to announce her lot. A personal commission by Laurie Rowe herself. So very generous,' she simpered. 'You wouldn't want her to notice you're missing.' She jerked her chin to me. 'I'll show her the way.'

In the granite-tiled loo, I set the glasses down and ran the tap full blast, rubbed Meredith's expensive bergamot hand cream into my palms. When I couldn't stall any longer, I made a show of flushing the loo, opened the door slowly.

She was waiting for me, as I knew she would be.

'I thought your name was Libby.' She spoke with no inflection.

I shook my head. 'I didn't want to be rude.'

I felt myself blushing with the mundanity of it.

She let out a nondescript interjection but made no attempt to move.

'Meredith, I—'

'You should get those glasses back to the kitchen, they'll need them.' She held my gaze. I squirmed under it but didn't look away.

'It's not what you—'

Again, she broke me off, raised a palm to silence me. 'I don't want to speak about this any further. I've known Charles and Laurie for a very long time, but I don't need to know everything that goes on in their marriage. Or outside it.' But then she cocked her head, took a step towards me. 'Wait . . . is that why you were asking me all those questions earlier? Using me as some pawn in . . . whatever it was I saw going on?'

I reddened. 'No, no, that's not it, I . . .'

'Listen.' She stabbed a finger towards me, her face pinched. 'Laurie and I may have our differences, but at the end of the day she's my friend, and don't think I won't be the first to tell her what's going on, if I think you're planning on making any sort of trouble. I am aware that Charles likes his dalliances, but at least the other girl had the decency to know when it was time to call it quits and move on. If I suspected for one moment that you had any sort of designs . . .'

The phrase caught in my ears. 'I'm sorry, you said "other girl"?'

She tilted her chin at me almost pityingly. 'Sweetheart,' she crowed, making me feel all of three feet tall. 'You don't really imagine that you were the first?'

I shook my head, trying to make sense of what she was saying.

'I—'

She cut me off. 'I always suspected that was what had gone on.' She scowled. 'Laurie said she'd left rather abruptly. That usually only means one thing. I assumed that she had the wherewithal to get out before things boiled over. Either that or Laurie got fed up and gave her the boot. She's never been one for showing her full hand. I just hope you're smart enough to realize when your time is up, too.'

My vision blurred. Something about what she said pulled at me: of something Joss had said, the day of Kynance Cove. *You wouldn't be the first.*

'I'm sorry . . . when you say, "she", you mean . . . was it the other nanny . . . Nina . . . ?'

'Was that her name?' And then, waving it off, 'Look.' She brought her face close to mine, so close that I could see the creases of foundation in her forehead as her expression morphed with threat. 'I know it must seem an attractive proposition, to a girl like you. The big house, the handsome boss, the wife who, let's face it, can often seem a bit "away with the fairies", but you really don't want to get yourself mixed up with things you'll regret having to extricate yourself from.' Here she paused, looked me over darkly as though considering whether to really say what she was about to next. 'And you certainly don't want to outstay your welcome. With either of them. You may think you know Charles. You may even think you understand him. But get too close, and you'll see the other side of him. And then you may wish you'd never met him at all.'

I opened and closed my mouth, catching air where words failed me. The sound of clapping burst from the living room and Meredith whipped her head towards it.

'That's my cue.' She turned on her heels, but before she left me, she craned her neck to look back. 'Think about what I've said. You girls think that everything is just there for the taking. But one day you'll wake up and realize that dignity is more important than whatever folly you're entertaining.'

When she was finally gone, I let out a breath into the silent corridor, pressed my back against the smooth grey walls.

I thought of that phrase Meredith used. '*A girl like you.*'

The words smacked.

They weren't unfamiliar. In fact, the phrase, or something like it, was one that had held elusive connotations throughout my life. Teachers at school, tutting at the pupils who wore too much make-up and were thought to be 'loose': 'Girls like you will end up nowhere.' Even Nan, taking me to the shops on the weekend, tilting her head at certain short-skirted college girls congregating outside Miss Selfridge: 'Girls like that are asking for trouble.'

I had always been led to believe that the way I behaved had a direct correlation to how I would be treated. It was just a truth that girls were brought up to understand: if something bad happened to you – a date went sour, you received unwanted attention – it was because of something you had done. You were asking for it. You were behaving knowingly, even provocatively. You were, to use one of Nick's favourite expressions, 'a prick tease'. You were a 'girl like that'.

And now here I was again: a girl like her, like Nina. I had been foolish enough to let myself believe Charles's rhetoric, become entranced with the thrill of it, a man who wanted me, needed me, so much so that the rest of the world didn't matter.

But it wasn't fair. *It wasn't fair.* Nick, Meredith – even Joss: they were all so quick to dismiss me, to assume that I had some sort of insidious motive, purely because of my sex. Even Charles, the night in the library, had led me to believe that I was somehow the driving force of our affair. It was something I had come to believe myself. Whether I denied, pursued, or encouraged, I was always the one at fault.

Alone in that corridor, I felt my stomach tighten in a fist of anger. I saw myself through Meredith's eyes. I recalled how Joss had looked at me when he realized my secret. Remembered too, the insults that Nick would hurl at me – slut, whore – the shame I felt, at assuming he was right.

I wouldn't stand for it any longer.

I had survived Nick, hadn't I?

And now I would survive whatever it was with Charles that I had unwittingly waded into.

I was done with allowing myself to play either the scapegoat . . . or the victim.

The auction was wrapping up. I heard the plucking of the string quartet start up, the burble of small talk rising, darted back to the kitchen before I could be seen.

I had seen what Charles was capable of with his own wife. And he had lied about Christine's death . . . due, I feared, to his own hand in her fate. Now that I suspected he had been involved with Nina, too, it made me wonder if there was something Charles had said, or done, to make the previous nanny's departure so abrupt.

Unless . . . the thought pressed against my temples . . . unless it wasn't a departure after all.

Charles seemed to leave a breadcrumb trail of women in his wake. And they all appeared to lead back to his sister.

If I wanted to find out what happened to Nina, I had to go back to the start.

I had to find Christine.

16

The waiting room of the Beverley Centre was much smarter than I had anticipated. I had expected something akin to Nan's hospice, full of fading floral prints and comfortable but practical furniture, but instead I arrived to discover a red-brick Victorian house covered with trailing ivy, a formal concierge desk that wouldn't look out of place in a country house hotel. There was a neatly coordinated lounge that housed a full-scale grand piano and French doors opening out onto a flagstone patio, manicured gardens below.

I had almost lost my nerve. I had called the day after the auction, cover story whispered repeatedly under my breath, waiting for the dial tone to be replaced by a crisp female voice, 'Hello, Meadow Lodge, how can I help?' I had explained who I was looking for, waiting impatiently as she checked the patient registers, fingers clacking on a keyboard, only to tell me, half-heartedly, 'I'm sorry, there's no patient here by that name.' I nearly hung up then and there, no attempt at courtesy, but then her voice cut in again, 'Oh, no, wait, Christine Rowe did you say?' I swallowed, my throat dry with anticipation. 'Yes, here are her records. She was a patient here until 2008. Meadow Lodge is for residents aged sixty and under. She was moved.'

I waited for her to say more, but when she didn't, I pressed, 'Can you tell me where to?'

A pause on the other end. 'It really is confidential information. Not something I should be giving out over the phone.'

'Please.' I tried to calm the urgency in my voice. 'I need to see her. It's the first step I can take, towards a reunion.'

The story I had fabricated – my 'father', how desperate I was to mend his relationship with his long-lost sister – dropped unyieldingly from my lips, but somehow, she bought it.

She clicked her teeth. 'If anyone finds out about this, my job is on the line. You're lucky I'm a soft touch.'

I wrote down the name she said. Thanked her profusely. And the next day I found myself standing at the front door of the Beverley Centre.

'Her niece, you say?' A woman with a gelled-back bun and a gold name tag with 'Josephine' on it looked me up and down. 'I didn't know she had any family.'

I fumbled my way through the same excuse I had given first time around, watching her features morph from disinterest to surprise, until finally she said, 'Well, it'll be nice, for her to have a visitor. She's in art therapy at the moment, but if you don't mind waiting, she should be out in about half an hour.'

She led me through to a living room that was stiflingly warm, a dry heat that made my cheeks radiate. It was dotted with residents, some alone, some in twos or threes, or with the occasional visitor or nurse. There was a large flat screen television against one wall showing a daytime chat show, and easy, upbeat jazz played over the speakers, but still the room felt strangely silent. The air smelled strongly of synthetic peach air freshener, with undertones of disinfectant, that made my eyes water; once the nurse left me alone, I unlatched one of the French doors and went out into the courtyard, gulping the cool, fresh air.

I scraped back one of the green iron chairs on the flagstones, took a seat. I felt painfully that I was a fraud. Taking up these nice people's time. I had little experience of people with disabilities, let alone severe brain injury, and I was aware of acting clumsily, saying the wrong thing. I managed to psych myself out enough to call the whole thing off, was already pacing through the doors and out to the lobby, when a voice called, 'Ah, there she must be,' and I turned to find myself facing Christine.

It took me a moment to realize it was her, so firmly was my mind fixed on the young woman in the photograph, but once I made the leap in time, I knew very definitely that it was her. The woman in the wheelchair before me was in her mid-sixties now, and although her dark hair still retained its thickness, it was now streaked with coarse silver strands, combed neatly and parted in the centre. She was dressed simply, in a coral-coloured jumper and soft, navy trousers.

Her nurse, a girl of about my age with frizzy hair in a plait and freckles that looked like they covered every inch of her body, rested a hand on Christine's shoulder.

'It was Elizabeth, you said, wasn't it? Christine is excited to meet you.'

I smiled weakly at her, wondering why I had been so bent on verisimilitude when giving the name, as if any future checks would find a eight-year-old's visit plausible.

'Yes. Bess.'

And then my eyes flicked to Christine.

She didn't seem to have acknowledged me in any way, but was staring straight ahead, not vacant, but fixed. It was her eyes that got me, large and dark – the unheimlich way I found myself staring into a set that both were and weren't exactly like Charles's.

I swallowed the feeling down. Rubbed my hands along the sides of my jeans, wondering if I should hold one out to shake.

'It's very nice to meet you, Christine.' I decided against it, fidgeting instead with the car keys I still had in my hands before depositing them in my back pocket. And then, to fill the silence, 'I've heard so much about you.'

There was a pause in which I cleared my throat, and then her nurse placed her hands on the bars of the wheelchair and motioned with her head back towards the garden. 'I thought we'd sit outside, seeing as the weather's so nice. There's a pond out the back Christine is fond of. We can have tea.'

We made our way through the French doors and past the courtyard, strolling through the herbaceous borders to the pond, a kidney-bean-shaped body of water, where a cluster of cafe-style chairs and tables huddled under the shade of a tree. As we walked, the nurse gave a rolling commentary of what Christine's days involved, described a recent animal therapy visit the week before that she had particularly enjoyed. Her small talk was easy; she seemed adept at smoothing over any ineptness unfamiliar visitors might display. Christine didn't speak – I had come to assume that she couldn't – but the nurse continued to involve her in the conversation, punctuating her speech with the occasional, 'Wasn't it, Christine?', 'No, silly me, you're right, it was Wednesday', and I subsequently noticed that Christine was responding with a series of nonverbal cues – tics or aspirations – which the nurse seemed to effortlessly decode.

She took us up to one of the tables where she reversed the chair, turning it to face the pond, and then clicked the brake with the heel of her foot, turning to me.

'So, tea? I'll go fetch it. Give you a chance to catch up.'

She turned to go without waiting for my response, and as she faded from sight, the ball that had formed in the pit of my stomach the moment I left the car grew hard and tight. I had no right to be here. I had no idea what to say to Christine; where to even begin. And what if my instincts were all wrong, if her injuries had really been a result of her own hand, as the doctor had said?

'It is a lovely day, isn't it?' Anxiety made me awkward, and my awkwardness made me verbose. 'I've loved seeing Cornwall this time of year, when all the flowers are in full bloom. Every time the wind changes direction you get a different scent on the breeze, don't you? When I was London, it was as though there was just one perpetual smell, whatever the weather: a sort of acrid metallic one, like money, and rainwater and tube tracks all mixed up together. I remember . . .' In my babbling, I had forgotten that I was supposed to be playing Christine's niece, that I wasn't supposed to have lived in London at all. I glanced over at her, but she was looking out towards the pond, not at me at all. A bird swooped down over the water, caused the surface to ripple as it skimmed the surface, took off again. I saw Christine's eyes flicker in its direction. I looked up the oak tree shading us, its branches pendulous with thick green leaves. 'I saw the tree in the walled garden, the one with your name on it.' I swallowed. 'At Kewney Manor.'

Did I see something? A spark of recognition? It was nearly eleven o'clock, and the sun was burning through the cloudless sky. Even though we were in the shade, a bead of perspiration worked its way from my temple down the side of my cheek. I wiped it away. Forged ahead.

'It's a beautiful home. You must have . . . it must have been a nice place to grow up.' I thought I heard something; a noise, soft and low in her throat; and when I looked again, she had turned her chin towards me. I felt a flutter of adrenaline. I looked back up along the path we had come down, but there was no sign of the nurse. I moved my chair in closer, the metal legs scraping sharply through the gravel, bent my head towards her. 'Christine, I have to confess something to you. I wasn't being entirely honest, when I said I was your niece.' I paused, giving her space, but she made no further sound. 'I am the nanny at Kewney. I have been there nearly three months. I look after the two children there: Bess and William. They're lovely children, they really are. You should . . . I wish you could . . .' The weight of all I knew of Christine's past stymied me, sat heavy on my chest like a rock. 'They're your niece and nephew, Christine. They're Charles's children. Your brother, Charles?' She made no further sound, but I saw her mouth twitch, twisting oddly into the corner of her face. Tentatively, I carried on. 'Although, I should probably say, they're not really your niece and nephew, are they? They must be . . . they must be your grandchildren. Because Charles . . . because Charles is . . . because Charles is your son?'

I saw it then, definite: the jerk of her head, a rough, angular movement, accompanied by a low groan. A tear rolled down her cheek and my chest tightened. I couldn't bear the thought of upsetting her, but what if this were my only chance?

'Christine, I am so, so sorry to ask this, but I need to know the truth. That night, the night of your injury: did you try to hurt yourself, or was it . . . did Charles try to . . . was it him . . . ?' Her groans were louder now, her head shaking back and forth – not as though she were denying it; as though she didn't want to hear it. Tears of guilt prickled at the corners of my eyes. 'I'm so sorry, I'm so sorry,' I murmured under my breath. But then, strengthening my resolve, 'I promise you I am not here to harm you, or to upset you in any way, but I think I might . . . that Charles could be . . . his wife, already . . .' My throat felt as dry as sand, each breath I heaved rasping through it as I tried to form the words. Christine's movements intensified then, a steady rocking back and forth in her chair, and to my alarm I saw the nurse approaching at the far end of the path.

'Christine.' I spoke swiftly, and in my fervour, I reached out, took her by the hand. 'I think I might be in danger. Real danger. It is possible others before me may have already been.' I looked down at my hands. The skin around my thumbnail was raw, where I'd been picking at it. 'He hurts his wife. I've seen him. I've become muddled up with it all and I don't know what to do. I'm scared, and I have nowhere to go, and I know this is difficult for you, but if there's anything you can do, anything at all to help me, in any way, I . . . I . . .'

She wrenched her arm free from me, and I watched aghast as she began beating her forehead with the palm of her hand, over and over again, as her groans become a wail. I tried helplessly to do something, to reach out, to calm her in some way, but I watched as the nurse saw us, shifting into a sprint, tea sloshing over the sides of the paper cups she was holding in each hand.

'What's happened? What's going on?' she asked frantically, setting down the now near-empty cups as she laid a hand on Christine's shoulder. 'Christine, love, what's the matter?'

Christine thrashed in her chair. The nurse turned to me, accusingly. I stood, knocking the chair backwards as I did so.

'I'm so sorry.' I backed away, terrified now, not only for what I had inflicted on Christine but that they might discover my lies. 'I shouldn't have come. I'll go, I'll go right now.' I held my hands aloft like a criminal caught in the act. 'Please, I didn't mean any of this to happen. Honestly, I didn't want any of this I just . . .' I turned to Christine. 'Christine, I'm sorry. I'm sorry for everything that's happened to you. I'm going to try . . . I'll try and put it right.'

Christine wailed, and the nurse glowered at me. 'Look, if you're going can you please just go? You're only making things worse.' She walked behind the wheelchair, unclipped the brakes. 'Come, now, Christine, let's take a turn around the gardens. I brought some biscuits with me; we can feed the ducks.' Her voice was instantly calm, soothing, as she rolled the chair away from me. But as they moved past me, she turned her head to me, cold as night. 'Go.'

I stood rigidly, watching them as Christine's cries faded. And then I turned on my heels and left.

Christine hadn't said a word. But she didn't need to. I was convinced she had told me all I needed to know.

17

I sped back from the Beverley Centre, convinced that at any moment I would be pulled over, that the staff would realize my lies and come after me. Pulled into the drive, half expecting that Charles would be there, waiting for me, and was relieved to see Laurie's car, remembering she had announced that morning that she was going to be in all day, painting, which meant Charles would stay away. 'The gallery are showcasing an exhibition of my work,' she'd told me zealously, a streak of sky blue already scored across one of her cheeks. 'It's the largest show I've ever had. This could be my chance – to show that I can do more than just souvenirs.'

I went into the parlour under the guise of asking if she wanted something to drink, found her there at the canvas, ear buds in, humming as she worked. Unobserved, I watched her, the sleek motion of her arm as she stroked the brush across the painting, paused, stood back to think, added another stroke. The French doors were open fully, letting in a soft breeze that blew across the room, teasing the loose strands that had escaped from the bun at the nape of her neck. She was barefoot, moving gently on the pads of her feet, and the scene was altogether one of blissful solitude. She had borne the brunt of Charles's anger: did she suspect what he was truly capable of? If so, how could she accept it? And how much did she truly know of what was going on in her home?

'Laurie?' I called. When she didn't answer, I went over to her, touched a hand to her shoulder.

She flinched. But when she turned, saw it was me, her features softened. She removed the ear buds and placed the paintbrush down on the easel.

'Lily! Isn't it a lovely day? Have you been off somewhere?'

I remembered her anger the day she had discovered me with Joss, spoke deliberately. 'Just into the village, to pick up some toiletries. It was such nice weather I stopped at that cafe on the corner and had a coffee. I've only just got home. I wondered if I could get you a drink, or anything else?' If I was babbling, she didn't acknowledge it.

'Ah, that's so sweet of you, but no, I'm fine thank you, I'm going to get stuck in here because we're leaving in an hour or so.'

I must have frowned, looked confused, because she widened her eyes, leaned towards me.

'Charles and I are going to London for a few days. You remember, don't you? The children break up at lunch. You'll be all right, won't you, on your own?'

Of course I remembered now that she said it. Laurie had been so excited, the day Charles had announced that friends of theirs were visiting from Singapore, had talked of nothing else for days. 'We haven't seen Tim and Cordelia for years,' she'd burbled. 'Remember when we all got kicked out of the Groucho Club?' Pulled Charles towards her, giddy. 'It'll be just like the old days.'

That night Charles had lain on his side, tracing the pattern of my spine with a fingertip. 'I can't believe I have to leave you for so long.' He'd kissed the space between my naked shoulder blades. 'It's going to be hell, to be without you. I don't know how I'll bear it.'

I shivered now at the memory.

'Yes, I remember.' My voice came out limp. I cleared my throat, pushed myself ahead. 'I was thinking of planning some fun activities to do with the children. What did . . . do you remember anything they did with their other nanny that was particularly successful?'

'The other nanny?'

She sounded almost deliberately nonchalant, her tone breezy, despite the speed with which she replied.

'Yes,' I pushed. 'The one who was here before me.'

I searched her profile, but no imperfection crossed it. 'Oh. Well. I'm not sure I really remember.' She absent-mindedly picked up the paintbrush from the easel, twirled it in her fingers.

'Did she leave a long time ago, then?'

'Why are you asking about other nannies, all of a sudden?' I could hear the annoyance creeping into her voice now, despite her aloofness. She wiped a strand of hair from her forehead with the back of her hand, leaving a slash of paint across it.

'No reason. You said about the holidays, and at the auction Meredith mentioned a previous nanny so I was just wondering—'

'*Meredith?*' she cut across me, brow furrowing.

'Yes.' I swallowed. 'At the fundraiser, the other night. We were talking and she said that you'd had a couple of nannies before me,' I fabricated. 'She said the last one was called Nina, I think? You hadn't spoken about her before, but I supposed . . .'

Any anger that had been rising in Laurie seemed to dissipate. She scoffed, shaking her head as though shaking the bile from her.

'Listen, Meredith is a dear friend but she's also a ludicrous gossip. She's always been fiercely anti-help, so she crowed when it went wrong.' She paused, as if searching for the right way to explain it to me. 'Nina was a bit wayward, if I'm honest, and ended up leaving us in the lurch. I didn't mention her to you before because I didn't want to give you the idea that it was anything *we'd* done, that would make her leave.' And then she touched a hand to my wrist. 'I know you're nothing like that, but Meredith would love it if we let another nanny go. "To lose one nanny may be regarded as a misfortune. To lose two looks like carelessness."' Her mouth loosened into a smile. 'Take anything she says with a pinch of salt. She had a childhood crush on Charles, and I think sometimes she still can't believe that she didn't end up with him.'

My head swam. Nina had left them of her own accord. Laurie had dismissed her. Charles had scared her away. Or worse. All these theories couldn't all be true. But were any of them? I couldn't deny that since leaving Nick, I had let a sense of paranoia fester inside me. Was I simply going mad?

I caught Laurie looking at me. When we locked eyes, she tilted her head to the side, cat-like.

'I've got a pile of costume jewellery I've been meaning to go through, to give to charity. Before we leave tonight, would you mind helping me sort through it? And see if there's anything you'd like to keep for yourself?'

I knew I was being placated, but what could I say?

'Yes, of course.'

'Perfect. Thank you. I've got an hour or so more to do here, but if you don't go too far, I'll come and grab you after that?'

I acquiesced, leaving before I was dismissed.

Charles came home, and there was a rush of activity that saved me from his presence, the two of them showering, packing, carrying bags to the car. And then the children arrived, high-spirited at the illicitness of finishing the school day early. We stood in the drive together, watching their parents' car as it cruised down the long drive, waving until the clink of the wrought-iron gates shut behind them. I tried to conceal my exhalation at the sound.

After I put the children to bed, I found myself wandering into the kitchen, idly rooting around the fridge, pulling together ingredients for a salad. I felt weighed down. The last thing I could think of was eating. But it was something to do, to occupy my hands with, my restless mind.

The room echoed with memories: dinner that very first night, the pop of champagne; Laurie's strange behaviour over the leftover chicken; Charles and my kiss. The events at Kewney pushed and pulled me in every direction: what did it all mean? It was as though I was trying to follow an invisible map, one that was constantly being redrawn.

I took a seat at one of the bar stools, pierced a tomato with my fork and brought it to my lips, but even the smell repulsed me. I chased the ingredients around the bowl before eventually giving up, tossing the whole thing down the waste disposal. Restless, I wandered the lonely hallways, pausing in the library but unable to focus on any book in particular, before eventually retreating to my room, shutting the door behind me even though there was no need.

I sat down in front the rickety antique dressing table in the corner, head in hands, trying to organize my cluttered thoughts. I was *so sure* that something was wrong at Kewney, but I had nothing concrete, no proof. How could I convince myself that my hunches were right, not just some delusion I had hooked onto because of Nick?

Beside me, almost touching my elbow, were the earrings Laurie had pressed on me, clusters of pink and green rhinestones in a loose flower-shaped setting. I held one against my earlobe, looked at my reflection in the tarnished mirror. The stones caught the light, sparkled. Why was she always so eager to thrust these things upon me? I had been so flattered, at first, but now I felt her attentions were nothing more than a way of dazzling me, keeping me on side. The thought of wearing them made me feel sick. I placed them back into the black velvet bag they had come in, pulled the drawstring tight, and then on second thought I reached out for the spindly handle of one of the desk drawers, planning to secrete the earrings away in there until an opportune moment would allow me to return them to Laurie. I hadn't used any of the drawers there, my personal possessions being relatively few, and now I was surprised to find the drawer seemed jammed, jarring with resistance when I tried to open it.

I pulled as hard as I dared, fearing I was in danger of yanking the handle off completely, and eventually the drawer yielded, the entire thing released onto my lap, an idle collection of biros separated from their lids, spare buttons, the odd safety pin. The odds and sods were inconsequential, but in the gaping eye socket the drawer had left behind, something else caught my attention, something that I assumed to be the cause of the initial jam: a piece of paper, folded several times, its leaves torqued from being stuck within the cavity. I plucked it, shifting the drawer and its contents onto the floor beside me, not quite believing it would contain anything of interest, but finding, even before I had smoothed its creases, that I was wrong.

The page had been torn from a notebook: under-scored with thin ruled lines, torn at two points on the side where the staples had been, like a vampire bite. On it, a series of names, doodled across the page at every angle. *Charles*, they yearned, a heart around his name. *Nina + Charles. Nina Blake loves Charles Rowe. Mrs Charles Rowe.*

My mouth went dry as my fingers searched the letters. Just a young woman's infatuation? Or something more?

Nina Blake.

Now I had her name in full.

My mind instantly went to my phone, lying some-where at the bottom of the sea at Charlestown harbour. Despite how practised I was at being without it, now I craved its instantaneous knowledge. Facebook, Google: surely I'd have been able to track her down there. And then I remembered: Charles's study. Laurie had mentioned it, when I first arrived: a computer, good Wi-Fi. She'd said I shouldn't go in there when Charles was out, but how would they know? It was worth the risk.

The study was on the ground floor, reached through a door off the drawing room. I had never been in it before, but I had warned the children off going in there, fearful they'd mess it up, enough times to know where it was. My skin prickled as I opened the door, flicking a switch to plunge the room into light. It smelled of him, despite it looking like it had been recently cleaned and tidied, not a book out of place, and I couldn't shake the feeling of his presence, as though somehow he was watching me.

I moved gingerly, as though the slightest jerk of a limb could upset something, betray me, took a seat at his desk, body sliding against the soft leather of the chair, steeling myself against rifling through the neatly stacked papers to the right of the computer. I agitated the mouse, watching the computer bloom into life. It was password protected, as I suspected it would be, but that didn't matter – I had already spotted the Post-it note tacked to the edge of the screen, typical of his age and general lack of awareness of cyber security, typed the words into the box provided, B3ssandW1lliam. Even if it hadn't been provided, any lazy hacker would have been able to guess it.

A beep, and then I was in, staring at the innocuous default wallpaper of his desktop. I hesitated for a moment, realizing what my fingertips had access to, the answers to my own secrets that a certain amount of searches and clicks could unlock. But I had to stay focused, had to concentrate on who I was here to find. Instead, I loaded up the internet, navigated to Facebook, logged in, shocked but not altogether surprised to see a slew of notifications from people I had forgotten or had convinced myself would have forgotten about me: I heard, is it true? Is it true, about Nick? Each one made the air inside my chest compress a little tighter, but I tried to ignore them, tried not to think what their missives meant as I touched the cursor over the search bar, typed.

NINA BLAKE.

As the page loaded, I let out sigh of frustration. There were at least fifty Nina Blakes, twenty or more without even a profile picture. Where would I even begin?

And then it struck me – where had Joss said she lived? Derbyshire? No, Durham.

My fingers flew across the keyboard, narrowing down the results, clicking through the remaining candidates, trying to find anything distinguishing about them to suggest it was her.

This was pointless. *Pointless*.

I smacked a fist against the table, unleashed a cry of frustration into the empty room.

Was ready to give up, had navigated the cursor to the top of the screen, ready to log out, leave.

Until a picture caught my eye.

I'd dismissed it at first. The profile picture was nothing distinct; a neat circle showing a girl with long brown hair, a half-smile. It could be her. It could equally not be.

It was the background image which stopped me. Clifftops, shot from below. The craggy coastline I had come to know so well. And there, in the distance, no bigger than a thumbnail, was Kewney.

It was her.

I scrolled down, frantically searching for an update, a sign that she was happy, and well. That my suspicions were all wrong.

Bile burned in my throat as I saw the single, most recent message.

A woman called Sally Blake, posted just last week.

We miss you, Nina. Please come home.

A scuffling at the door made me spring back, gasp into the silence as I minimized the screen in haste.

I whirled around to see Bess's face appear in the doorway. Her voice small, frightened. 'Lily?'

'Is everything all right?' I breathed, trying to regulate my heartbeat.

'I had a bad dream. I went to your room to find you, but you weren't there.'

'Oh, darling. I'm sorry, I was just looking something up. Come on, I'll tuck you back in. There's nothing to be scared of.' I swallowed, a thought pervading. '. . . Do you often have nightmares? Have you . . . have you come to find me before?'

She shook her head and inwardly I collapsed with relief – the thought of her discovering me and Charles. 'Mummy won't let us out of our rooms at night. She says it's dangerous. We could trip and fall with all the stairs. She locks us in before she goes to bed.' My hand froze on the doorway as I led her out. 'I thought perhaps she'd forget to tell you to. And I was right.' She looked up at me. A cautious smile. 'You won't tell?'

I shook my head, reading the plea in her face.

I tucked her back into bed, checking under it for the requisite monsters. Fetched a glass of water.

'You're not going to leave us, are you?' she asked as I turned off the bedside light, her voice already starting to slur.

'No, no, of course not.' I whispered, heart constricting at the two of them bound up in this mess.

'Good.' She murmured, nestling her head into the pillow. Yawned. 'Mummy and Daddy seem so much happier with you here.'

When I closed the door behind me, I saw my hands were shaking.

Any thought of running whilst I had the chance flew from my mind. I couldn't leave the children here alone. What was I going to do?

Kewney Manor was supposed to be my sanctuary. It was fast becoming my jail.

18

The summer holidays had brought with them another heatwave, although this one minus the sun; the clouds choking the sky with a muggy humidity that made your skin itch, caused rasping flecks of pollen to catch in a dry cough in the back of your throat. And I don't know if it was this, or the open-endedness of the holidays, making the children lethargic and moody, but together they gave the suffocating sense of things coming to a head.

The first two days passed by in a flurry, though, and having both children in my sole care gave me no time to act on what I had found. It was too hot, Bess whined. Too hot to get in the car, too hot for the beach, or for a walk into town. William became irascible, disrupting furniture, kicking up cushions, throwing Lego over the balcony of the first-floor landing, watching it explode in pieces onto the Great Hall's chequered floor. At night, when they were both finally asleep, I sank alone in my bed, exhausted, a tightness in my chest I couldn't shake. Even if I wanted to escape, how could I ever leave them like this?

In the days, I placated them with ice lollies, with hastily arranged playdates, similarly sticky-necked children they roamed the grounds with, looking for something to do or destroy. When we were alone, I tried to ask them about Nina. Seizing the window of opportunity, with no parental ear to overhear – that perfect sweet spot of fed, watered and entertained – to pepper questions into conversation I thought were subtle enough to fly under the radar.

Did your other nanny let you have this many ice lollies? Mock indignation. What was her name again? Nina?

Gosh, it's so hot today, was it this hot when Nina was here? A well-timed pause. How long was Nina your nanny for? Where did she go, when she left?

Each attempt was met with a response curt enough to let me know my questions were entirely uninteresting – 'Yeah,' 'Don't remember,' and that classic childhood retort, 'Dunno.'

Until, after lunch on the second day, Bess threw down the daisy chain she'd been working on, scowled. 'What do you keep asking about Nina for? We told you: mummy doesn't like us talking about her.'

When I found I couldn't answer, she ran off in a huff.

On the third day it rained. Great, thick droplets of the stuff that knitted the sky and churned up the sea. It was still warm, and so a subtropical humidity rose, making the air feel thick, close. The sheets of rain fell like bars, making Kewney seem even more like a prison cell, and the children pressed their noses against the windows, dismayed. They had loathed going outside whilst it was fine, but now that they were prevented from doing so, of course it was all they could think about.

'Let's play a game,' I chirruped eagerly after lunch, having just about managed the mood since breakfast and now counting down the long stretch of hours until dinner.

'Like what?' William moaned, chin in hands.

'Monopoly?'

'Ugh, I hate Monopoly.' With the full exasperation of a six-year-old, he sank his face into the kitchen counter.

'Scrabble, then.'

'William can't even spell.' Bess, my hoped-for ally, crossed her arms. 'It's boring with him.'

'OK, I've got it: hide-and-seek.'

They turned to me in unison, their faces twinned with horror, as though I'd just suggested doing maths homework.

'Hide-and-seek?' Bess picked out each syllable, redolent with disgust. 'We play it all the time. That's *boring*.'

I looked at my watch. Charles and Laurie weren't due back until early evening, but with the rain, and British transport being what it was, they would most likely be delayed. The me of two days ago may have given up, moved on to another idea more easily, but after forty-eight hours of battling with their moods, the thought of eking out the fragment of solitude the game would provide was too good to pass up.

'Come on!' I coaxed. 'It'll do you good to stretch your legs. Let's just play one round each and then I promise we can watch movies all afternoon. With popcorn and everything.'

They groaned, but rose from their chairs, acquiescing. I volunteered to go first, relishing the relative silence as they mooched into the Great Hall and pressed their faces to the wall either side of Steve-the-suit-of-armour. Their counting voices grew softer as I retreated from the hall, wending back through the library, and pressing against the secret door which led into my conceived hiding place: the billiard room. The wall-to-wall panelling made the room pleasantly cool, a relief from the rest of the house, whose large sash windows and lack of double glazing created a greenhouse effect. A faint smell of chalk still lingered, lending a further feeling of dryness in the air. I settled with relief into one of the brown leather armchairs arranged on either side of the fireplace, waited.

The silence was short lived. Before I had the chance to fully relax my muscles, the door barged open, and Bess and William fell into the room.

'I knew it, I knew it!' William, so hyped by the scream he'd elicited from me that he developed hiccups, pointed a triumphant arm towards me. 'I told you she'd be in here. It's the first place everyone goes.'

I shrugged. 'You got me. You're too clever for me.' Whatever mild annoyance I felt at having my freedom disrupted vanished the moment I saw their faces: the funk had gone; they were finally having fun.

Bess went next, a mildly more in-depth search which lead to her recovery underneath William's bed. And then it was William's turn.

'OK, you're up, buddy.' I rubbed his shoulders as Bess and I took up position in the Great Hall. 'Make it a good one. But no going outside, please. I'm not going traipsing through the rain to look for you.'

'I wouldn't go outside, silly. You'd hear the front door.'

When we reached the count of sixty, I turned to Bess. 'First bets?'

'Mummy's dressing room, behind the screen. He always picks there.'

We made our way upstairs and into Charles and Laurie's wing, calling William's name as we went, in the hope that we'd rouse a noise from him. The dressing room was empty.

I looked to Bess, who twitched her shoulders together.

'I guess he found a better spot.'

I followed her along the corridor to her parents' bedroom, hesitating slightly as she pushed the door open. I had never seen inside their room; it seemed too odd, too intimate. I didn't want to see the bed they shared together, to be reminded of the marriage I lived in the shadows of.

Bess frowned at me slightly as she saw me hovering at the threshold. 'I don't think he'd go in here, but we may as well rule it out.'

'That's fine. I'll listen out for clues elsewhere.' I made a show of tilting my ear into the corridor, ignoring the soporific grey and blue tones of the matrimonial suite, the glimpse of one of Laurie's bras hanging over the back of an occasional chair.

'Empty.' She re-emerged, shutting the door behind her.

We continued on, scouring the rooms on the first floor: the guest rooms and bathrooms, an airing closet, the children's bedrooms, even my room. We even looked in the attic at Bess's behest, the smell of mothballs bringing back memories of my own treasure hunt. No sign of William.

'That's funny.' The corner of Bess's mouth wrinkled as we stood at the bottom of the stairs. 'I was sure he'd be up there somewhere.'

His prolonged absence was giving me the faintest flutter of trepidation too, but I didn't want to alarm her unnecessarily.

'He's obviously outsmarted us.' I gave her a wink. 'Let's speed up and prove he's no match for us.'

Together we stomped through the ground floor, opening cupboards, and peering under furniture, scouring every corner of every room. With each room, I felt my anxiety mount, the flutter becoming a thud. Where had he got to?

'William!' I honed my hearing, determined to make out the tiniest cough, the faintest scuffle of a shoe. The sky was beginning to darken, the deep grey of late afternoon hanging heavily on it. I pictured Charles and Laurie's faces, fighting through the driving rain to get home, on being told I had mislaid their youngest child. 'You don't think he's gone outside, do you?'

We had been searching for over an hour now. I would have thought he'd get bored, come to find us by now. My mind began to race through potential disasters – slipping in the mud and twisting an ankle; climbing a tree and falling, breaking an arm; losing his way in the labyrinth of gardens and trying to fight his way back through all the rain. I had just about placed him sprawled at the bottom of the cliff, having lost his footing, when Bess's face brightened.

'I bet I know where he is.'

Bess took me by the hand and guided me back

through the house to the kitchen, taking me past the body of the room and through to the sloped-ceilinged open pantry at the back. There, she turned to a door I'd never thought to notice before, a low, wooden door set into one of the white-washed stone walls, grasped the handle and pulled.

'Coming?' she asked, challenge in her voice, as she ducked inside.

'Coming.'

Bess disappeared into the darkness. I poked my head and shoulders inside, trying to adjust to the gloom, but moments later a pool of light illuminated my way: she was standing at the bottom of a narrow flight of wooden steps, pointing a torch at me. As I creaked my way down the steps, hands either side to steady me, my fingers brushed a wooden hook stuck into the walls where she must have taken it from.

'What is all this?' My voice echoed back at me.

Bess held the blunt of the torch to her chin, and I saw the adventure in her eyes as it lit up her face in a ghoulish white glow.

'Smugglers' tunnels,' she said, turning her attention back to the path.

I followed behind her in a mild daze, now imagining William trapped between two rocks, knocked out by falling debris. The tunnels were hewn out of the rocks, the walls rough to the touch and damp as I repeatedly brushed against them, trying to pick through the narrowness. The air smelled damp, too, musty, and dank, and I might have been imagining it, but I was sure I felt a tightness in my chest, suggesting that the oxygen levels weren't the best. I had to fight the urge to turn back, to ask Bess to find William on her own. Ignored the voice in my head that wondered if my sudden claustrophobia was because I was reminded of what happened with Nick.

'They go right under the house.' Bess's voice ricocheted around me. 'All the way down to the cove. We're not allowed down here on our own, but Daddy took us here a few times, years ago.'

'Who used them?' I held my arms out at either side, shielding myself as the tunnel thinned.

'Smugglers.' I could hear the shrug in her voice. 'One of our great-great-great-great-grandfathers was helping them bring in stuff like alcohol and tobacco. Daddy says he was probably keeping some of it for himself. Or selling it to his friends for more money. Smugglers,' she added keenly, 'are like pirates.'

As the passage curved and went on, Bess began to call out for her brother, sending her voice out into the void ahead of us. My vision adjusted to the beam of the torch, so that when I turned back, all I could see was black.

'Will?' I called out, treading closer to Bess to seek out a reply. 'William, come out now, game's over!'

No reply.

As we journeyed, I felt that we were growing closer to the sea, the damp smell of rock infused increasingly with the scent of iodine. From somewhere in the distance, I heard the hollow *ping* of water dripping into puddles. Presently, the path opened up, became a cave, and I listened gratefully to the shush of waves and roar of rain, saw the cracks of light between boulders revealing the muted grey outside. The space was now as wide as a small room, and I tried to place whereabouts on the cove we were – wondering how I could have missed it all the times we had been out there, although in truth it was so well masked by the landscape that I'd never thought to look.

'William?' Bess called again, pirouetting to look for him. We were greeted with silence. 'Funny.' She was nonchalant. 'I thought for sure he'd be here.'

Up until then, I had been so focused on the tunnels that the full reason why we were down there had been softened. Now, the reality sharpened.

'William?' I called, the tightness in my voice betraying my anxiety. 'Please come out now. Enough.'

'Forget it, he's not here.' Bess twirled the torch in her hand, pointed it back in the direction of the tunnel. 'Let's go.'

At that moment she let out an almighty scream, and I turned to see a body launching itself on her back. A body that, I saw gratefully in the dancing torchlight, had the form of a young boy.

'William.' Bess shoved him off her, dusting off her knees. 'You're so annoying.'

He collapsed into a ball on the floor, hugging his stomach as he laughed.

'Oh my gosh, that was so funny. You were so scared. Aaaah.' He jumped to his feet, mimicking her screams.

'Go away, I wasn't scared, you just surprised me. She shoved him lightly, folding her arms in annoyance.

'Ow, that hurt.' He responded by give her a push of his own.

'Did not.' Again, she retaliated.

'Did too.'

'Guys.' I tried to call time as he gave her a shove so hard her torch went flying, rolling into a corner of the cave. 'Come, cut it out now.' I stalked over to retrieve it, following the beam of light it emitted until I found the crevice it had got wedged into.

I bent down to pull it out, resting my left hand on the wall over the cave, but as I did, my fingertips brushed something surprisingly soft, material. With the torch retrieved, I stooped to see what it was, letting the children's arguing voices drown out in a blur of sound as the blood drained from my body and I saw what it was.

A backpack. Large and hardwearing. The sort you'd use for hiking, or travelling. Wedged into a gap in the rocks at such an angle that no one would spot it unless they were looking for it. And on the handle of the backpack, a luggage tag, neon yellow with a clear plastic window. And as I shone the torch over it my blood drained further still, as I saw the name that was written on the tag.

Nina Blake.

19

Nina Blake.

The words were handwritten, block capitals. Exactly like the ones on the note she had written. The letters merging into illegibility as my vision blurred, as I reached out, pressing a hand against the rough walls of the cave to steady myself.

'Lily, are you coming?' Bess's voice pulled me back into focus.

William had retrieved his own torch, was turning it on and off with a methodical click. 'Yeah, come on, Lily, we did the game like you said, so now we can watch TV?'

'Yes, yes.' I backed away from the backpack, not wanting to alert them to what I had found. 'Come on, let's get going. I'm sure your parents will be back soon.'

We retraced our steps back into the pantry, where the sheer ordinariness of it made me feel numb. Bess and William descended on the living room, all argument forgotten, and I followed them, trance-like, grateful to the primary colours and cacophonous music emitted from the television for acting in loco parentis when I could barely speak.

But although I was silent, internally my thoughts blared. As the children fought for control of the television, I felt the walls of the living room closing in on me;

as though the white China roses on the living room wall-paper were growing in size, blooming out of the paper, and suffocating me with their scent.

Nina was missing. The message on her Facebook page was clear. I could clutch at straws, argue that she'd simply just run away, didn't want to be found. But that didn't explain the backpack. Didn't explain the thought that made my breath catch in my lungs, that made me clutch at one of the Rowes' velvet throw pillows until my knuckles turned white: if Nina's backpack was here, where was Nina?

Laurie and Charles returned, angry and exhausted from their lengthy journey. I couldn't quite bring myself to look either of them in the eye, and my fear of detection manifested itself in a certain mania, a burst of verbosity and overt helpfulness that I felt certain they both noticed yet couldn't make myself stop.

That night I lay in bed, waiting for him to come, as I could only assume he would, anticipation making me toss and turn against sleep.

Charles had killed Nina. I was sure of it. Just as he had tried to kill Christine. What would it take, for him to come for me?

The words of an old Emily Dickinson poem rattled in my ear. Something about not stopping for death, but death coming for her anyway. I had thought that, by leaving Nick, I had cheated death. Had I instead stumbled right into its hands?

I fell into something resembling sleep, woke with a start to see the clock had already struck midnight and assumed with relief that he wasn't coming – he had never come past midnight before – but adrenaline prevented me from finding rest, and so I roused myself, went to the window. I peeled back the curtains, searching the landscape for some hint of Laurie's presence, certain that she was out there, somewhere.

The grounds extended beyond my eyeline, silent and still, giving nothing away.

Finally, at just past one, he came.

His smell asserted itself on the room, as it had done so many nights before. Changing it, making it his. Wood and warm spices, like a very expensive bonfire. I breathed it in, couldn't help the wrenching inside me, at the thought of the nights I had drifted off happily with that scent on my skin.

'I've missed you.'

'Charles—'

'You're more beautiful than I remembered.' He came further into the room, and I felt his presence in it as though he were already on top of me. The smell of bonfire grew thick, choking.

'Charles.' I felt detached from my body, like those near-death experiences where people describe watching themselves from above. I would give him one chance. One chance to prove me wrong. 'Where did your last nanny go?'

I watched him, carefully, saw the frown grasp hold of his face before a look of bemusement fought it down.

'What do you mean, "Where did she go?"? Home, I imagine?'

I squeezed my eyes tight, trying to keep hold of the thread of my thought.

'You saw her? You saw her leave?'

He laughed. 'Well, I wouldn't say I personally accompanied her home. But yes, she left.'

His voice was even, coaxing, like he was taming a horse, and for a moment, I wanted to believe him. He came right up to me, brushed the curtain from where it still rested in my hand. Stroked my cheek with his fingertips. I thought of the same fingertips I had seen, pressing around Laurie's neck. Imagined them around Christine's. Nina's. Wrenched myself away.

I knew I was playing with fire but I couldn't stop myself. I had to know. I had to hear him say it.

'So you watched her? You saw her leave this house, get in a car and . . . and . . .'

'What are you suggesting, Lily?' He was still maintaining the sing-song quality to his voice, but I heard the annoyance curling around the edges of it, the sharpening of his consonants that told me he was on edge.

'I'm not suggesting anything. I just want to know. If you saw her. Why she left.'

'Why do you care so much about why she left?'

'*Why won't you tell me where Nina is?*'

The words ripped from me and I froze, suddenly wary. The name prickled through me, the first time I had said it to him, out loud. In my mind's eye, I picked out the letters of her name. On the paper. On her backpack. And I saw it startled him. Saw his expression turn sour, even as he tried to hide it.

'I don't know what it is you're asking.' When he

spoke, his voice was toneless, cold. 'I don't know why Nina left.' He moved towards the bed, sat. Ran a hand through his hair. 'We woke up one morning, and she'd just . . . gone. She was always a little flighty, probably on drugs. She wasn't even a proper nanny, anyway.' As he sank into the story, his speech gained pace, momentum. 'Laurie met her in the village, looking for work, and she wanted to help her out. She'd fought with her parents. Was on the road, travelling. Laurie felt sorry for her. But neither of us were surprised when she didn't stick it out.' I stared into his eyes, trying to search out the truth behind them, but they were totally clear. Charles was so talented at placating me, but I knew it must all be a lie. Why would she just leave without saying goodbye? Why would she leave without her bag? And if she had left on purpose . . . why was she still missing?

'There now, does that answer all your questions?'

It didn't, not by half.

'Were you having an affair?'

I saw it then, although he quickly made it vanish. The flinch. Momentary, but exact.

'*Lily.*' He rose, came towards me, hands on my shoulders as I trembled beneath him, light kisses on my cheeks where the tears had begun to fall. 'Is that what this is about? Don't worry any more about Nina. She was nothing to me. *Nothing.*'

'What did you do to her, Charles?' My voice came out gummy and hoarse, unable to stop the dread in my heart. I had strayed too close; I couldn't turn back now. Fear exhausted my limbs, and I felt the physical size of him, my body wrapped in his limbs. I was powerless against him. Was this it? Was this how it ended?

'I don't know what you're talking about, my love.' He released me, took my hand, pulled me lightly in the direction of the bed. 'I don't know what's happened to you. This is *madness*. Stop all this talk. Please, just come to bed. I've missed you so much. Don't spoil it.'

Madness. Exactly what I had accused myself of. But I couldn't ignore what I had found. I couldn't ignore the truth that was staring me in the face.

'Tell me, Charles.' I snatched my hand back. 'I have a right to know what you did.'

'Are you listening to yourself?' He gave me a strange, crazed smile. 'To what are you accusing me of?'

'Tell me.'

'For heaven's sake, stop this. Come to bed.' He reached for my hand again.

I twisted away. 'No.'

'Come to bed, Lily.'

'I won't.'

I realized too late how much the exchange reminded me of Laurie.

'*I said come to bed.*' He was across the room before I took a breath. Had me around the waist, threw me so hard against the wooden headboard that, as my head connected with it, the room seemed to turn on its axis.

I cried out into the darkness, feeling the release of his hands as I tightened myself in a ball away from him, waited for the pain to pass, for him to show himself fully, for who he was.

'*Lily?*' When he spoke into the silence I heard the

sudden change overwhelm his voice, the fear and sorrow. *'No, no, no. Oh God, no.'* He came beside me. Fingertips running through my matted hair, the antithesis to their touch just moments before. 'Lily, I'm so sorry. I'm sorry. I didn't mean to do it. You have to believe me. I don't know what came over me. Please, Lily, please.' Kisses along my spine, hands stroking, touching, trying to unfurl me. 'I didn't do anything to Nina. I promise you.' He paused. 'I did sleep with her. It's true. But it wasn't like this. It wasn't like us. She left. That was it. She even left Laurie a letter. I can find it for you in the morning.'

I sobbed into myself. My temple throbbed. My mind ached, trying to parse the truth and the lies.

'Darling, darling girl.' He shushed into my neck. 'You have to understand. I can't lose you. I just can't. I let my anger get the better of me but you know I never meant to hurt you. You know that, don't you?'

I was trapped. I felt myself nodding.

'Forgive me. I'll kill myself if you don't forgive me.' His voice ached.

I said nothing, but I let him wrap himself around me, fighting the tears that stung my eyes.

Realized how much his words reminded me of Nick.

I'll kill you, if you ever try to leave me.

I'll kill myself.

20

Charles stayed with me that night.

He had never stayed.

Fell into a sleep of such stillness, such grace, that any impartial observer would assume he didn't have a care in the world.

I didn't sleep, though. I remained supine, half sitting, half lying against the headboard, watching the darkness from the crack in the curtains, a thin sliver of yellow moon just visible. As my vision was beginning to blur, I saw the motion sensors blink on, edged myself out from beside Charles, went to the window, looked.

She was there, as I knew she would be. Picking her way barefoot across the lawns. Her hair was loose, falling in tendrils down another silken robe tied tightly around her body. Several yards from the house, she paused, gave a languorous stretch, limbs reaching to the sky, wrists curling inwards, wrapping around her body and down her back, a lioness greeting the day.

And then she straightened. I could just make out her expression, the certain set of her jaw, her shoulders squared, determined. Powerful and proud.

She inclined her head sharply upwards. Looking directly up at my window.

I pivoted my body round. Pressed my back against the bedroom wall. There was no way. No way she could have seen me. Not from that angle. Not through the gap in the curtains, it would be impossible.

It seemed foolish now, to think she didn't know about us. All the times he had been here, the nights he had spent in my room, I had told myself that he knew of her comings and goings, had things cleverly timed. Because it was easier. Because I had wanted to believe it.

But if she knew, was this all part of some plan?

Had she known about Nina?

Made me a distraction, ensuring she wouldn't be next?

When I dared to look out again, fingertips barely touching the edge of the curtain, she was gone.

I turned to Charles. Saw the rhythmic rise and fall of his chest. Could hear the stillness of the country air. Elsewhere, deep in the house, the metronomic tick of the grandfather clock matched the pulse of my heart against my torso.

'Charles?' I whispered. He didn't stir. '*Charles?*' Again, louder. He was still.

I couldn't stay at Kewney Manor any longer. And I couldn't let Charles get away with what he had done, risk him hurting anyone else.

I had to go to the police. I had to tell them what I knew. Even if it meant risking everything. Even if it meant exposing myself to all that I had run away from.

But if I went to the police, I needed proof.

I needed to get the backpack.

Slowly, slowly, I stole from the room. Closed the door millimetre by millimetre until I felt it release into the frame, shut.

As I moved through the dark house, I remembered with an ache that first day, all the promises it held, Laurie's glee as she showed me around. Steve-the-suit-of-armour stood sentry-like as I slipped through the Great Hall and into the kitchen, ghostly with the breakfasts I had made there, the glasses of wine I had drunk, the stool where I had let Charles kiss me for the first time. I acted methodically, passing the kitchen's slick surfaces and into the pantry, to the wooden door at the back.

I wrenched it open, my body stiffening, unwilling to re-enter that dank space, but I forced myself through, feeling for one of the torches that hung beside the stairs. I trod the passageways a little easier this time, holding the beam of light directly in front of me as I tried to ignore the tightness in my chest as the air thinned. As the passageways curved, narrowed, I heard the sounds of rain, knew I was getting closer to the cave itself. Finally it opened out, and I breathed in the fresh air source with relief, flashing the torch around its interior until I found the backpack.

My fingers were shaking as I went to it, fumbling as I tried to hold the torch and keep my adrenaline in check. I dropped it, the thing spinning a laser of light as it clattered to the floor, rolled into the distance. I cursed, retrieved it, and then with renewed determination I found the zip of the bag, opened it.

The thing had been packed in a hurry. Even in the dim torchlight I could see that. Clothes stuffed any which way, toiletries spilling out from an open bag. My hands delved into it, feeling amongst the tangle of cotton for anything more concrete, fingers stumbling eventually on something rigid, cool.

I knew what it would be before I had loosed it from the folds of clothing, recognized the familiar size and shape, although my own had been unused for quite some time. A passport. Swallowing dryness, I opened it, knowing whose name I would read inside, but as I did, a piece of folded paper fell from it – the same ruled lines, I saw as I unfolded it, as the paper in my room.

A letter.

But my surprise at finding it was soon replaced by shock as I began to read it, saw who it was address to.

Dear Joss,

A wash of vertigo overcame me. *Joss?* All the times I had asked him, cajoled him, about her, and he had acted like they had been nothing but passing acquaintances. Why, if they hardly knew each other, would she be writing to him?

I read on, my brain processing what I was reading faster than my eyes could capture it, the writing increasingly hurried, scrawled, not the neat curls on the paper I had found in my room.

By the time you read this, I will be gone.
I can't stay here any more.
When Laurie offered me this job, I was so grateful. I was happy, at first. I thought I had finally found a home. But things have become so weird, Joss. I don't understand these people, or their fucked-up marriage.

*You did warn me, about my relationship with
Charles. About getting involved with the goings-
on at Kewney Manor. Maybe I should have
listened to you. But it's too late now.*

*All I know is, there is something wrong with
these people. Very wrong. And I'm not sticking
around to find out what it is.*

*Thank you, Joss, for all that you have done for
me. I won't forget it.*

Your friend,

Nina

The letter fluttered from my fingertips, coming to rest on
the dank cave floor.

Nina had tried to leave. She had been planning her
escape, but she had somehow been prevented. And if she
hadn't managed to get out, if all her belongings, and her
passport, were still here, then I could only assume that
something must have happened to her. Something awful.
Something that meant her backpack remained hidden
here, in this cave, where only the owners of the house
would ever go.

And Joss. Joss *had* known her, more than he'd let on.
What was it he had said to me, that horrible day at
Kynance Cove? '*You're hardly the first.*' He had known
about Charles and Nina. And he knew about me and
Charles. If I could go to him, *explain*, surely, surely he
would help me? He had been so angry with me after that
trip that I wasn't sure he'd ever want to speak to me
again, but without him I was totally alone. I had to try.

Moving before I had the chance to change my mind,

I felt my way back out of the cave and into the body of the house. Pausing in the Great Hall, I held my breath, listening cautiously for any unwelcome sounds. Hearing none, I padded across the hallway to the front door, closing it with my fingers laced around the edge so that it closed with barely a sigh.

It was raining, a fine spray that misted my head and shoulders as I stepped into the open. I tilted my face to it, welcoming it. The jasmine smelled strong tonight, nurtured by the rain, and I could smell the roses too, their sweet, cloying scent. Every sense felt heightened, after the suffocation of the house.

I picked my way past the house, keep close to the wall to avoid setting off the motion sensors until I reached the edge of the gravel drive. Kewney village was only a five-minute drive down the hill. Twenty by foot. Shorter if I ran.

Once I passed through the side gate, heard the wrought-iron squeak shut behind me, I ran.

I had never been to Joss's house before, but I knew which one it was. Since our trip to the cove, the number had stuck in my memory. I had remembered how he had marked it out: his parents were number 3, and he was number 8. And he was right, there weren't many houses in the village.

The streets were quiet as I passed through, but nevertheless I slowed to a walk. There wasn't much to recommend it – a pub, a post office, a Co-op and a cafe – less so now, all shuttered and silent, but it was a pretty sort of place, the lean row of shops marked out by neatly kept flower-beds. I knew the lane of semi-identical fishermen's cottages that meandered downhill past the shops, the cul-de-sac that led to a footpath, which in turn took you down to the sea. I knew, too, that Joss's parents' house was the one with the red door, his opposite, with the blue. They'd moved there from further up in the hills when the children had grown and his parents had decided to downsize, had helped Joss with the down payment when a place became available opposite them. I got the impression that he was the favourite.

The house with the red door was dark as I reached it, his parents long gone to sleep. But as I approached the short driveway to Joss's house, I saw the yellow glow of lamplight from the window to the right. He was awake.

I reached the front door, trepidation and anticipation fighting within me, and balled my hand into a fist, ready to knock, when movement from within stopped me. There was Joss, in what I saw was a kitchen, closing the fridge door and emerging with a bottle in his hands. He stooped over a counter for a moment, pouring, and when he turned around I saw he was holding not one but two glasses of wine.

A sense of foreboding began to throb in me as I watched him, enthralled, walk into the room beyond, a living room, I could see as I edged my body closer to the window, the source of the lamplight. I tuned my ears to the gruff timbre of his voice as he handed over one of the glasses, heard then the melodic reply of a woman's voice, saw the stretch of a pale arm reaching to take it, slender legs crossing and uncrossing on a sofa. Laughter.

This was a mistake, I panicked, already planning my

retreat. This was a terrible idea. I shouldn't have come here. What would he think of me? I backed slowly away from the door, part of me desperate to stay, when the higher voice caught, turned in to a confused cry.

'Hey.' And then in a flash she was up, staring directly through the window at me. 'Hey, Joss, there's someone there.'

For a moment I froze, watching in horror as his face joined hers, but then right before we locked eyes, before I could be certain he'd got a good look at me, I turned and ran.

'Hey, come back here!?'

Before I had made it out of the front gate I heard the door opening, the sound of his, calling, refused to look back.

'Lily?' he called as I turned onto the lane, and then, louder, 'What are you doing here? Lily, come *back*.'

I'd made it halfway up the lane before he caught up with me, hand reaching for my wrist as he wrenched me to a stop.

'Lily, what's going on?'

'*You knew.*' Despite myself, I couldn't help the anger breaking free, the unfairness of it all. The rain had thinned to a stop, but been replaced by a stirring wind that made me shiver in my T-shirt, hug my arms around one another.

'Knew what? I don't know what you're talking about.'

'About Charles and Nina. You knew.'

He opened his mouth as if about to defend himself, but then paused, looked down at his feet. 'Yes, I knew.'

Anger clenched tighter. 'Why didn't you tell me? That

you were friends with her? That you'd talked about it. About them.'

'For God's sake, Lily. What's this all about?' He huffed, and I could hear his trademark annoyance creeping into his voice. 'Yes, we were friendly. We talked, in the grounds, same as you. I knew about her and Charles. But as I've said before, it's none of my business what goes on in that house. It's none of my business who she was sleeping with. Or you, for that matter. You're both as idiotic as each other.'

The anger morphed into a stab of pain. I looked up at him, tears threatening to fall, and could see as soon as he said it he regretted it.

'So, what, you think we're all just the same?' He reached for me, but I batted him away. 'No. You think we're both just "dumb sluts", is that it? Jumping into bed with the boss at the first opportunity?'

I saw Joss grimace at the phrase. It was a signature of Nick's: coupling stupidity and a sexist slur. My stomach curdled even repeating it.

'No. I would never think something like that. That's not what I meant, Lily, you know that.' He worried his head, moved the hair from his face where the wind had tussled it. 'I just—'

'She's missing.' I cut across him. 'And I think Charles had something to do with it. I think . . .' I let out a ragged sigh. 'I don't know what I think.'

'What?' Joss's eyebrows knitted together.

'I found her bag. In the tunnels under the house. There was a letter in there, to you. I think she was trying to run away, but something stopped her.'

'What? What letter?' He shook his head, frowned. 'She already gave me a letter.'

'Nina already gave you a letter?' I echoed, numbly. I had seen the letter myself. Why would she have one in there, when she'd already given him another?

'Yes. She said she couldn't live with herself, for breaking up a marriage. That she was an awful person, for taking Laurie's kindness and throwing it in her face. That she was leaving, to give a chance to put things right.'

'What?' It didn't sound anything like the letter I had seen. Why would she have given him this one, and stashed something entirely different? 'Where is it? Can I see?'

He shrugged, helpless. 'I have no idea where it is. It was six months ago. I probably threw it away. Lily – what's all this about?'

'No, no.' Like the interlocking jewels on one of Laurie's necklaces, pieces were starting to fit together.

Laurie's kindness. An awful person.

It didn't sound anything like the letter I had seen. There, Nina had been defiant, not remorseful. Why would she have changed tone so dramatically?

But that wasn't the only letter Nina had supposedly left, was it? Charles had said she'd given Laurie a letter, too. He'd said—

All at once I felt as though a trapdoor had opened. That I was freefalling through it. *Laurie.*

She had been so angry, the day of Kynance Cove. Did she wonder how much Joss knew, what he would tell me? How much I would piece together myself?

The clams. The dinner party. The midnight walks. Laurie's incessant, confounding behaviour.

I had thought that Laurie was using me as a shield, throwing me at Charles to protect herself. A part of me had even pitied her, worried for her fate.

But what if it wasn't Charles I should be scared of?

What if it was Laurie?

I swallowed. Looked up at Joss.

'When? When did Nina give it you?'

'Nina didn't give it to me.' He shook his head, confirming what I had already guessed. 'Laurie did.'

21

'Laurie gave it to you?'

Joss nodded, and my head started to feel light. 'She said she knew we were friendly, but that Nina had had to leave in a hurry, and she'd asked Laurie to give it to me. It wasn't opened, so I figured Laurie had no idea what was inside. When I read it, I was relieved. Assumed Laurie didn't know.'

The wind grew stronger now, whistling in my ears.

'What's all this about, Lily?'

'I have to go back to the house.' My muscles jerked, already prepared to run. I still didn't understand the full truth of what I had discovered, but I needed to get back to the cave. I needed to get the backpack, before she realized that I had gone, and what I knew. I owed it to Nina. To both of us.

He looked up the hill, and then back towards me. 'I don't understand.'

'I can't explain.'

'Lily.' He worried his head. Used his forearm to wipe the hair from his face, where the wind had blown it into his eyes. 'You've come to my house in the middle of the night. Ranting about Nina and Laurie and letters. I'm worried. Please. Tell me what's going on?'

I almost told him. I came so close to breaking down and revealing it all: my true self, how I had come to be at Kewney, and everything that had happened to me since.

But I wouldn't drag him into it. Couldn't risk something happening to him, too.

'I . . . can't.'

I held his gaze, saw him wrestling, fighting the hurt of a second rejection as quickly as I saw him hardening himself against me.

'Joss, I'm so sorry.' I whispered. 'I wish I could explain all this to you. I wish we could . . .' I shook my head, letting the thought escape into the wind. 'I know I haven't been a good person. There are things I will never be able to put right. But this one, at least, I can try to.'

'Lily . . . I . . .'

'You should go,' I urged. Added, with a pinch in my heart, 'Your friend will be worried.'

He looked down, murmured. 'I'd forgotten about her.'

'It's OK.' I touched him lightly on the arm, meaning it in so many ways. 'You go. I'll be fine. I'll . . . I'll talk to you in the morning.'

'I can't just . . .'

My touch became a push. 'Please. *Go.*'

I made it back to Kewney through the wind that now howled, pressed my back against the front door, catching my breath. Inside I moved cautiously, alert to any sound that might indicate another presence. I scanned the shadows in the upper corners of the house. Deciding them empty, I made my way to the cave.

The myopia of the tunnel gave me no relief, nothing to fix my eyes on or soften my mind to but the thoughts that swirled around inside me, as violent as the wind outside.

What an idiot I had been. Throwing myself at the first man who would have me. Disregarding Laurie – not just her thoughts and feelings, but the warning signs that now seemed so obvious.

If I went to the police, I risked exposing everything about myself that I had worked so hard to keep hidden.

Staying silent risked a fate far worse.

There was danger on each side of the coin toss.

I would be ruining everything. My anonymity. My self-preservation. But in the end my fear of Laurie won out.

I pushed my tumbling thoughts aside, tried to focus solely on the beam of the torch, the rhythmic tread of my feet against the tunnel floor. *Press on, press on. Get the backpack and go. Don't think. Do.*

Finally I heard the persistent *drip, drip* that told me I was nearing the cave's dank walls, the faint white noise that told me I was nearing the sea. As the space opened up, I swung the torch around the walls, searching the dingy crevices for the backpack when something caught its light, something that made me scream, the torch falling from my grasp and skittering across the floor, me collapsing after it, groping the cold stone floor wildly.

A figure.

'Lily?'

The torch reclaimed, I thrust myself to my feet, brandishing the light in front of me like a weapon.

It was Charles.

22

'Stay away from me.' I agitated the torch in his direction, heart cantering against my chest. I still didn't know if he was entirely innocent. And even if he was, I had experienced myself what his anger could do.

'Lily, just calm down . . .' He held his hands up in a gesture of submission.

'*I said stay away.*' My voice ricocheted off the stone walls.

I swept the torch wildly across the cave walls, mind speeding through my next movements: the agility I would need, to take the backpack and run. I could get the passport alone. Surely that would be enough? But it turns out my plans were fruitless: the backpack was gone.

'*No.*' I breathed, my throat tight. Wielded the torch to face him, fear replaced by urgency. 'Charles, where is it?' And when he didn't answer, '*Charles, where is it? Tell me where Nina's backpack is.*'

'I . . . woke up,' he began to babble, took a step towards me as I took one away from him. 'I saw that you were gone. I was worried . . . I thought maybe . . .' He shook his head. 'I went looking for you. I knew you'd been down in the caves with the children – they can't keep anything a secret. When I saw the door to the pantry open, I assumed that's where you'd gone. But you weren't here. And then I found the backpack open, I knew you must have seen it. That you'd be back for it. It was too dangerous, leaving it here. I had to get rid of it, I couldn't let you have it. I . . . I . . . I . . .'

I balled my fists, trying to calm my racing adrenaline. 'Charles, for once and for all: just tell me the fucking truth.'

'I . . . I can't.' He took a step towards me. 'You don't understand. I—'

I shone the beam directly into his eyes, blinding him. '*Don't come near me.*' Despite what I believed of Laurie, I still didn't entirely trust Charles, or what he was capable of.

He stopped. Swung his upper arm against his face. 'I'm not going to hurt you, Lily. Just put that damned thing away.' I hesitated. 'Please.'

Slowly, I lowered the torch.

'Why are you here, Charles?' I had no weapon, nothing to fight him with. I had already felt the force of his rage once tonight. But I was done. Done with all the lies, and the secrets.

He exhaled into the musky air. Hung his head. 'I came to hide Nina's backpack.'

'Why?'

'Because . . . because she's dead.' The word hung in the space between us. I let it fall, not giving him the satisfaction of a reply. 'I knew that you'd figured it out, that you'd tell someone. And I couldn't let that happen.' He dared to look up at me, search the meagre light for my reaction. 'I always knew you were sharp.'

I turned away, disgusted by his pathetic attempt at

flattery. 'Who killed her, Charles. Say it, or I'll say it myself.'

A silence, as he searched himself. And then his shoulders slacked, admitting defeat.

'She did it.' His voice broke. 'Laurie killed Nina.'

It was true.

This whole time, it hadn't been Charles.

It was Laurie.

I pressed a hand to my core. Even though I had known it was true, hearing it out loud was like a punch to the gut. I looked up at him. 'And you knew?'

He began to shake his head vehemently. Paused. Slowly, slowly, began to nod. I doubled over. Wretched dryness at the thought of him in my bed, his lips on my skin. Knowing. The whole time, knowing.

'Not at first. She found out about me and Nina. Confronted me. And then the next day, she told me that Nina left. There was a letter, I saw her things had gone, I . . .' He held his palms up, useless. 'What else was I to believe?'

His eyes sought me out, but I jerked my head away, disgusted by him. I clenched my teeth. 'When, then . . . ?'

'I followed her.' He let out a hollow sigh. 'The night after she told me Nina had gone, she left our room in the middle of the night. She thought I was asleep, but I . . . I followed. She went over the cliffs, down and onto the cove . . . I couldn't understand what she was doing.' Mentally, I retraced the path I had watched her make myself. My own confusion. 'She came down here.' He inclined his chin towards the back of the cave. 'Through the rocks. There's an entrance there. Out to the sea.' The smugglers' tunnels. I wondered if that was why I didn't always hear her come back in. Why the motion sensors hadn't always woken me up on her return. She'd come inside through here. Charles pressed a hand to his temple. He looked older, even here in the dim light, all the jaunty charm leached out of him. 'She was there. With Nina's body.' He moaned. 'She'd strangled her. With the cord of her dressing gown.'

My stomach contorted. I pictured Laurie's kimonos, the beautiful silk I had so admired. Imagined the twist of silk around my neck, slowly tightening. Pressed a hand to my throat as I saw Charles look away.

'But she was trying to leave. Why? Why didn't Laurie just let her go?'

'I don't know.' He shook his head. 'I realized a long time ago I could never begin to understand Laurie fully. Or what goes on inside her head. I told you once that she was "complex".' He sighed deeply, the noise echoing across the dank walls. 'It's much more than that. When I married her, I thought that she would change, that I could save her. But it's only gotten worse. She's manipulative. She's utterly fearless. I don't think there's any limit to what she will do to have the perfect life she thinks she's owed.' He looked up at me, his eyes boring into me. 'Nothing and no one can stand in her way.'

His words gripped at me. Laurie had murdered Nina, even though she had been trying to leave. And she knew about me and Charles. And she was here, somewhere, in the grounds, in the house.

'Charles, I have to go.' Panicked, I raised the torch once more, praying I'd spot the glimpse of nylon hidden in the cracks of the wall. 'Just tell me where the back-pack is.'

He shook his head. 'I can't do that.'

I felt tears springing to my eyes, sniffed them away, knowing that what I was about to say would be betraying Nina for my own sake. 'Then let me go. Say nothing of this and you'll never see or hear from me again.'

'I . . . I can't risk that . . .' He shrank away from me, pressing his back into the walls of the cave. 'I helped her get rid of Nina's body.' He looked into the body of the cave, towards the sea. 'Out there. Took the rowboat out in the middle of the night, and let the waves take care of the rest.' I saw him reading my thoughts. 'That's why she comes down here at night . . . she says she's . . . I don't know, "paying penance" . . .' There was a bitterness in the way he spat the plosives, and I saw him turn his eyes heavenward. 'I don't know if I believe it's that, or if she's just . . . checking for the body.' My stomach flipped. He looked back at me, urging, imploring. 'Either way, you see, don't you: I can't help you. I'm part of this.'

Anger coursed through me, electric.

He had used me. He had let me fall for him, *knowing* what had happened with Nina. Knowing that I may well be next.

And like an idiot, I had allowed it.

'You *coward*.' Hot tears pierced my eyes. I had to get out of there. I needed the backpack and I needed to *go*. Why was he doing this? 'You could do this. You could tell the police what you've told me. Explain. Explain everything you've just told me. You made a mistake. You thought you were protecting your wife. They'll listen.

They'll understand. *Please*, Charles: this is your chance to put things right.'

'I *can't*.'

I shook my head, hot tears stinging my eyes. 'I don't understand.'

'I just can't,' he said, weaker now.

'*Why?*' My frustration echoed back at me against the cave walls, *why, why*.

And then another noise merged with it. The sound of rock on rock. Scraping. A low laugh that ballooned into the cavity of the cave.

'He won't go to the police.' And with horror, I saw Laurie emerge through the gap in the rocks, stalk silently towards us. 'Because I'm the one person alive who knows the truth about Christine.' As she stepped into the body of the cave, the torchlight picked up the glint of a knife. 'And he knows, if he does, I'll tell.'

23

Christine. The name ricocheted inside my brain. In my fervour over Laurie, I'd almost forgotten her. Charles may have been innocent of injuring Nina, but what about her?

Laurie spoke, snapping my attention back. 'Come on. Both of you,' Laurie commanded when neither of us spoke, raising the knife – from the block in the kitchen, I recognized its grooved handle now – and pointing it back in the direction of the house. 'I think it's time we all had a little chat.'

I felt frozen, my limbs unwieldy, incapable of movement, but when I didn't move she came towards me with the blade, stopping just inches from my chest.

'*I said come on.*'

I lowered my head, began to move through the tunnels, Charles behind me, Laurie at our rear. As we soldiered back through the tunnels, and up into the bowels of the house, I realized that she smelled of the sea. She was barefoot, her tread making a soft shuffling sound across the cave floor, and her hair was wet, matted tendrils of it clinging to the shoulders of her kimono. I had lost all sense of time down in the cave, but as my eyes adjusted to the thin light in the kitchen, I could tell dawn wasn't far behind us. How long had she been waiting out there, listening? How long had she had the knife?

We moved up into the body of the house, and traversed across the Great Hall towards the parlour, where she bade us to take a seat on the gilt-edged sofa. We did. Silently, compliantly.

As I sat, something pricked at my senses: an oddly familiar smell I couldn't quite give a name to. All around us, the room was littered with canvases – the spoils of Laurie's frenetic painting. Big and small, resting on easels or propped against furniture, they all carried with them the same dark energy I had come to recognize in her work, but, unlike the previous paintings, these weren't tempered by touches of light, but were dark, brooding things; angry slashes of sky and inky, furious sea. All along the white marble mantelpiece, altar-like, a dense row of pillar candles danced, their flickering flames making the paintings seem to come alive. The effect was claustrophobic, and the smell grew stronger, stinging my eyes and nose, as I realized what it was: turpentine. I looked around, trying to locate the source, and saw the floor was littered with discarded painting rags, the spoils of her creative flurry.

She walked over to the sideboard, just out of my peripheral vision, but then I heard the soft clink of the knife being set down and the release of a decanter being unstopped and poured. It was then she reappeared, holding three heavy, crystal glasses whose copper liquid was reminiscent of her hair, offered a glass to each of us.

'Cheers.'

She waited, watching us, and so obligingly I pressed the glass to my lips. I thought it would burn, taste chokingly of peat, or ethanol, but my mouth was oddly numb, and so I found myself drinking more, thirstily, gulping it back, inciting Laurie to cup her hand on the outer rim, urge, 'Steady.'

'Right then,' she began, when my glass was empty. 'I think perhaps we should start with a history lesson – isn't that your area of expertise, Lily?'

'Laurie, don't do this.' Charles, beside me, reached an arm out towards her.

His fingertips just grazed hers before she swatted him away. 'No, no. Lily always seems so *keen* to learn about Kewney's past. And there's one story she doesn't know.'

'Laurie—'

'I know Christine's alive.' I felt both their eyes on me; spoke before I could think not to. Heard the breath catch in Charles's throat. 'I . . . I visited her.'

For a moment, neither of them spoke.

'Well,' Laurie smoothed a hand across the lapel of her kimono, ridding it of some imperceptible speck of dust. 'I really should give you more credit. So, you've worked it all out, have you?'

I shook my head. 'Not all of it, no.'

Couldn't bring myself to look at Charles.

'In that case, I'll continue.' She wet her lips with her glass, raising an eyebrow at her husband over the rim. 'Once upon a time, there was a girl called Christine.'

'Laurie.' Charles warned.

She ignored him. 'Her parents were strict – cruel, even. Shutting her in the smugglers' tunnels for bad behaviour. Making her stand out in the sea, naked, on the coldest night of the year, because she'd wet the bed. Only . . . as she got older, she began to push back. She began to disobey. Sneak out at night. Made friends with the wrong crowd.' She paused, inspected the corner of a nail, flicked a fleck of paint from the shiny pink gloss. 'It wasn't any wonder, really, that she wound up pregnant at fifteen.'

'*Laurie, enough now.*'

Before I had a chance to process her words, Charles had moved to standing, arms outstretched towards her. The scene jerked. Laurie's body torqued, the liquid from her glass sloshing over her hand and down her wrist. When I looked up, she holding the knife.

'No, no, Charles,' she warned, pressing the blade towards him. 'Let me finish. You're always spoiling my stories.' He backed down. Sat, compliant, as she raised the knife upwards, inspecting its sharp point. The motion allowed the sleeve of her kimono to slide down, and I saw the underside of her wrist for the first time, the criss-cross of scars. She caught my eye, inclined her head towards me. 'Don't worry, Lily, we'll come to you next.' She lowered her arm. The sleeve slid down, obscuring it. '*Any*way. They sent poor, tarnished Christine away. Six months later, Nancy had her "miracle baby". And you'll never guess what they named him?' She let the sentence land, but I couldn't bring myself to answer her directly.

'Christine was your mother.' I spoke plainly. Angled my body towards him. Watched him, slowly, nod.

'They punished her by sending her away. Even more so, by raising me themselves – the pain of watching on the periphery.' He sniffed. Shook his head. 'And they tried to poison me against her, too. But they couldn't.' Stared down at the drink in his hands, swirled the orange liquid around but didn't drink. 'I loved her. And she loved me.'

His voice was tight. I almost felt sorry for him.

'Poor Charlie.' Laurie cut through the moment. 'That wasn't enough though, was it? Because she'd got a job in Newquay. Became involved with a group of people that Nancy was *still* convinced until her dying day was a cult. Fell in love with one of them and decided to move to India.' She pouted. 'Guess Mummy couldn't have loved you that much, huh?'

'*It wasn't like that.*' Charles's whole body clenched. I thought of the man I had fallen for, bright and intelligent, brought so low. Almost subconsciously, I felt my fingertips unfurling, my arm moving to close the gap between us, to offer comfort. But then I stopped myself.

Charles had slept with me, despite knowing what Laurie had done to Nina. He had hurt me, as I had seen him hurt Laurie. If I had been right about Christine being his mother, did that mean I was right about what he had done to her, too?

I balled my hand into a fist, shrank away.

Laurie finished the rest of her whisky. Wiped her mouth with the back of the hand holding the knife. Placed the glass on a side table with a loud clink. 'Go on then, what was it like?'

Charles pulled himself even tighter inwards, staring down at his hands. 'That's what she was coming to tell me. The night she . . .' He swallowed thickly. 'I was a schoolboy by then, busy digging up dirt and causing trouble. We didn't have as much time for one another any more, but she was still the best thing in my life. I'd live for the moment she came back from work. But that night was different. That night she came home to get her things. And she told me that she was leaving. And that she was my mother.'

'And then what?' Laurie goaded, licking her top lip.

Charles shook his head, and I saw the tears openly fall. 'I was angry with her. And devastated. I begged her to take me with her, but she said she couldn't. We fought, and . . . and . . .' He balled his hands into fists, pulled at the tufts of hair at his temples. 'Why are you doing this to me, Laurie?'

She smirked. 'I think it's important Lily knows who you really are.'

He turned to me then, shifted his body so that he was facing me fully. His face looked grey. When he spoke, it was little more than a groan. 'I don't know how it happened. It was so long ago. All I know is that one minute, we were shouting, and the next I was on her.' He squeezed his eyes tight.

My stomach twisted into knots. Part of me wanted to press my hands over my ears, to block him out. I had wanted to know the truth, but I hadn't wanted to be right.

'*No, Charles, no . . .*'

But he was lost in the memory.

'There was screaming, I think. Mine or hers, I don't know. And then my parents were pulling me off her. And then there was noise, and an ambulance and . . . and I . . .' He let out a strangled cry. 'It was too late for Christine. But my parents . . . their reputation . . . everything they stood for in this damned place . . . they decided it was best, for everyone, to cover it up. To say that she'd died. Forbade me from visiting, from ever mentioning her again. I was only a child . . . you understand, don't you, Lily? Please, say you forgive me.'

My body felt as though it was on fire. I thought of the woman in the photographs in the attic, her whole life before her. The one I had visited at the Beverley Centre. To do what he had done, and then abandon her like that . . . it was unthinkable.

The privilege of these people, to cover up for their mistakes without being plagued by the consequences.

I pressed a hand to my mouth, swallowing down bile. 'No. I don't forgive you, Charles. For any of it.'

Charles worried his head. When he spoke, he sounded as though he'd aged a decade. 'I've spent the rest of my life trying to make up for what I did. When I saved Laurie from the hospital all those years ago . . . I thought it would be a form of redemption. For Christine. I confided in her. She's the only one left who knows the truth. I thought . . . I wanted to bring us closer together.' He shook his head. For a moment, none of us moved, spoke. But when he looked up at Laurie, I was surprised to see not pain, but anger. 'Instead, she used it against me. Taunted me. Told me I was evil. Tried at every opportunity to elicit that same madness in me again. Like she wanted it. She even used it to blackmail me after . . . after Nina. Assured me that if I ever said anything, she would bring me down with her.' And then he turned to me. 'Lily, it was wrong of me to drag you into this. In being with you, I clung on to some stupid hope that things would be better . . . that you would, somehow, save me.' He tightened his lips. 'But I know I don't deserve to be saved.' And then I saw his fists flex and curl. 'And I'm done with your games, Laurie. I don't care any more. I'll take whatever fate I deserve, if it brings you down, too,' he spat. 'I was only a child. I didn't know what I was doing. You're the evil one, Laurie: what you did to Nina, you did in cold blood.'

We both watched Laurie, anticipating her response. She inspected the tip of the knife, ran her finger along its fine edge. And then turned to me with a strange expression.

And in that second, I realized there was one more truth that was about to be unearthed in Kewney.

'Well then, Charles, I guess you have a type.'

I felt a dull ringing in my ears, the blood draining from me as I raised my eyes to meet hers.

'*What?*' I breathed in, believing, not believing.

'You seem to have convinced my husband that you're some sort of holy saviour.' She looked down her nose at me, haughty, cruel. 'I think it's time he knew you for your true self.'

I bit my lip, feeling the room grow hot around me. 'I don't know what you mean.'

'Oh, Lily, don't be shy. We're all sharing.' She pointed the tip of the knife towards me. 'Now, be a good girl, and tell us both what you did to Nick.'

24

'I don't know what you're talking about.' The words stuck in my throat.

'Oh, I think you do.' Laurie crowed. 'Tell Charles. Tell Charles all about how you killed your boyfriend and took advantage of us. How you have used our home and our good will to hide your guilt.'

'No, it wasn't like that. I . . . I . . .' I sank my head. I felt as though I was falling. As though the floor had been removed from beneath me.

'Go on,' she bade me. 'What was it like, then?'

And as Laurie glared at me, I felt the parlour slip away from me as I was plunged back, back, back. To the night I had been running away from. To the memory I had been trying so hard to obliterate.

To that night.

That final night in the flat.

To Nick.

I had told him it was over. I had had my bag packed, hidden in the cupboard. I had tried to leave, just say my piece, walk out of the door. And then he had pressed a knife to my neck, a knife not unlike the one Laurie was holding now. Told me he would kill me, that he would kill himself.

And I believed him.

I backed down.

We made it to bed, I don't know how. I thought he'd fallen asleep, but I couldn't. I lay rigid beneath the sheets, listening to the life outside our window, and I couldn't see how I would ever be free. And then I saw him get up, leave the room. When he came back, I don't know how much later, he kissed me on the cheek although I lay stock still, pretending to sleep. Whispered in my ear, 'It's better this way.' I could smell the alcohol on his breath. Dread swept through me as he turned around.

Time ticked by: I listened to the seconds click past on his watch. My head felt tight. A ball of sickness sat in the pit of my chest. Something wasn't right.

'Nick?' I whispered. Louder, '*Nick.*'

When he didn't stir, I went into the kitchen, spotted the stove.

On the kitchen table, I saw one of the big medical textbooks he left all over the flat for me to trip over, blaming my poor housekeeping when I did. It was open.

The Effects of Carbon Monoxide Poisoning
Mild exposure to carbon monoxide can induce headaches, fatigue, and nausea, similar to flu-like symptoms. Medium exposure causes extreme headaches, drowsiness, disorientation, and an accelerated heart rate. Extreme exposure may lead to unconsciousness, and eventually death.

I walked back into that room, looked at Nick's sleeping form. Then I lay in bed beside him, hand pressed to my chest. Felt the growing pinch inside my skull. And then, as the nausea swelled and the dizziness took hold, I stood up. Made a choice.

And

I

left.

'How? How did you know?' I struggled to take a breath, the memory of that night pressing into my lungs. The truth of what I had been running from finally catching up with me.

Laurie tutted. 'I knew there must have been something you were running from, to accept this job in such a hurry, no questions asked. There was something off about you from the first time we spoke about him. The way you closed up, avoided eye contact. I knew his job, his first name, where you lived. So I did some searching.' She paused, as if for effect. Stalked over to the side table where she picked up the decanter, refilled her glass. 'You're not the only one who can go digging around places where they don't belong.' I saw the small smirk on her lips, knowing she had me on tenterhooks. 'There wasn't much out there, to be honest. But it's amazing what you can discover, with the right amount of money, knowing the right people to ask.' She flinched her shoulders lightly, took a small sip and set down the glass. 'Our trip to London was the perfect excuse to find out for sure.'

'I had no choice.' A tear escaped from the corner of my eye, slicked down my cheek. Another joined it, pooling in the crease of my neck. 'So he's . . . ?'

'Suicide, they claim,' she said piously, as I felt myself

go weak. 'Poor lamb. The stress of being a junior doctor can really get to you. Plus a girlfriend who left him in his hour of need.' She raised an eyebrow. 'Luckily for you, they don't know how close that hour was. Because I'm certain there must be more to it than that, why you've skulked around from the day you arrived. Jumping at the slightest knock on the door. Am I right?'

I hung my head, confirming. Couldn't bring myself to look at her. I hadn't known for sure. I hadn't looked, in the papers, online. Hadn't wanted to know. Thought perhaps there was a small chance he might have survived.

That night, I had acted almost unthinkingly, as though in a trance. But in the cold light of day, I knew what I had done. But also what I had saved myself from.

Suicide. That's what Nick intended. For the both of us.

If he had survived, I knew he would find me.

If he was dead, I had killed him. Or at the very least, let him die. I was convinced, either way, I would be discovered.

All those months I had spent looking over my shoulder, not knowing which fate I would rather catch up with me.

Was it wrong, the relief I felt now, that no-one had been looking for me after all: not Nick, not the police; no-one. I was safe. Or, at least, I had been.

'It's true.' I whispered, unable to look at either of them. 'I knew what I was doing. And I ran.'

Laurie aspirated, a loud 'hah'. 'Do you see, Charles? What sort of a woman you have chosen to debase our marriage with? She's no better than me.' When she turned to me, I saw the glee dancing on those thin lips, the pleasure at having won. 'I took pity on you. Even after I suspected what you had done. I gave you every opportunity to be my friend. I gave you dresses, gifts. The most beautiful things. I was kind to you. And yet you still betrayed me, didn't you? You repaid my kindness by sleeping with my husband. Just like her. Just like Nina.'

'No.' I listened to her words, the memories of that time, of my escape from Nick and arrival at Kewney. Something still wasn't right. She had shown me kindness, yes, but it hadn't been unfettered. That wasn't all there was too it.

I thought of Laurie out there at the cove. Bearing her naked body to waves. She had told Charles she was paying penance. But she hadn't looked penitent. She had looked defiant. I raised my chin to face her. 'You're not sorry at all, Laurie. You wanted this.'

I remembered how she had gleaned my relationship status, the whereabouts of my family, friends. '*A position best suited for people without a whirling social life.*' Charles had said Nina was alone too. Had Laurie shown these same 'kindnesses' to Nina? I had once suspected that Laurie knew about my relationship with Charles. But it wasn't simply that she knew: she had *planned* it.

'You groomed me.' Slowly, I began to rise. 'All those dinners, those smart clothes. Every time you complimented me, raised me up in his presence.' The realization hit me with the clarity of one of her crystal glasses. 'Is that what you did to Nina?' She turned away, jaw set. 'You wanted us to be with Charles, didn't you?' Even as she twisted away from me, I saw the panic in her eyes, the truth it gave it. 'I'm right, aren't I? We were just part of some sick game of yours.' I shook my head. 'But I don't understand – why? Why did you do it? Why did you kill Nina, if she was doing exactly what you wanted?'

'*It was the only way to make him stay*.' Without warning she lunged towards me, hand clenched hold of the knife so tightly I saw her knuckles whiten.

'*Laurie, no*.' Charles leapt to his feet, palms raised, holding her back.

They locked eyes, and for a moment neither one made a move, blinked an eyelid.

I held my breath. At last, she brought the knife down to her side.

'You know, he was the nicest he'd ever been to me, with Nina?' She snatched the whisky glass from the side table, brought it to her lips. I listened to the pulse of her throat as she drank thirstily. 'Always by my side, always checking in on me. It was almost like he really loved me.'

'Laurie, don't.'

'Oh, shut up,' she snapped at Charles, her consonants crisp. 'Do you know what it's like to love someone so painfully that you would do anything to keep them?'

I considered it. For a while, I really believed I loved Nick. I let so many things fall by the wayside to keep him happy. But looking back I could see it wasn't love, not at all.

'No.' I shook my head. 'No, I don't think I do.'

'Charles is everything to me. I would do anything for him – *anything* – even at the sake of my own health, my sanity. I kept the truth about Christine all these years, didn't I? I hadn't planned it with Nina, at first. But I saw how he acted around her. It's funny.' There was a glint in her eye. 'It reminded me of how he was at first, with me. He became intoxicated with her. He would hang around the house all day, saying all the right things. Being as charming as we all know Charles can be. It wasn't hard to work out what was going on. And for the first time in as long as I could remember, he was sweet to me. He came home early from work when I asked. Attended all the events he always said before were so "boring". Took me for dinners out, weekends away.' She gave him a sardonic grin. 'I guess it's what you'd call a guilty conscience, right, Charlie?' Her glass emptied, she tossed it to her side. 'I didn't have a choice in what was going on, but it didn't mean I liked it. I was . . . a little crueller to her than I should have been. But that didn't mean I wanted her to leave. That would have ruined everything. I couldn't have him moping about, or worse, going to find her. I *tried* to get her to stay. Did everything I could to convince her. And when she refused, I got angry. I didn't really know what I was doing, at first. And then I tried to find someone else. To make it up to you. I . . . I did it for *you*, Charles, don't you understand?'

Beside me, I saw Charles's fists clench, the slow shake of his head. 'No, Laurie. You did it for yourself.'

Laurie's face torqued. Slowly, Charles rose.

'I thought I loved you, once.' His voice gained momentum. 'And I thought that you loved me, too. But I can see now it's never been about that. You never loved me; you loved the idea of me. You have manipulated me from the moment you set eyes on me. You used me, as your ticket to freedom. I pitied you, what your parents did to you. But they were right. I should have left you where I found you.' He raised his chin. 'And I don't love you. I *hate* you.'

It was then that the world exploded.

'*No!*' Laurie cried out. But instead of Charles, it was me she lunged for, slashing wildly with the knife. I felt a ripping across my stomach, so fast and so unexpected that I almost didn't feel the pain, couldn't quite believe it when I saw the bloom of red.

'*Laurie, no!*' Charles went for her, both hands at her wrist, trying to wrench the knife away from her as she jerked, resisted.

I backed away, hands pressed to my stomach, the shock of it making me numb, inert, as together they fought, what she lacked in physical strength made up for by mania. He backed her up against the parlour wall, hard – I heard the sound of her back connecting solidly, her yelp of pain, saw her retaliate with the knife, plunging it into the top of his chest, eliciting a roar from him that ripped through the room, that I was convinced, partly hoped, would wake the children and end this.

In a burst of strength, he rescued the knife from her hand and threw it to one side, barely took a second before he wrestled her against the wall beside the mantelpiece, forcing his full weight against her chest.

'It's over, Laurie.' Blood pulsed from above his breastbone, and I saw the way he adjusted his weight, imagined the pain he was in from the way he spoke through gritted teeth, his breathing forced. The cut she had inflicted on me was shallow, but I saw how deep she had plunged the knife into him. 'The life you've tried to manipulate. Everything you've built on lies. It's finished. You'll never step foot in this house again.'

'This house?' To my surprise, she laughed, low. 'Do you know, I've always hated it?' Watching from where I was, frozen in place, I was surprised at how in control she seemed, so calm. '"Kewney Manor."' Her voice curled around the name. 'There's a similar word in Old Cornish. It means "rancid".' She chuckled. 'I saw it once, in one of those relentless books about Cornish heritage in the library. Not sure if your ancestors realized it or not, but it's always tickled me.' Out of the corner of my eye, I saw where she had loosed her left arm from his grip, from the elbow up, fingers moving, crawling up, to the corner of the mantelpiece

'*Charles*,' I warned, the words getting stuck in my throat. He didn't hear me.

'"Rancid".' She tilted against the knife's edge, eying him defiantly. 'It describes this whole place to a T. It's rotten. You, your whore of a mother.' She smirked, and I saw Charles's fingers tense around her throat. 'Her parents. All of you. You think you're such a saint, but you drove me to this. Cheating. Lying. You have your wicked ways, your temper. Don't pretend you're any better than me.' She gave a ragged sigh. 'So no, thank you. I've no interest in this house. As a matter of fact, I've always fantasized about destroying the place.' All at once I saw the glint in her eyes. A tiny, almost imperceptible movement as her fingers stretched. 'I just never thought I'd get my chance.'

A twist of her wrist, her hand grasping.

And I realized, too late, what it was.

'*Laurie, no!*'

At the sound of my voice Charles released her, turned to face me.

And in that moment, seizing his distraction, she moved. Gripped hold of one of the pillar candles on the mantelpiece, raised her arm to throw.

'No!'

I felt wrenched in two, caught between wanting to run and feeling compelled to stay, to stop it.

Before he could stop her, Laurie let her arm drop. Let the candle fall into an open metal bin just out of her reach.

A bin I knew from memory held the used painting rags she discarded throughout the day.

Painting rags that I knew would be covered in oil paint.

And turpentine.

I had the strangest sensation then, as though I were watching us from above, like those reports of people having near-death experiences.

I saw myself screaming, body bent double, hands reaching; it was as though it was happening outside of me, as though I couldn't hear it, feel it.

Watched, as Laurie stretched her foot, touched the side of the bin.

Kicked.

I watched it teeter. Flames sparked from its centre as it rolled, tipped onto its side.

Fell.

'Laurie, no!' Charles turned from her, the knife falling

from her hands as he reached out, flailed uselessly towards it, shrinking back against the heat.

The bin exploded onto one of the canvases that lay scattered about the room, and quickly the flames soared, tearing through the canvas and spreading to others, sunsets and seascapes melting, and curling, and coming alive in a wash of gold. Racing through the discarded rags that lay in our wake.

She watched, mesmerized, as the fire took hold, catching on the soft furnishings, twirling like orange vines up the silk curtains, the flames rising, three feet, five feet, black clouds of smoke engulfing the ceiling. I thought I heard her laugh.

Furniture caught, wood cracking, splitting around.

I turned to Charles, who had staggered to the ground.

'Charles, we have to go.' I leaned over, trying to grab hold of his upper arm. He stared dazedly around the room, taking it in, and, I realized now, incredibly pale. Blood had soaked through his shirt, turning it dark brown. When I pulled, he was like a leaden weight. I couldn't lift him.

'Charles, come on. Help me.' The feeling seemed to rush back to me with the smoke that choked my lungs, made my eyes stream.

Finally he looked directly at me, and, with an expression that still pierces my thoughts, he shook his head.

'Go. Save the children.'

I was about to move when I stopped, stock still. Looked across at Laurie, who seemed lost in a reverie. 'She locks them in,' I said, my voice hollow.

Charles's face contorted. '*The keys, Laurie,*' he

breathed, and I could hear the effort in his voice. '*Tell her.*'

She huffed, looked at me one last time. 'It wasn't true. It was just a warning. An idle threat.' Then, with a purse of her lips. 'I thought you'd be pleased. You wouldn't have run the risk of being caught . . . *in flagrante.*' She slurred the phrase. Couldn't help a salacious smile. 'I was only trying to help you.'

I wanted to say so many things, but in the end, none of them mattered.

Instead I nodded. Looked to the double doors behind us.

Ran.

Out into the cool hallway, the door slamming shut behind me before I could stop it. My mind a mess of thoughts, trying to jigsaw together all that had happened.

The children. Oh, God, the children. I raced up the stairs, taking them two at a time, passing through the landing and entering their wing as alarms began to sound.

I roused William, fumbling for him in the dark and pressing his sleep-hot body against mine. Bess, more alert – 'What's happening, what's going on?' – as I clutched her to me, dragging them back along the landing and down the stairs to the Great Hall, into the Great Hall, already thick with smoke, where I swerved my eyes away from the parlour, the halo of fire around the door frame, couldn't look, didn't want to see.

We moved to the underscore of beams bending, snapping, fire crackling, the heat on our faces, their bodies trembling, cries rising, louder, as realization threw them into wakefulness. The sound of glass exploding triggered me to drop to my knees, hauling them with me, remembering some long-forgotten school fire-safety practice about smoke rising, keeping to the ground. Together we crawled, bodies low, over the stone tiles towards the thick front door and out, finally.

Out into the cool, fresh air. I sucked it in as the wind howled, blew the smoke from me.

And then Bess's voice, then William's joining her – the sound that will forever reverberate in my memories – 'Mummy! Daddy!'

Holding them back. The wrench of their sobs as we stumbled, my knees threatening to buckle under the weight of them as I turned to look at the house, saw the billows of smoke already escaping the top floor windows.

And then, another figure, or maybe it was just a hallucination.

'*Joss?*'

His mouth opened and closed, and I tried to make out what he was saying although dizziness was starting to take hold of me, my vision going fuzzy around the edges.

'Oh God, oh God, Lily, what happened?'

'What . . . what . . .' I tried to force the words out, but must have forgotten how to talk. 'What are you doing here?'

'I couldn't get you out of my head.' He squeezed his eyes shut and I saw a thousand unsaid things pass over his face. 'I'm just glad . . . I'm glad I wasn't too late.'

He continued through my silence as I reached for his hand, took hold.

'Joss . . .' I began. 'I'm so sorry. I . . .'

'Shh, shh,' he comforted, his fingers lacing into mine. 'Forget that now. Tell me what I can do.'

Finding my voice, at last. 'Just be my friend, Joss. That's what I need. A friend.'

In the distance, deep in the valley, sirens.

The sound made my body relinquish the last of whatever strength it held. Collapsed onto the lawns, felt the cushion of dew-drenched grass beneath me, the smell of fresh earth against my skin.

The children beside me, their whimpers swirling into the howling air.

Blackness threatened, but as I lay back against the grass, feeling Joss's arms reach to support me, I looked up at Kewney Manor, the place that should have been my refuge, and had so nearly become my grave.

I didn't know what would happen in the next hour, let alone tomorrow, or the long days after that.

But for the moment, I had survived.

Nick, Charles, Laurie. I had survived all of them. And for now, that was enough.

Laurie had said that the manor was rotten; that there was something in its very foundations that made it wrong.

But as the dawn broke, streaks of pink searing the sky, fighting through the growing smoke, the glow of orange flames that broke free from the manor's facade, I wondered how she would paint it.

I had a feeling she would find it beautiful.

2023

The sign on the gates said 'Sold'.

I hadn't believed it, when I'd heard.

MILLIONAIRE BUYS MURDER MANOR: the papers once again dredging up that unlovely title.

But now here it was in ink and card, chained around those floral filigreed gates.

Beyond, the familiar gravel drive, drawing the eye to where the facade had once stood. To where all that remained now was rubble. Scorched earth.

And here I was, in front them. Needing to see for myself. Wanting . . . wanting what, exactly?

Forgiveness? A sign?

A chance to explain?

I knew she was in town. Kewney village remained unchanged in ten years, particularly in its capacity for gossip. As soon as we'd arrived I'd asked around. Barely finished my question before I got the full report.

'*Oh* yes, *she's here. Come to dot the i's and cross the t's.*'

'*Quite the little lady, now. Goes by "Elizabeth", not "Bess".*'

'*Beautiful, like you'd expect. Looks the spitting image of . . . well, you know . . .*'

They'd gone to America, I knew. A distant second cousin or aunt with the money and patience to take them in. She was going to Yale, someone said. '*She was always a bright spark.*' And William to military school. I tried to picture my rambunctious little tree climber taking orders.

I had written, at first.

Sent them the details of where to find Christine, wishes that they would visit. Hoping, I don't know, that it would give her some sort of ending. Maybe all of them. A couple of trite back and forths between us, which soon faded into nothing.

I gripped hold of the gate, feeling the cold iron hard against my skin.

Maybe I should have tried harder.

But the truth about Nick had been buried with Charles and Laurie; hidden in the debris of Kewney Manor. And so, perhaps selfishly, I took the opportunity to bury all of my pasts in one. I move on.

I couldn't save Bess and William, any more than I could save Laurie, or Charles, or Nina. That didn't mean it didn't hurt. It didn't mean that I didn't still wake in the night, the memory of that time as present to me as the scream threatening to rip from my throat. But I have learned with time that there are no white knights, that people aren't inherently good or bad, and that if I wanted to save other people, I first of all needed to save myself.

I walked down the lane and into the village, to the ice-cream shop on the corner. They were waiting for me, as I knew they would be, fingers and faces sticky with the residue from the cones they had long since finished. I spied them before they saw me, and I felt the smile radiating almost subconsciously across my face, the warmth of love that seemed to tingle through me so naturally now, at the very sight of the two of them, together like this.

'There she is!' he cried, his voice a song, and on seeing me, she beamed, reached her chocolate-stained hands towards me as I backed away from her in mock horror before relenting, pulling her close.

'Mummy, I had two scoops,' she sang into my neck, and in response I tapped her nose and chin lightly.

'I can see. And I bet now you'll have nothing for dinner.'

'Sorry,' he said gruffly in response, standing. 'I didn't know how long you would be.'

'It doesn't matter.' I reached for him, burying myself in the comfort of his familiarity. It was easy to wave away the trivial, when you had faced the profound. 'How was your mum?'

'Glad to see us.' He shuffled his feet. 'Misses us. But she gets it. Why we've chosen to stay away.' He coughed into his hand. 'How was it?'

'It was hard,' I murmured, the nothingness of Kewney still bright in my memory. 'But I'm glad I went. I'm glad I had a chance to say goodbye.'

I looked into his eyes, the eyes of a man I had slowly learned to open myself up to over the past ten years and could keep no secrets from. He said nothing, but he didn't need to.

He understood.

It was a different sort of love, this love with Joss.

It was quiet, and gentle, and yes, at times, it was dull and mundane. It didn't burn hot and bright, like with Nick, or lurk in the shadows, like with Charles, but was as steady and enduring as the waves, whose ebb and flow greeted us each morning as we pulled back the curtains on whatever town or village we'd arrived in. Travelling the world, as we had once talked about. Somehow lured, always, by the sea.

For a while, I didn't think I wanted such love.

For a while, I didn't think I deserved it.

But if there is any advantage to being broken, it is that it allows the cracks to show, and, slowly and patiently, Joss is trying to find a way to seal them.

I am not sure I will ever be able to fully forgive myself for what happened, for allowing myself to fall into the same web of control that I had done with Nick. Shame is a difficult thing to unlearn. As Laurie once said to me, I have done things I am not proud of, things I will always regret. But I don't believe that means I am incapable of love, of being loved in return. And so I look at my family, my imperfect, perfect family. And I try each day to be the best person I can be for them.

The world has pivoted in the years since Kewney Manor stood proud, and I am trying to tell myself that the things that happened to me were not my fault. I was not, as Meredith had once so disdainfully cast me, 'A girl like that', but rather, just a girl; simply that; no better and no worse.

I picked up our daughter, kissed the top of her head, and took Joss's hand in mine.

'Come on, family. Let's go home,' I coaxed, as we walked into the light.

Acknowledgements

This book began with something of a 'dream come true' for an author. Driving down a Cornish country road during a long Covid summer, the plot and its characters presented themselves to me, almost fully formed, urging me to tell their story. Inevitably, what began at a sprightly pace became murkier and sludgier as 'the plot thickened', so I am particularly delighted to be sitting here now on the other side of it, giving thanks to the many people who got me through it!

As always, thank you to my steadfast and generous agent, Luigi Bonomi, whose encouragement and words of wisdom I so value, and to the whole team at LBA for their continuing support.

To Wayne Brookes, my editor: you are a champion! Thank you for your searing insight, for being such wonderful fun, and for steering the course when 'it all got a bit Dynasty'! To Lucy Hale, Hannah Corbett, Jamie Forrest, Charlotte Tennant and anyone in the wider Pan Macmillan team I may have missed: it is a privilege to continue to work with you; thank you for the dedication you show to your authors. To Bella Bosworth for her keen copy-editing eye, and Tiana-Jane Dunlop for stunning cover artwork: thank you, thank you.

A particular thank you to Dr Rachel Thornton at Addenbrooke's Hospital for your valuable guidance on the character of Christine (and the tone of Dr Thirsk's letters): I hope that I have done your sensitive words justice. And to Helen Millward, for such a helpful introduction, and for proving that the social media hive mind is a wondrous thing!

To the friends who have once again listened to my heart-rending and hair-pulling: to Hannah, for Cornish colour; Sharan, Charlotte and Brenda for getting me out of tricky plot holes (literally out of caves . . .); to Paula and Shirley, for knowing most problems can be solved with a glass of something sparkling; to Debra and Steph, who I am constantly grateful to have in my life. I owe you all (several) drinks.

To the writing friends who keep me both grounded and sane: Vic Watson, Emma Hughes, Charlotte Duckworth, Emily Freud, Liv Matthews, Lauren North and Mira V. Shah: I'm so lucky to have you!

To my extraordinarily supportive family: Mummy, for begrudgingly learning to like Laurie, and Sheron for listening to me painstakingly explain an entire plot to her on a sun lounger without batting an eyelid. To 'my boys': George and Marlowe – you are my world.

And finally, to all the readers, booksellers and book bloggers for such continued enthusiasm and spirit: it is an immense privilege to keep doing this job, and you are the reason we are able to do it. Thank you.